I0565616

POSTED
FOR MURDER

Virginia Rath

POSTED
FOR MURDER

VIRGINIA RATH

COACHWHIP PUBLICATIONS
Greenville, Ohio

Posted for Murder, by Virginia Rath
© 2019 Coachwhip Publications

Published 1942
No claims made on public domain material.
Cover image: MacLean tartan © MadSci

CoachwhipBooks.com

ISBN 1-61646-485-2
ISBN-13 978-1-61646-485-1

POSTED FOR MURDER

PART ONE

I

"And so," Hallie Durdan said, her fat, flabby voice and her flabby, soft face quivering with indignation, "with simply no warning at all he told Adela their marriage had been a mistake. That's the reward she gets for making him a perfectly wonderful wife for seven years!"

"The same thing has happened to a good many women after twenty-one years," Antonia Jordan said.

"Yes, I reckon it does happen, men being what they are. But if you knew Adela!"

Hallie Durdan's pudgy fingers strayed to the plate of pastry on the tea table. Somehow, when she looked down at her plate there was a chocolate eclair on it. She cut into it quickly, looking anywhere but at her guest.

Antonia shrugged and put her own half-eaten pastry on the tea table. It's Miss Halide's diet, not mine, she thought. Let *her* keep it. She said:

"But I don't know Adela Maclean, Miss Hallie.
I take it that you're expecting her and her husband
tonight and I thought I heard you say that they
are coming from Wisconsin, but—"

"I've told you all about Adela time and again.
People don't listen to what I say," Miss Hallie
complained. "Adela's mother and I went to board-
ing school in Virginia together. Then Adela went
to the same school with my daughter Rosalie."

Miss Hallie's eyes watered as they always did
when she mentioned her daughter, and two fat tears
rolled down the petulant creases in her cheeks.

"But I reckon I forget that Adela is twenty-nine,
and so would Rosalie be if she hadn't been taken
from me. And as you're four years or so younger,
you never really knew Rosalie."

Antonia made sympathetic sounds. "Adela visited Rosalie here, didn't she?"

"She stayed with us three months when she was
twenty-one. She was hardly back home in Wisconsin again when Rosalie passed away."

Miss Hallie dried her eyes with an embroidered
napkin and a brave, sweet smile.

"Then Adela married Ian Maclean," she went
on. "I've never met Ian, but it was such a suitable
marriage. His grandfather and Adela's were old
friends. Both their families wanted them to marry,
and Ian had a good position in his grandfather's

lumber mill. I reckoned, from Adela's letters, that their marriage was simply ideal. And now—this!"

"Does Adela," Antonia inquired dryly, "make you her confidante in all matters relating to her marital happiness?"

"What? I wish you wouldn't be satirical, Toni. Adela is too proud and ladylike to write me about Ian wanting a divorce. But Adela's mother wrote me just what Ian said. She thought they should have a second honeymoon. She said she and Adela have no idea who the other woman can be—"

"Must there necessarily be another woman?"

Miss Hallie's dingy blue eyes widened. "Maybe no one that really matters—but what other reason could Ian have for wanting a divorce?"

Antonia started to say that she could think of many reasons why either a man or a woman might be fed up simply with marriage in seven years and without loving any other man or woman. She didn't because she had long ago decided that Miss Hallie's mind was as soft and bottomless as a large stretch of quicksand.

You could throw facts and ideas into it—even the mental equivalent of a cow—by the hour, and the only result would be a few air bubbles. Of course, Antonia thought, enlarging on her fancy, there were a few humps of solid ground dotting the quicksand. These represented what Miss

Hallie referred to as her "principles" or her "beliefs."

All of these were heirlooms. What had been good enough for Hallie Durdan's mother would last her own lifetime. Though she had lived fifty of her fifty-five years in California she was self-consciously Southern. Wife, widow, mother, and bereaved mother, she had always insisted on being called "Miss" Hallie.

"Adela just wrote that she and Ian needed to get away for a while," she continued. "So I invited them here because Adela's mother asked me to. And I will try to be polite to Ian, though when I think of anyone treating a wonderful girl like Adela that way my blood just boils—"

"So the wife beater hasn't arrived yet?" said an indolent masculine voice.

Mr. Fredric Carter lounged into the room and kissed his aunt's cheek. She reached for his hand, settled it on her shoulder, and patted it reprovingly.

"Auntie would rather you didn't joke about such serious subjects, Freddie."

Miss Hallie had been one of three Carters. The older brother, Dr. Breck Carter, had hung out his shingle in Berkeley thirty-five years ago. He had never married: perhaps because Miss Hallie had been widowed at thirty and took it for granted that she and her child would make their home with "Uncle Doc."

A younger brother, Freddie's father, had died before Freddie was twenty-one, and Miss Hallie had insisted that Freddie make his home from then on with her and Dr. Carter.

Freddie winked at Antonia across his aunt's head. "Well, Miss Hallie, though I've never met Ian Maclean, I do think he should be warned that his reputation has preceded him here."

"Has it?" Antonia said.

Miss Hallie fidgeted. "Adela will want to see all her old friends, and I may have just—well, I reckon I've hinted to them what the situation is, because we must all be mighty nice to poor Adela—"

"While making Maclean feel like he's inhabiting a well-refrigerated doghouse," Freddie finished cheerfully. "Why don't we ask Toni to stay to dinner? You know how it is when strangers come to stay a spell. Polite conversation, and if they've been traveling all you need is some magic-lantern slides to make it a lecture on the scenic beauties of America."

Antonia laughed. Miss Hallie considered her nephew's remark seriously.

"It might be a good idea. I'll want to talk to Adela myself, and since Toni doesn't know Adela either, she won't mind being polite to Ian."

Freddie chuckled. "There is logic in that remark if you untangle it. I don't mind Toni's being polite to Maclean at dinner, but I will make it clear to him that I have an option on Toni's future breakfast-table conversation."

He eyed Antonia expectantly and then said aggrievedly:

"Can't you blush, woman? Just the faintest rosy flush to indicate a maidenly consciousness that I've been paying you marked attentions and that you do not find them wholly displeasing?"

"Freddie, you idiot," Antonia said.

"That's what they all say."

"No," Antonia said hastily, seeing Miss Hallie draw in the corners of her mouth, "they don't. People tell me you are really a very good lawyer—"

"Though not yet a very prosperous one?"

Miss Hallie patted Freddie's hand again. "You mustn't be impatient, dearie. You know we love to have you here until you build up your legal practice and go to a little home of your own."

"Still, it will be several years before I can support a wife, so why don't we get married and live on your money, beautiful?"

"I don't mind sharing my thousand a year with the right man," Antonia said calmly. "But why do you always make your declarations in form when

Miss Hallie is present, Freddie? It reminds me of the *Five Little Pepper* books."

"All I know about the five little Peppers is that they grew. And a public proposal is proof that my intentions are honorable."

"I know young people have changed since my day," Miss Hallie said mournfully, "I can't think it's quite nice to talk so even if— Can you see the clock, Freddie?"

"It's a quarter of five."

"Well, Adela sent me a wire from Willits saying they would positively arrive this evening but not to wait dinner for them. Adela is always so thoughtful. But— Is that the doctor? He should be— No, it's only Loretta."

II

Loretta Van Horn stopped for an instant in the doorway. She'd never, Antonia thought, seen Loretta enter a room without that momentary hesitation and a look half questioning, half apologetic. You felt that if someone said "Boo!" very loudly Loretta would scurry quickly away.

She was very thin, with dreamy brown, spaniel eyes and fine, bodiless brown hair that never held a curl or wave. She always wore serviceable dresses that were too large for her and hats that were too

small for her—and a variety of long and short
necklaces, clips, pins, and bracelets that usually
had a dozen or so small charms dangling from them.

Miss van Horn was usually determinedly
sprightly, but she had taught music for so many
years that this might be excused as being part of
her professional manner. For her occasional girl-
ishness there was no excuse except that she had
never overcome a slight lisp that sometimes made
her sound absurdly infantile when she was most
in earnest.

She put a bulging brief case on one of the many
tables in the overfurnished living room, took off
her coat, and sat down without removing her gloves.

"Well, aren't we cozy this dweary afternoon?"
Loretta also found it difficult to pronounce the
letters *l* and *r* correctly. "Tea and all—"

"Will you have tea?" Miss Hallie said perfunc-
torily. "It's cold now, but it's too late to send to
the kitchen for more hot water. That is, unless
Freddie wants tea. Do you, dearie?"

"No, thank you," Freddie said rather shortly.
He was never rude to Loretta, though to Antonia
he dismissed her as "a goon." Loretta flushed but
said promptly:

"No, thank you, Cousin Hallie. I had a cup of
tea at Drake's before I started home."

"So that's why you're so late. I wanted you to be home before this. Adela and Ian will be here for dinner tonight."

Sitting or standing, Loretta always drooped slightly, like a vine that should be tied to a trellis. But now she sat erect.

"You mean—they're really coming, Cousin Hallie?"

"Goodness, Loretta, you're far too old to be so moony and absent-minded. I told you—"

"You told me you'd asked Adela to break her trip here. I thought it was Adela's mother who suggested that, not Adela. I know Adela said they would try to take Berkeley on their way, but—"

"I do wish you wouldn't mumble, Loretta. It's all nonsense to say I don't hear as well as I used to. I can hear perfectly well when—"

"I didn't think Adela would care to come back to Berkeley," Loretta said with unusual crispness.

"Don't be silly. Of course she wants to come back, and all her old friends are mighty anxious to see her again."

"I doubt that," Loretta said. Fortunately Miss Hallie did not hear her. She went on triumphantly:

"And they are coming. I had a wire from Adela after you left this morning and I've been waiting for you to come home to tell you—"

"I know." Loretta rose quickly. "I'll pack my things at once. Fortunately my little apartment hasn't been rented."

Loretta was fond of saying that she "managed very well" with what she earned as a teacher and accompanist. Miss Hallie was equally fond of saying that she always gave Loretta "something substantial" on Christmas and birthdays. In that connection she would point out that Loretta was "only a second cousin, you know."

But when Miss Hallie enjoyed poor health, as she had this winter, she would remark: "After all, we are cousins, Loretta. Real nurses cost so much and you'll do quite well and get your room and board free." So since December Loretta and her meager belongings had occupied the least desirable bedroom, and it seemed that Miss Hallie did not want her to vacate it now.

"You are so selfish, Loretta," she said. "Of course you won't leave just when Adela is coming. You'd almost think you wanted to avoid her. Of course you don't—"

"Oh, don't I!" Loretta muttered. Then: "Adela and I were never close friends," she said mildly, turning to Antonia. "She and dear Rosalie and I were all of an age, but I was already teaching when Adela visited here, so though Rosalie was always sweet about asking me to parties and so on—"

Miss Hallie murmured something to the effect that her daughter had been too good for this wicked world and put the tea napkin to her eyes again. Then:

"But if you weren't so thoughtless you'd know you could be useful and not want to move out, Loretta," she complained. "Goodness knows what the excitement will do to my heart, and it's not as if I'd ever put anyone else in that little back bedroom but you. Adela was dear Rosalie's best friend—"

"And I was—was very fond of Rosalie," Loretta said slowly.

She hesitated and then sat down, reluctantly, it seemed to Antonia. Miss Hallie was babbling about flowers in the guest room now. Antonia thought Loretta was not listening to her. She sat still, frowning for an instant before she began, very carefully, to strip off her left glove.

"But I'll be deserting you very soon, Cousin Hallie," she said abruptly. "You see, I'm going to be married."

She dropped the glove into her lap and put out her hand. A flame shot up in the fireplace and caught the sparkle of a diamond that was, conservatively speaking, the size of a large pea.

"Cripes!" said Freddie elegantly. "Will you take a look at the headlight! But who—?"

"I am going," Loretta said, "to marry Richard Prince."

Antonia gulped down her instinctive "You're joking!" She had met Richard Prince. That was part of the social education of most Piedmont debs. He was approaching forty but had so far escaped all the traps set for him by fond mammas of marriageable daughters or by the daughters themselves.

He had inherited money and made more by his management of Berkeley's best music store. He had an impressive bass voice and, as Loretta was a very fine accompanist, she had often served him in that capacity, even going to his home when he wanted to practice. Loretta had bored all of them with her descriptions of that hillside home.

But the idea that Loretta might ever be mistress of that home . . . No, Antonia decided, in spite of that hunk of ice on her finger, it's too much to swallow except in installments. Miss Hallie was still staring at Loretta blankly. At last she smiled pityingly.

"My dear Loretta, are you perfectly certain that you aren't deceiving yourself as to Mr. Prince's intentions? I have your interest at heart and—"

"And you can't understand why Richard chose me? Neither will anyone else. I'm sure I don't, myself," Loretta said with a sweet humility that verged on mockery when she held her thin hand

out so that the light from the fire caught the gleam
of the great diamond again.

"But you don't need to worry, dear Cousin Hallie. Richard announced our engagement to the
Oakland and Berkeley papers today. I—I didn't
know he was going to or I'd have told you before."

"Well," said Freddie, rallying, "my hat's off to
you, Loretta. The family fortunes may yet be re-
trieved. You know I'm only joking. I really mean:
felicitations and all those things."

Loretta smiled. "I know, Freddie."

"I'm sure I hope you will be very happy," Miss
Hallie said grudgingly. "I do think it would have
been nice if Mr. Prince had come to meet us and
certainly more correct if I or your cousin Doc had
been permitted to announce your engagement."

"Richard has no use for social customs, and I
didn't know he'd made the announcement until I
met him at Drake's this afternoon. He gave me my
ring then because he has to go to Los Angeles tonight. But of course he will call when he gets back."

"I hope," said Miss Hallie gloomily, "that he
will not be gone longer than you think. I reckon
I'll lie down now if you'll excuse me. I seem to be
very tired."

"Then I'll just come along and make you com-
fy," Loretta offered. "You'll have a nice rest and be
all fresh for your company."

"No, I mustn't impose on you. I'll do very well alone," Miss Hallie said mournfully and left the room, pausing only three times to rest one hand on a convenient chair while she pressed the other tenderly over her heart.

Loretta stood watching her until she had disappeared.

Then she laughed—a short, ugly sound that made Antonia flinch. Freddie's pale eyebrows shot up before Loretta turned and smiled at them in her usual diffident fashion.

"Well, three's a cwowd, so I'll run upstairs and tidy a little before dinner," she said and followed Miss Hallie out of the room.

"Well!" Antonia said. "Why did your aunt act like that?"

"She's sore," Freddie said succinctly, "because after being a poor relation for ten years Loretta is going to marry Richard Prince."

"But that is just mean and—and childish."

Freddie shrugged. "Yes, but it's true."

III

"I suspect you're right," Antonia said finally, "but I still think it's disgusting."

Freddie shrugged again. "Aunt Hallie has liked having Loretta around to give charity to and pity, though I was never sure Loretta knew that until just now."

"I suppose that subconsciously Miss Hallie always resented the fact that Loretta lived while Rosalie died. What was Rosalie like, Freddie?"

"I was only eighteen when she died, but I thought she was the prettiest girl I knew. She was small and dimpled and blue-eyed, but I suppose in time she'd have changed along the same lines as Aunt Hallie has. I don't suppose Rosalie was strong on brains either, though she wasn't pig-headed, which Aunt Hallie is sometimes."

"How well you know your aunt."

Freddie flushed. "I know how to handle her, you mean? But if I do use the very best butter on Aunt Hallie what harm does it do? She's been good to me since Rosalie died. She has money, yes, but she must love someone in a maternal way, so why not her nephew instead of some other young man who'd play up to her? Because she would be a push-over for any guy who would, you know."

"I suppose she would. I imagine she'd have loved to have sons. Freddie, I got the impression that Loretta doesn't like Adela Maclean, isn't glad she's going to be here for a while, and doesn't think some of Adela's old friends will be either."

"I agree with you. As I remember Adela, she was a nice-looking girl with what Aunt Hallie

would call 'pretty' manners. But while Rosalie and
Loretta always put up with my jokes or teasing,
Adela had a very firm way with her and a sort of
lion-taming eye."

Freddie stretched and yawned. "Maybe that's
why Bruce Ferrell didn't marry her. Everyone here
thought they would marry, but Adela just went
home very suddenly and Bruce didn't follow her
to Wisconsin. He stayed here and married someone else, so maybe Bruce will be glad to see Adela
again, and then again maybe Bruce won't."

A door slammed and slow weary footsteps came
along the hall. Miss Hallie's brother, Dr. Breck
Carter, entered the room, put his ancient black bag
on a table, and sat down with an explosive sigh.

Antonia frowned at him affectionately. "I
thought that when you took Dr. Maybry into
partnership you weren't going to work so hard.
You were going to improve your golf game, and
goodness knows it needs improvement."

The old doctor chuckled. He was no taller than
his sister, but his fat was hard, healthy fat. He
looked a little like Mr. Winston Churchill and
even more like a slightly exasperated Kewpie. He
was rather asthmatic and given to snorting or
puffing his words.

"You always were an impertinent wench, Toni.
You arrived in this world two weeks early. But I
don't make as many house calls as I used to—"

"No," Freddie said, "now that he has a partner he only keeps the same old office hours and makes calls half the morning and all afternoon."

"Don't go out nights any more," Dr. Carter said testily. Freddie grinned. "Well, not often. I dare say I'll die in harness though. I've the highest opinion of Jimmy Maybry, but when they're bad off my old patients want the old doctor, not the young one. Did you come to dinner, Toni?"

"No, it's blue Monday, so I made a few calls and ended up here. Miss Hallie insisted on ordering tea—"

"So I judged," the doctor said with a disgusted look at the tea table. "And that you ate half a pastry while Hallie ate three or four. Pretty soon she'll be complaining about her heart and be insulted when I tell her it's gas on the stomach. And her blood pressure will go up after a few more tea parties and company dinners."

"Miss Hallie is upstairs lying down. She seems to be very tired very suddenly," Freddie remarked noncommittally.

His uncle grimaced. "So? Loretta with her?"

"She didn't want Loretta," Antonia said bluntly. "She— Doctor, do you know about Loretta?"

"About her and Richard Prince? Yes. I dare say you youngsters can't believe it. Well, it's rather like mating a lion with a dove."

"I always thought Loretta looks more like a sparrow in a high wind," Freddie muttered.

"But you think it's a good thing?"

"Well, Toni—" Dr. Carter took off his glasses, held them six inches away from his nose, and squinted through them thoughtfully.

"Well, Toni, it's a fine thing for Loretta. I dare say she's going about like Cinderella at the ball, wondering when the clock will strike midnight. I hope it never does. Loretta's a good girl. *I* know. Not a mean bone in her body. If there had been she could have—"

"Could have what?" Antonia said.

"Eh? Oh, I was going to say there's more to Loretta than most people think. Unfortunate manner and mannerisms, of course. But Richard Prince has self-assurance enough for two."

He stuck the glasses back on his nose. "I've seen other odd marriages turn out to be very happy ones simply because two people happen to see something in each other that's never visible to anyone else. I hope it's like that with Loretta and Prince."

"I suppose," Antonia said innocently, "that you are looking forward to seeing Adela Maclean again after all these years."

Dr. Carter glanced at her sharply and removed his glasses again. "No, Miss Bright-Eyes, I am not.

I don't think anyone but Hallie is looking forward to seeing Adela again. But that doesn't mean I—"

"I think a car's stopped outside." Freddie sleeked down his already sleek pale hair and got up.

"Maria isn't too quick about answering the doorbell, so maybe I'd better take a look. It might be the Macleans. Come along, Toni. . . ."

The doorbell rang before they reached the front door. The woman standing outside it was, as Freddie had remembered her, "nice-looking." You might even, Antonia admitted, stretch a point and call her pretty if you wanted to be charitable.

But for no good reason Miss Jordan decided that she was not going to like Mrs. Maclean. Her features are all good, but they're screwed too tight, Antonia thought.

Wonderful teeth—of course she sees her dentist four times a year. Correctly dressed for traveling: buys a good suit one year, a good coat the next year, a good black dress every six months. . . .

"Yes, this is little Freddie," Mr. Carter was saying with an unusually inane smile. "Adela, this is Antonia Jordan. Aunt Hallie wasn't feeling very well and she's lying down. I'll call her."

"Indeed you will not," Adela said. "If she is sleeping she must have her nap out. One minute."

She walked back toward the front steps and called into the darkness: "Ian! Just leave the car where it is. The garage is hard to get into when you aren't familiar with it. Freddie will put the car in later. Bring the bags and don't scuff them."

"I'll go help," Freddie said hastily. "Uncle Doc is in the living room. I'll be right back."

"Oh, don't bother, Miss Jordan," Adela said as Antonia made a polite movement toward the living room. "I can find my way. I know this house well."

She doesn't approve of me, Antonia decided. I wonder why? I didn't think this dress was too tight across the breasts, but from the way her eyes flicked me up and down . . .

Freddie, babbling cheerful nothings, held the door open for a tall lean man: six feet two, big-boned and muscular, handling his tall body and three heavy pigskin bags adroitly. His hair was sandy, his eyes bluish-gray, and only a long expressive mouth saved his face from austerity.

He said in an unusually attractive voice that Antonia felt resembled some other voice she knew but couldn't immediately identify:

"I hope we haven't upset any plans you had for this evening. We've driven almost steadily since eight o'clock this morning, but tires are precious now and speeding isn't encouraged."

"I saw your car is a swell job and almost new. You're lucky. My old heap and the tires on it won't last the duration, even with coddling."

Mr. Maclean looked at Mr. Carter with a marked lack of sympathy. "You may congratulate my wife on her foresight," he said bleakly. "On the tenth of December last Adela persuaded her mother to stump up the money for this car as well as six new tires."

"I take it you didn't approve? Well, cheer up. Give the government time and maybe they'll commandeer your car."

"Nothing," Ian said concisely, "would amuse me more."

A door slammed upstairs, and Miss Hallie appeared at the top of the stairway wearing a pea-green negligee foaming with rather soiled laces.

"I did so hear people talking, Loretta! I guess I know when I— Adela!"

She lumbered down the stairs as Adela and Dr. Carter came out of the living room.

"Dear Adela! After all these years—brings it all back—my precious Rosalie—so glad," Miss Hallie said incoherently and dissolved into tears and Adela's arms.

Dr. Carter grinned cynically while Freddie shuffled his feet and passed his hand over his hair. Ian Maclean stood watching his wife and his hostess with, Antonia thought, a completely detached look that encompassed boredom and disillusionment and went deeper than either. I've seen someone else look at people that way, she decided. But who?

Miss Hallie mopped her eyes on her sleeve. "So silly of me."

"No, but you mustn't upset yourself," Adela said. "You and I will have time to talk over everything that worries you."

"Of course. Loretta! They're here!"

There was a definite and distinct silence. Then Loretta's voice floated down the stairs. "Yes, Cousin Hallie. But I'll say how do you do later on." A door closed upstairs, also definitely and distinctly.

Miss Hallie blinked. Adela said hastily:

"This is Ian, Miss Hallie."

"Oh. Oh, of course."

Miss Hallie gathered up her negligee and advanced toward Ian. Her uneasy smile and timidly outstretched hand were exactly those of one confronting a large growling dog.

"I'm so glad to meet dear Adela's husband. What lucky children you are to be on a second honeymoon."

The blue faded out of Ian's eyes, and his jaw muscles tightened at the words "second honeymoon." But he said courteously:

"And I have looked forward to meeting you."

"I dare say these people are starving," Dr. Carter said abruptly.

"Yes. Yes, I reckon they are," Miss Hallie fluttered. "Come right upstairs to your room and we'll have dinner in just a little while."

Antonia watched the procession climb the stairway: Adela with her arm protectively about Miss Hallie's dumpy waist, Ian with two bags, Freddie with one. She turned and addressed Dr. Carter.

"'Wife beater?'" she said. "Oh—rats!"

IV

"Sit wherever you want to," Miss Hallie said. "Adela, you sit next to me and Doc in his usual place and Ian here and Antonia— Oh, I wanted you to sit next to Freddie."

"Sorry." Antonia sat down beside Ian. "Does it matter?"

"Well, of course—" Miss Hallie looked at Adela, and Adela's eyebrows rose sympathetically. "No, it doesn't matter. Sit where you want to, Loretta."

They gave their attention to the soup. By the time the roast beef was before them Adela and Miss Hallie were deep in a series of inquiries after old friends on Adela's part and detailed answers from Miss Hallie. Antonia turned to Ian.

"Shall we begin by my asking you if this is your first visit to California?"

He grinned. "It is. And what will happen if I say disgustedly: 'Sunny California! Hah!'?"

"I would only say that you must have been reading the literature that used to be put out by the
Los Angeles Chamber of Commerce. The war must
hit them very hard since we are no longer allowed
to advertise the weather. But we in San Francisco
and the East Bay have never claimed that our
weather is anything but pretty bad. Besides, this
is only the ninth of March."

"The East Bay being what?" Ian asked.

"Oh, Oakland, Berkeley, Piedmont, Hayward.
We're rugged individualists. We won't let Oakland
or San Francisco swallow us up like Los Angeles
swallowed up Santa Monica, Venice, and so on.
We're in Berkeley now. In case you don't know, it
is the seat of the University of California."

"I do know. And I believe that I may have a
cousin in San Francisco."

"Don't you know?"

Ian shook his head. "I haven't seen him for
fourteen years. I fancy it would be foolish to ask
you if you know a Michael Maclean?"

"Mac—Michael?" Antonia planted her elbows
on the table, her green-blue eyes sparkling. "Of
course! The voices! What does he look like?"

"He was the darkest white man I've ever known
and had the bluest eyes I've ever seen. Slight, wiry,
with a way of walking and holding his head that
some people called arrogant."

Antonia nodded. "Beautiful hands, the longest eyelashes in captivity, a tongue that biteth like the serpent and stingeth like the adder. Well, your Michael Maclean is known to San Francisco as Michael Dundas."

"Dundas? That was our grandmother's maiden name. But it's like Michael to change his name and proceed strictly on his own. You see, after he was sixteen our grandfather was *in loco parentis*. But when Michael was twenty one night he was there and the next morning he wasn't. How has he gotten along in the world?"

"We-ll—do you like this dress I have on?"

"Hmm? Yes, I definitely do. Why?"

"Because Michael designed it. He is an extremely successful *couturier*."

Ian snorted and choked on a morsel of potato. He hastily swallowed some water, leaned back in his chair, and laughed. Adela broke off her conversation with Miss Hallie.

"Miss Jordan must be very witty," she remarked. "Mightn't the rest of us be amused too?"

"No, Della, I don't think you'd be at all amused," Ian said pleasantly.

Freddie looked at Antonia quizzically and with reproachful eyebrows. But he very obligingly began talking across the table to Adela and Miss Hallie. Ian turned back to Antonia.

"I wasn't laughing because Michael is a couturier and I'll wager he makes a very good thing of it."

"Yes. He's well known all up and down the Pacific coast, and lots of women prefer his things to Mainboucher's. Why were you laughing then?"

Ian grinned. "Our grandfather only met one person in his life who was more stubborn than himself, and that was Michael. But Grandfather's pure Scotch, whereas Michael's mother was an Argentinean, so he had also a sort of Latin flexibility that always baffled Grandfather—and all of us.

"I always suspected the old man secretly admired his guts though," Ian said. "I'm fairly certain he put detectives on Michael's trail after he skipped out. He'd never let any of his clan starve or lie in a pauper's grave—"

"But neither would he pass along the word to the Maclean clan that their stray lamb had become a couturier and a dabbler in crime?"

"A—what?"

"An amateur detective. He is always getting mixed up in murder cases. He met his wife during one."

"He's married? Happily?" Ian said with unnecessary intensity.

"Very happily and has a son. You'll find him in the telephone book: Russian Hill Place. Valerie, his wife, and I were sorority sisters at Cal. You see, I'm a completely useless member of society," Antonia said. "I went to college, made my debut, didn't marry. I should be doing war work, but there is nothing I can do that others can't do more efficiently."

"I'd have thought," Ian said, smiling, "that you'd have wangled some sort of job that would allow you to wear a tricky uniform."

"Not me. You should hear Michael on the subject of the type of female war worker who doesn't volunteer unless she is certain there'll be a uniform and it will be becoming. That doesn't mean some women aren't doing hard, thankless work. And of course Michael's the sort who's saddled with all sorts of defense work and doesn't talk about it."

A rawboned maid with a long face whose features seemed to have been left over from at least four other faces began slapping portions of lemon pie, heaped with whipped cream, down before them. Antonia grimaced, ate two mouthfuls, and pushed her plate away.

Miss Hallie, she saw, was devouring her dessert as if she expected the old doctor to snatch it away from her at any minute. Loretta was still pecking at her food as she had all during dinner, though usually she had an astonishingly hearty appetite. I don't believe she's said one word since we sat down, Antonia thought. She turned back to Ian.

"You speak as if you and Michael had been rather good friends. So why—?"

"Why did I never try to locate him? I was only twenty when he left Wisconsin, and young men are self-centered brutes. I let things drift. I had several very uninformative post cards from him in San Francisco, so I knew he was alive. Then after I graduated from college I was a Rhodes scholar. That's no excuse, of course, and tomorrow I will certainly go over to San Francisco—"

"Now, Ian, please don't begin making plans for excursions so soon," Adela said. "Of course we want to see San Francisco, but we've had a long, tiring trip and we'd better rest tomorrow."

"I'm not tired," Ian said curtly.

"But poor Adela is," Miss Hallie said. "Besides, tomorrow night we will have some of Adela's old friends in, and I reckon that will be excitement enough for one day. And I'm afraid I'm a little tired again, myself. So if you don't mind, Adela and I will just go to my room. We can talk a while, dear. I have so many worries, and you are so sensible."

PART TWO

I

Adela was sleeping soundly when Ian left his bed, her hair pinned into a wave-preserving net, her firm mouth a little open. But even asleep, her fingers curled into the palms of her hands.

He had noticed last night that Miss Hallie and Adela had the same kind of hands. Oh, Adela's were firm and smooth while Miss Hallie's were pudgy and flecked with brown spots. But even in moments of idleness and relaxation the short thick fingers curled instinctively into the palms, making tight, possessive little fists. . . .

Ian got into slacks, a warm sweater and sport coat, and went downstairs. The glum maid, Maria, was throwing knives and forks at the dining-room table. She said ungraciously:

"Breakfast at eight."

Ian nodded and went on out of the house. He wanted, like a cat in a strange place, to investigate his surroundings.

Yesterday evening there had been a slight drizzle that Adela had called a "low fog." It had been dark by the time they passed a fantastically gabled building, set in enormous grounds, that Adela said was the Claremont Hotel. And, always instructive, she had pointed out the courts and unpretentious clubhouse of the Berkeley Tennis Club near the hotel.

Afterward they had followed streets that climbed, twisting and turning about the hills, until Adela told him to stop the car. He had said: "But this is the end of nowhere," and Adela answered in her usual literal fashion:

"It's the end of Vincentino Road. Once there was no house nearer than a block away."

Even now there were only two houses close enough to Dr. Carter's to be called neighbors. The doctor's home was, as Ian had suspected, built next to a small ravine. He walked down the front steps, along a path bordered with cacti and shrubs, to where it met and merged with the driveway into the basement garage.

On the other side of the driveway another path disappeared around the left side of the house. Ian followed it and found that it suddenly dipped down a steep bank to a small stream that was probably dry by early summer but gorged with winter rains now.

Trees of a variety he couldn't identify locked fingers over the stream. The path beside it was distinct, and the ravine evidently ran a long way up into the hills. As far as he could see there was nothing except leafless, dripping trees and thick, dripping underbrush.

Ian shivered. This would be very pleasant in summer, but right now it was damned damp, moist, and unpleasant. But he walked on until he came to a small rustic bench tucked into the brush where the path curved and widened.

The back and arms of the bench were scarred with initials, some of them sentimentally encased in crude hearts. Ian bent to look at them, smiling, thinking that this bench must have been here for years.

He looked more closely at one set of initials and then laughed shortly. "A. D.—B. F." Adela Douglas and Bruce Ferrell that would be. He tried to picture Adela sitting here eight years ago watching Bruce Ferrell hack out their initials. But the picture didn't fit in with anything he knew of Adela. It suggested a certain frivolity that he had never detected in her, even before they were married.

But, he thought, walking back along the stream, I always suspected that at least Adela's pride took a fall as the result of knowing Ferrell out here.

She has never talked much about him. It was always Adela's mother who told me that Adela might have married Ferrell. I wonder. When Adela first came home after her visit out here she was— well, say that she was less sure of herself than she ever has been since then. . . .

He reached the driveway and stood absently taking stock of the Carter house. It was a large two-storied, brown-shingled building, garage beneath, an extra half story like a cocked hat in front. There were a few empty flower beds on the right side of the house, in front of a wooden fence with pointed palings. Beyond that was only a rolling hill, skewered with the signs of various real-estate companies, untenanted except for a few scattered houses, lonely against the sky on the hill's crest.

Some other street must lead up to them, Ian thought idly. I don't know why anyone would want to build up there.

He walked to the end of the driveway and stood looking at what he could see of Vincentino Road before it curved away down the hill. There was one house, surrounded by vacant lots, directly across from Dr. Carter's: a white stucco affair with a red tiled roof and a wooden balcony across its upper front.

Around the corner of this house two small figures in Indian suits appeared suddenly and headed for Ian. "Yah, yah! You can't catch me!" the taller of the two chanted. "Yah, yah! Tan't tatch us," the smaller boy echoed.

Ian stopped them with a sweep of his long arms. "Who can't catch you, Sitting Bull?"

"Mummy," Sitting Bull said, pointing.

"Mummy," loping across the street, was dressed in shabby slacks and a faded sweater, neither of which detracted in any way from what Ian instantly labeled "an *Esquire* figure." But the face above the sweater, with its red, red mouth, magnolia-petal skin, and black eyes with a suggestion of a slant, called for more exotic garb. It was inevitable but, in her case, becoming that her blue-black hair should be parted in the middle and knotted at the back of her neck.

"Thanks for grabbing the kids before they got up in the canyon," she said. "They love it up there, but it's too damp now. Little Brother, don't kick the nice man on the shins."

Ian winked tears from his eyes and shoved Sitting Bull, a square-faced, black-browed child, toward his mother. Little Brother, who was a tow-headed cherub, he tucked under one arm.

"You're Adela's husband, aren't you?" the woman asked. "Adela and I are old friends and I'm looking forward to seeing her, though I always thought she was kind of a stinker."

This was said with a calm placidity that left
Ian at a loss for an answer. He finally murmured
something fatuous about young people not always
getting along as well as they should and added:

"But haven't I seen you before?"

"My face on magazine covers and my figure in
Esquire and both in advertisements. More in ads
than anywhere else. Bruce Ferrell's drawings in
Esquire, you know, or little cartoons in the *Post*
and *Collier's*—"

"Then you are Mrs. Ferrell?"

"No, I'm Judith Maybry. My husband is old Dr.
Carter's partner. I just pose for Bruce. Billy, if
you pinch me again I'll slap you. I really will. My
husband doesn't know Adela. He's very anxious to
meet her, though I told him he won't like her, and
he hates to go to dinner at Miss Hallie's. Have you
and Adela any children?"

"No," Ian said briefly.

"That's too bad, though I can't imagine Adela
having a baby. It's not a very ladylike process. I
want a girl next. Bruce and his wife have an awfully cute little girl. They live over there."

Judith pointed toward the first house on the
other side of the ravine. It also stood off to itself,
with the trees that bordered the ravine on one side
and a vacant lot on the other.

"It belonged to Bruce's folks," she remarked. "Most of the older houses in Berkeley are brown shingle with lots of vines. I lived a block or so down when I was a girl, and so did Loretta when her folks were alive."

"Down!" said Little Brother imperatively.

"I want Lulie Mae," Sitting Bull whined and added conversationally: "Bruce."

"What's that, lover? Oh—Bruce. Yes," Judith agreed, looking toward the Ferrell home again, "here comes Bruce."

The man approaching them was tall and he still had several years to go before people would no longer call him "a big man" and pronounce him "fat." But the danger signs were there, Ian thought, though now Ferrell merely had a little too much chest and a faint suggestion of a second chin.

He also had a good deal of carefully disarranged curly light brown hair, light eyes of no particular color, a dimple in his chin, and white teeth which he displayed frequently. "Cock of the barnyard," Ian reflected, perhaps unreasonably, but like most men he could usually recognize the type of male who is dedicated to the proposition that no woman can resist him.

"Well, how's tricks, old-timer?" Mr. Ferrell said jovially.

Sitting Bull answered this inquiry with a rude noise, and Little Brother stuck out his tongue.

"Charming brats, aren't they?" Mr. Ferrell said. "I have an idea you're Adela's husband."

"Yes," said Ian with uncalled-for emphasis, "I am Adela's husband."

"And I'm Bruce Ferrell. Of course Adela has told you all about me, but don't let that prejudice you. I mean to say I'm not a bad guy when you get to know me."

"The name Ferrell is vaguely familiar," Ian said maliciously. "Is there something I should know about you?"

"Bruce meant Adela must have talked a lot about him because they almost got married," Judith said.

Bruce scowled at her. He collared Little Brother, who was trying to climb his leg, and held him out, wriggling and squalling, toward his mother.

"For God's sake, Judy, take this. If I ever saw two kids who were born to be hung—"

"I like them to be happy," Judith said placidly. She scooped Little Brother into her arms. "If you pull Mamma's hair she'll slap you. I mean it."

"Where's their nursemaid?"

"She's always late nowadays. She's going steady with a young man who drives a grocery wagon. He brings her here every morning, but I guess they

park and talk for half an hour first. Lulu Mae's
supposed to come at eight-thirty—"

"Eight-thirty?" Ian repeated. "Good lord! It's
nearly nine and I was told breakfast is at eight. If
you'll excuse me. . ."

Bruce laughed. "You'd better prepare some very
pretty excuses for Miss Hallie."

He waited only until Ian had walked a few steps
away from them to lower his voice and then did
not lower it quite enough.

"Can't you try to make it this afternoon, Judy?"
Ian could not hear what Judith Maybry said, but
he caught Bruce's "No, Evelyn won't be home. She
has some shopping to do. So why does your husband have to know?"

Ian had deliberately stopped in the middle of the
graveled driveway on the pretext of scraping mud
from his feet with a small stick. He thought he
heard Judith murmur something about "Adela." But
before Bruce could answer a car came up the hill.

Ian turned in time to see a slim, childish figure
in a woolly beret and sport coat get down from
the front seat of a grocery truck. Little Brother
and Sitting Bull tore away from their mother and
ran to her.

She put an arm about each of them, said: "Hello,
kids," and went on talking to the truculent-looking

leather-jacketed young man who was driving the truck. Watching her, Ian began to suspect that though she was talking to the delivery boy the smile that brought out the dimple in her cheek might be aimed at Bruce Ferrell.

Lulu Mae was, he thought paternally, a pretty child, but she was also as demure as a drawing-room-comedy maid. Mr. Ferrell was grinning appreciatively, and the young man in the truck was beginning to scowl when Lulu Mae finally dismissed him.

"Thanks for the ride, Jerry. You'd better go on or you'll be late for work."

The grocery truck lumbered away. "You're late, Lulu Mae," Judith Maybry said.

"Yes'm. Do you want I should take the kids out as soon as I get them in warmer things? You see which one of you can get to the house first, boys."

Sitting Bull tore away instantly with Little Brother chugging after him. "Yes, take them out before lunch too," Judith said. "But not up in the canyon, Lulu Mae. It's too damp."

"Yes'm," Lulu Mae said and followed the Maybry offspring into the house while Judith lingered in the street a few minutes longer with Bruce Ferrell.

Ian's last glimpse of them showed Bruce frowning, talking rapidly, while Judith regarded him with a faint provocative smile. . . .

II

Miss Hallie said stiffly that it didn't matter at all that Ian was "over an hour late to breakfast, though Maria says she told you when we always have it, and poor Adela has been worried."

After five minutes of this Ian decided not to insist on carrying through his own plans for the day when he found that Adela already had that day mapped out for him. He was turned over to Freddie for a personally conducted tour of the University of California grounds, Piedmont, and Oakland.

They lunched in Oakland, and after Ian had won an amiable argument regarding the luncheon check Freddie remarked:

"The women wanted us out of the house. I think Adela is looking into the housekeeping. Aunt Hallie always has trouble with servants."

"Our servants never stay with us very long," Ian said candidly. "According to Adela, they are a most immoral and ungrateful lot. So you may have no cook by this evening."

"I wouldn't break down and weep if there was no cook and no jolly get-together of Adela's old pals," Freddie said with equal candor.

"Why?"

"You'll find out. When this bunch gets together there are—well, undercurrents. And maybe they'll all be glad to see Adela again."

"But perhaps they won't? Oh," Ian said as Freddie flushed and made embarrassed noises, "I know that people thought Adela would marry Bruce Ferrell. Having met him, I've been wondering if his wife will be especially delighted to meet Adela."

"You would, naturally. But Evelyn Ferrell isn't jealous, even though she's older than Bruce. You'll understand when you meet Evelyn. This gang sees a lot of each other and Uncle Doc and Aunt Hallie, but they—well, you'll see," Freddie prophesied. "And I've got to get to my office. I can't risk being late for dinner tonight."

Ian grinned. "I fancied you were also in the doghouse this morning."

Freddie grimaced. "I made Aunt Hallie ask Toni to dinner tonight. I don't know why she objected. I thought I'd finally picked out a girl that she approved of, but since last night . . . Well, I'll drop you at Uncle Doc's office first before I go home to pick up some papers. You know lawyers get quite a lot of income-tax work."

"Perhaps your clients think it is safest to consult a lawyer before they file their return instead of having to consult one afterward?"

"That used to be the idea, though people are being pretty patriotic about it this year. You and Uncle Doc are going to play golf together, and I warn you, you'd better watch him like a hawk.

Don't take his word for how many strokes he took on a hole. . . ."

Nevertheless, Ian enjoyed the hours he spent on the Berkeley links with Dr. Carter. The old man would have been indignant if you had accused him of cheating. He expected his opponent to follow suit and lop a few strokes off every hole, and his remarks during his frequent excursions into the rough were pleasingly lurid. They reached home a little after four. Dr. Carter beckoned to Ian with an exaggerated air of stealth and led the way down the hall, past the stairway, into a small room crammed with medical tomes, tattered classics, a large desk, and several cabinets with glass doors. He unlocked one of these and dug a bottle of scotch out from behind a jar in which someone's gallstones had been preserved.

"My room," he said, pouring whisky. "Hallie calls it the library when she wants to impress strangers. Drink up, my boy."

They came out into the hall again just as Adela descended the stairs from the second floor. Her nostrils widened disapprovingly.

"Yes, we just had a drink," Dr. Carter said robustly. "Could I give you one? You look tired."

"I am. I'd meant to rest today, but there are so many little things that have been worrying Miss Hallie. What a pity Loretta hasn't made herself

more useful. A house like this is a great care, and
Miss Hallic is so anxious that her menfolk should
be comfortable and—"

Ian cut sharply across Adela's smooth voice.
"Have the servants given notice?"

"Ian, that sounded almost rude, though I know
you didn't mean to be. The cook has given notice.
Well, what do you expect?" Adela said reasonably
as Dr. Carter snorted. "Do you know that I discovered a dozen empty rum bottles in the pantry?"

"Rum? Well, I'll be damned."

Ian grinned. Briefly, the picture of Adela un-
earthing rum bottles in the pantry amused him.
He might guess that Adela's research would
affect tonight's dinner. He could not be expected
to guess that the cook's fondness for rum would
vitally affect his life.

"Yes," Adela said, "the creature reeked of it this
morning. She drinks it in tea. Miss Hallie can't
have a woman like that in the house even if she
does have two sons in the army."

"She had three," Dr. Carter said. "The third
one was at Pearl Harbor."

"Oh. Well, that is very regrettable but quite beside the point. I've persuaded the maid, Maria, to
stay, though there are two silver spoons missing."

"I dare say Maria is staying on because she needs
this job so badly that she can't afford to resent the
suggestion that she has pocketed two spoons."

"Really, Dr. Carter! It's the family silver, and I did not accuse Maria of stealing it," Adela said. "I am convinced she was only careless and threw the spoons out with the garbage. And I wanted to tell you that Miss Hallie doesn't feel well and I've persuaded her to lie down."

"Oh—damn! Well, I'll take a look at her."

Dr. Carter stumped heavily up the stairs. "I don't believe," Adela said thoughtfully, "that it is wise to consult a member of your own family when you need a doctor. . . . Ian, I know you don't realize it, but lately you look at people in such a peculiar way sometimes. I'm sure it gives them the wrong impression of you, and you don't want that—"

"Having fun, Adela?" Ian asked.

"Really, Ian! Dr. Carter must have given you a very strong drink. I don't—"

"Adela!" Dr. Carter called. "Come up here. . . . Hallie had better lie down until she has to dress for dinner. She's been overeating lately."

"She said," Adela interrupted disapprovingly, "that she felt dizzy."

"May I do the doctoring for this family, Adela? Naturally her blood pressure is up. Also, your activities this morning have excited her. Let her have a good nap, and if she has any more worries to unload on you please don't do anything about them until tomorrow. That is, if you don't want me to call off this dinner tonight."

He went back into Miss Hallie's big front bed-room which was directly across the hall from the one Ian and Adela occupied. Adela waited until they were in it before she said regretfully:

"Poor Dr. Carter has failed so much in the last eight years. You have no idea—"

"I have an idea that Judith Maybry was right when she said you're rather a stinker, Adela."

"Judith said that! About *me!*" But Adela never dispersed her energies by anger, though her eyes narrowed. "That's very amusing and very unwise of Judith. She should remember that I knew her before she ever married this Dr. Maybry. Will you want a bath, Ian?"

"Yes, I think so. I had a rather sketchy shower when we finished playing golf."

"Then do take it now and put your towels in the clothes hamper and don't lie and soak for hours and get the room all steamed up—"

"And don't forget to wash behind the ears," Ian finished.

Adela gave him the blank look she kept for his jokes or any facetious remarks he might make.

"Don't be childish, Ian. Your shirts are in the second bureau drawer. Take the one on top."

"Good God! Would it be a world-shaking calamity if just once I took the bottom shirt or the one in the middle!"

"Ian, you are shouting. You know it's much better to rotate one's clothing."

Ian struggled with the laces of his heavy sport
shoes and finally managed to unknot them. When
he spoke again it was, with a conscious effort,
more pleasantly.

"And what are you going to do, Adela?"

"I'll go for a little walk. I've been in the house
all day, and you know how I depend on my daily
walk to keep me fit. I'll take a stroll around the
neighborhood now.

III

Returning from the bathroom, Ian laid down
across his bed, still in his bathrobe. He did not
intend to sleep, but when he jerked upright again
it was six o'clock and there were voices outside
the door that he apparently had not quite closed.

"So," one of them was saying, "if you want an
explanation, that'th it. Of course you wouldn't
understand. I didn't expect that. So let'th not discuss it."

Ian recognized Loretta's lisp and then Adela's
determinedly well-bred Middle Western voice.

"But I think we must discuss it again. Not now,
but—"

Ian did not hear Loretta move away, but Adela
didn't finish her sentence, and after an instant

a door slammed toward the back of the house. He got up, tiptoed to the guest-room door, and looked into the hall.

Adela had moved too. She was standing near the top of the stairway now, turned half away from him, forefinger pressed against her lips. That always meant that Adela was making some decision.

Finally she smiled: a small complacent smile. Ian saw her nod briskly before she turned in his direction as if she felt someone was watching her. He dodged quickly back into the bedroom.

When he ventured another look into the hall Adela was gone. He could hear the murmur of voices now in some other bedroom. But he supposed that, with dinner at seven, everyone must be dressing now.

When he had finished dressing he opened the door again. At first it seemed that Adela might never have moved. She was standing in the same place near the stairway, directly under one of the hall lights.

Then Ian saw that she was studying something— the palm of her own hand, apparently. After an instant the palm curled shut and the hand went into a pocket of the sport coat she was wearing. She saw Ian and hurried down the hall.

"I was just seeing how Miss Hallie is."

"Were you?"

"Why do you use that tone of voice, Ian? She is much better now. And I must hurry or I might keep people waiting. Fortunately it doesn't take *me* very long to dress."

Ian could not deny that, but after fifteen minutes or so it struck him that Adela was taking unusual pains with her dressing tonight. He said, with no other thought than to establish pleasant relations:

"All this for Bruce Ferrell?"

"What vulgar minds men have. I hope that I am always well groomed. Naturally I don't want any of my old friends to be able to criticize my looks."

"I was only joking, Della," Ian said wearily and sat down in a chair by the big front window.

He did not smoke: you didn't in Adela's bedroom. Yet she considered separate rooms the first step toward the divorce court. Respectable married couples used the same room, though as a concession to modernity it might contain twin beds. This in spite of the fact that Adela was the complete prude. She called it "being modest."

She was very well pleased with herself tonight, Ian realized suddenly. The last hair was in place, the small string of "good pearls" clasped about the "good black dress," but she still sat at the dressing table with her nail file in one hand.

Ian found himself watching the hand and the silver-handled file. Adela balanced it across her

palm, staring at it, moving the hand ever so slightly up and down as if calculating the weight of the
object across it.

For perhaps five minutes she made no other
movement. Then the tenacious fingers tightened
about the nail file and Adela smiled to herself.
Not so much complacently this time as regretfully.
But Ian knew that smile too. It meant that Adela
saw her duty and meant to do it.

He was never certain what he might have said
to her if Miss Hallie had not rapped on their door
just then. Adela got up quickly.

"Yes, we're dressed. We— Oh, Ian! *Not* that tie
with *that* shirt."

"Go ahead then. I'll change."

"The plain blue one," Adela specified. "And perhaps your suit could do with a little brushing. . . ."

Ian took his time yanking off the offending tie,
knotting the plain blue one, using the clothes-
brush, asking himself: "Who has Adela got her
knife out for now?" When he reached the living
room everyone was holding cocktail glasses filled
with tomato juice.

Judith Maybry, in a nearly backless white gown,
was admiring Loretta's engagement ring. "Who'd
have expected you to do so well for yourself, Loretta? But it's nice you have after all these years."

Ian heard someone chuckle and found Antonia beside him: Antonia in a sage-green dinner dress with a flaming red girdle.

"You are probably wondering," she murmured, "if Judy is deliberately malicious or merely says what she thinks. That's a moot question. Have you met everyone?"

"Everyone but Mrs. Ferrell and Dr. Maybry."

"He isn't here yet," Judith said. "We'd better not wait for him. He's on a baby case, and babies are a long time coming sometimes."

Miss Hallie blushed, giving the impression that she considered Judith had been slightly obscene.

"We certainly will not wait for Jimmy," she declared. "He must take what is left when he gets here."

"I'm very sorry Dr. Maybry is late," Adela said. "I am looking forward to meeting him. I believe I saw him this afternoon when I was out walking. A man with a doctor's bag came out of the house opposite this one and got into a car. Of course he didn't know who I was. I hope he won't be so tired that he will decide not to come over after all."

"There won't be anything for him to eat at home if he gets back so early that he hasn't eaten somewhere else. So he'll probably come over, though otherwise he'd rather go to bed," Judith said simply.

Miss Hallie looked mortally offended. Antonia said quickly:

"Ian hasn't met Evelyn."

Adela's cold eyes impaled her briefly. "I was just going to introduce my husband to Mrs. Ferrell, Miss Jordan."

Antonia returned the look with interest and a derisive grin. "Just call me Toni, Mrs. Maclean. Evelyn, this is Ian."

For no good reason Ian had expected to see another Adela in Evelyn Ferrell. And Evelyn was wearing what would also be called a "good black dress," in contrast to Judith's revealing, shabby evening gown, Antonia's creation by Gisele, and Loretta's limp, beruffled chiffon that was not quite a dinner dress and not quite an evening gown.

On the other hand, though women would probably suggest that Evelyn Ferrell was a shade too plump, any normally speculative male would decide that she would look very well wearing no clothes at all. And though her voice was also low and controlled, it had a warmth that Adela's would never have.

As her dinner partner Ian had opportunity to observe Evelyn closely. Loretta, on his other side, was monosyllabic, but Evelyn was an expert dinner conversationalist.

Ian let himself be borne easily along on the smooth tide of her small talk. He realized, with a slight sensation of surprise, that she had red hair. But it was so dark a red as to look almost black in some lights, and her way of wearing it, in a thick braid pinned firmly around her head, did nothing to enhance its color or texture.

She's a very restful woman,. Ian decided. Her eyes, roving over the table, often smiled when her lips did not. Detachment: that's what she has, he thought. And she looks at Bruce the way I find myself looking at Adela sometimes.

The food was nourishing, uninspired, and not so well cooked as it had been last night before the cook was under notice. Spring lamb, green peas, marbly new potatoes, jelly with a slight mint flavor.

They talked of taxes and black-outs; of sugar and tire rationing; the fall of Java and Rangoon. They wondered what would happen in Russia in the spring. They spoke of Douglas MacArthur and Bataan Peninsula and the possibility that he might be sent to Australia. . . .

The only laughter came from Freddie and Antonia and from unspecified causes in spite of Miss Hallie's frequent, plaintive "Something funny? Why not tell us all so we can laugh too?"

But except for the presence of a couple as young as Freddie and Antonia, the dinner was cut from the same piece as hundreds of others, stodgy and sedate, that Ian had sat through in his own home. Until, that is, upon Adela's referring to something that she must do "when we get home," Judith inquired interestedly:

"Oh, then you and Ian aren't going to get a divorce after all?"

IV

Adela looked, Ian decided impersonally, as if she had just discovered a fly in the gravy. And that his nerves must be a trifle frayed when his only reaction was a strong desire to laugh. He realized that Adela had given him a chance to wither Judith before she said:

"You are both misinformed and impertinent. If you weren't— I don't believe in divorce."

"Even when you were young you had that 'till-death-do-us-part' idea, didn't you?" Judith said reflectively. "You even actually thought that no nice girl ever went in for necking or anything like that. You haven't changed."

Judith's question had thrown Miss Hallie into a flutter she couldn't pull out of. Miss Hallie realizes that now Adela will know that she has told everyone here why we've gone through this

nauseating farce of a second honeymoon, Ian
thought. I might have guessed that Adela's mother
would write Miss Hallie all the details. . . . He
realized that Judith was speaking directly to him.

"Don't you believe in divorce either?"

"I think," Ian said, "that it might be dangerous
not to, Mrs. Maybry."

"Dangerous not to what?"

"Dangerous not to believe in divorce," Ian said.

Fortunately at that moment Maria ushered Dr.
Maybry into the dining room. Dr. Carter indicated the chair next to his own.

"Sit here, Jimmy. Maria will bring your soup."

"No, Jimmy doesn't deserve any soup, getting
here so late," Miss Hallie said. "He will just have
to put up with roast lamb and try to catch up with
the rest of us."

"That will do very nicely," Maybry said, and to
the old doctor's "How did it go?" he returned a
brief "The child died."

"Too bad," Dr. Carter said sympathetically. "It
was her or the child? I was afraid of that."

"Now we just won't have that kind of talk at
the table," Miss Hallie broke in. "If Jimmy wants
you to tell him what he did wrong you can do it
later, Doc."

"Don't be a damned fool, Hallie," her brother
said rudely.

Dr. Maybry shrugged despondently. He was a slight man of thirty-five or so: the type that merely shrinks with the years, becoming more spare, more dry, more lined. His black hair was already gray over the temples. He had deep-set brown eyes, a small black mustache, and at times a nervous trick of trying to catch it between his teeth.

He and Dr. Carter were soon engaged in low-toned professional talk. Ian turned to Evelyn Ferrell.

"I can't remember if Adela has told me anything about you." That was seizing conversation by the throat but the best he could manage. Evelyn laughed.

"Very little, I imagine. I'm not one of the neighborhood gang like Bruce, Loretta, Judith, and Miss Hallie's Rosalie. I'm older than Bruce and I was married to someone else when Adela was here before. I don't think we met more than twice.

"You see, Miss Hallie's Rosalie and I had been friends: the way a young girl and a young married woman often are friends. But that didn't last after Adela came here to visit Rosalie."

Adela would see to that, Ian thought. He said: "And Dr. Maybry isn't one of the old gang, I believe?"

"No, Jimmy practiced in Oakland for a while. None of us knew him until he began working with

Dr. Carter, moved to Berkeley, and married Judy. But Adela seemed quite anxious to meet Jimmy," Evelyn added thoughtfully.

"Don't you think," Loretta said unexpectedly, "that women usually want to see what sort of man the girl they were always jealous of has married? Hoping she's just thrown herself away, as they say? Of course I don't mean just Adela. We were all a little jealous of Judy when we were girls."

Evelyn smiled. "I can easily understand that. But Judith isn't vain, you know. Loretta, if you'll come over to see me whenever you can, I'll help you plan your trousseau."

"Oh," Loretta said with her diffident smile, "it will hardly be a trousseau, but I do want to do the best I can with my poor little savings."

Ian stuck a smile on his face and kept it there as they went on talking across him, but he was watching his wife again. She had had two distinct jolts within the last few minutes: his own and Judith's remarks about divorce. Ordinarily that would have turned Adela to a frigid statue of martyred womanhood for the rest of the evening.

But Adela was still pleased with herself. She was done eating and for an instant let herself forget her social responsibilities. She looked slowly about the table with a small tight smile.

As Ian translated that smile it was triumph savored beforehand. This was one of the rare moments when Adela was not giving a performance based upon her conception of Adela. . . .

Ian drank his coffee quickly and tried to believe he was being fanciful. When he looked at his wife again she had remembered what was due to her spotless character. Her smile was now nobly sad, sweetly regretful. She is thinking, Ian decided, "But I must do my duty, no matter how unpleasant it is."

Miss Hallie rapped on the table with her coffee spoon. Bridge was the next order of the evening. Antonia promptly refused to play, and Loretta was as quickly excused by Miss Hallie.

"Loretta can't keep her mind on cards, so she doesn't need to play. But that still leaves nine. Maybe Freddie and Antonia would play three-handed with Loretta, though I like to play with Freddie."

"Count me out," Ian said, "and that leaves you just two tables."

"Oh, of course you want to play," Adela said. "He is only being polite, Miss Hallie. He loves bridge and would rather play—"

"My dear," Ian said with elaborate courtesy, "would you allow me, this once, to know what I would rather do? I would rather not play bridge."

"I don't like bridge, but I'll play," Judith said. "But not with Jimmy. He's too good for me."

"Evelyn's more his style," Bruce said. "You play with me, Judy."

"If Jimmy doesn't mind playing with me," Evelyn said quickly.

"What? Oh." Maybry gave up biting at his mustache and smiled briefly. "Of course not, Evelyn. Bruce is right: a husband and wife shouldn't play games together. It's much more amusing to play games with someone else's husband or wife."

"Regular love feast, isn't it?" Freddie muttered to Ian, escorted his aunt hastily to a chair at one of the card tables, and was so solicitous for her comfort that Miss Hallie had no time to analyze Maybry's remark.

Antonia, invited to kibitz, sat down at Freddie's elbow. Ian retired to a chair near a window and pretended to read a newspaper after Loretta wandered away to the piano at the other end of the room.

It was a large room and needed to be, to contain eleven people and all the furniture necessary to Miss Hallie's happiness. There were three big front windows and on one side of the room double glass doors covered with heavy black curtains.

Miss Hallie had gone that far in blacking out the room before she decided that it had too many windows and that it would be less expensive to put Bristol board over the one window in the doctor's little study.

Presently Ian threw down the newspaper and sat listening to the cardplayers. Loretta was playing the piano very softly. She played well, Ian thought, and then, after watching her for a moment, that she did not look at all ineffectual now. . . .

The room was growing uncomfortably warm. As if she guessed his thought, Antonia got up.

"Come out to the balcony and get a breath of fresh air," she suggested.

"What balcony?"

"Here." Antonia opened one of the black-curtained glass doors. "See? Shall I close the door, Miss Hallie?"

Miss Hallie, trying to make six no trump, said absently: "Yes, there's quite a draft."

Antonia pulled the door shut after them. "There. I wish I could furnish a moon, but even if it wasn't foggy it wouldn't have risen yet." She put her elbows on the balcony railing. "It's nice here when the honeysuckle is in bloom. Did you see Michael today?"

"No. I wanted to go over to San Francisco, but I found that my day had been planned for me."

"I know," the girl said sympathetically. "I haven't mentioned Michael to anyone. I got the idea last night that you wouldn't be telling your wife you'd located your long-lost cousin."

"I haven't. Adela probably wouldn't remember Michael if they ever met, but she has heard of the family black sheep and she doesn't approve of black sheep. So . . . ." Ian shrugged. "And since we are being frank, when are you and Freddie going to be married?"

"You're taking more for granted than Freddie does. And Miss Hallie doesn't think I'm worthy of him, though I had thought she'd decided I'd do, since nothing better has come along. But I've detected traces of frost in her manner this evening. Would your wife have anything to do with that?"

"If Adela doesn't like you she could have a great deal to do with it," Ian said honestly. "She and Miss Hallie have certainly had at least one long confidential talk since we arrived. But does it matter?"

"What Miss Hallie thinks of me? Not that much!" Antonia snapped her fingers. "And sometimes I think I'd better marry Freddie since I'm twenty-five and have nothing better to do."

"For God's sake, don't!" Ian said harshly. "Don't ever marry anyone to be obliging or because it is expected of you!"

"Oh? So that's the way it was?"

"That's the way it was. And of course the situation as it stands is absurd in this day of easy divorce. But there have always been complications that— Don't you think we'd better just inhale the night air?"

"Well . . ." Antonia turned so that her soft shoulder was against his and her hair brushed his cheek. "Look at the shadows."

Ian pulled her close to him and kissed her roughly, almost impersonally. Then: "I don't know why I did that," he began. "I—"

"I do," Antonia said coolly though her lips trembled a little. "I almost asked you to and you are unhappy and I'm pretty and you haven't kissed anyone like me for years. Any pretty girl would do. It's all right—and a fair exchange is no robbery."

She put her arms about his neck and her mouth against his. Ian grasped her eagerly. If he kissed her more gently this time he also kissed her more thoroughly and not at all impersonally. When he let her go she smiled ruefully.

"Well, maybe that will teach me not to be impulsive. Because wasn't it just our bad luck that Freddie should decide to join us?"

"What!" Ian turned toward the doors into the living room. One of them was not quite closed now.

"Yes," Antonia said, "I opened my eyes, just coming up for air, and at least half the assembled company saw us before Freddie closed the door like a little gent. Well, after a decent interval we'll go in, very blasé and nonchalant."

V

Ian saw at once that Freddie was still pink, that there was an ugly purplish flush over Adela's cheekbones, and that Dr. Carter was frowning heavily at his cards. Well, that makes three who saw us, he reflected.

Then Bruce Ferrell grinned at him like, Ian thought unreasonably, one amorous tomcat to another. So that makes four. Thank God Miss Hallie's back is to the balcony. . . .

Antonia sat down, making no attempt to be too offhand. It takes a woman to carry off this kind of thing, Ian thought. He was sure that he had re-entered the room with all the aplomb of a dog just caught sucking eggs.

Judith's back had also been to the balcony. She put down her hand for Bruce to play, yawned, and spoke to her husband.

"Jimmy, I think we'd better be getting home. Lulu Mae is with the children, but I want you to take a look at Bobby."

"What tree has Bobby fallen out of now?" Maybry inquired.

"He hasn't. I think he's getting a cold. Lulu Mae brought him home with damp feet this afternoon. She said he waded in a puddle. Of course he does do that," Judith admitted, "but I'm not sure Lulu Mae didn't take them up to the canyon even though I told her not to. She kept them out too late too."

"Well, my dear, I'll look at our youngest." Maybry finessed a ten-spot. "But there's no sure preventative for the common cold. Oh yes," he added as Dr. Carter chuckled, "I give cold shots if people want to take them, but—"

"You don't give your own children cold shots," Judith remarked. "Isn't there a saying about doctors' wives dying young?"

"You needn't worry," Maybry said dryly. "I've never known a healthier human than you, Judith."

"But I meant the children. You never know if there's anything wrong with them."

"It's a wise child that knows its own father," Bruce said with the laugh that Ian had already noticed was so abrupt as to be nearly explosive. Then he turned an unhealthy red. "I mean: it's an unusual doctor that pays any attention to the ailments of his own youngsters."

"Why, Jimmy!" Miss Hallie cried. "You trumped Evelyn's ace! Whatever on earth made you—? Why, you look sick. So pale and—"

"Aunt Hallie, I know you want a drink of water," Freddie said hastily. "Let me get you one."

"Well, if you would, dearie." Miss Hallie preened herself. "You do look after your old aunt, don't you? Would anyone else like a drink? I reckon there's some ginger ale and— Good gracious!"

The lights went out. Freddie shouted from the general direction of the dining room: "Is someone being funny or is that the fuse?"

"It must be the fuse!" Dr. Carter shouted back. "You'll have to put in a new one."

"Then where the hell are they?"

"Freddie! There are some fuses in the dining-room sideboard," Miss Hallie said. "Haven't you a flashlight, darling?"

"Oh, I always carry one in my pocket," Freddie returned rather sulkily. "No. Where are all our flashlights? We bought four after Pearl Harbor. I don't seem to have any matches."

"Candles!" Miss Hallie shrieked. "In the sideboard, Freddie. And matches in the kitchen."

"O.K. I'll— Damn!" There was a sound that suggested that Freddie had blundered into a chair and knocked it over.

"I'll come help you," Dr. Carter said. "I left my flash in my car."

"It's funny your fuse blows out so easy," Judith said. "It went out another time when we were playing bridge here. . . . I don't like sitting still in the dark. I bet I can find my way upstairs."

"Oh no, Judith," Miss Hallie fluttered. "All of you just sit still. Oh, dear, I wish you would all sit still and not wander around! And don't strike matches! I'm so afraid of fire. Why don't you—? Freddie! Freddie dear!"

"I can't find any spare fuses," Freddie shouted.

"I'm perfectly sure they're in the sideboard, dear, but maybe they're in the kitchen linen closet, and I suppose we may not have any— Ow!" said Miss Hallie protestingly. "Who was that?"

Ian heard a succession of the small jingling sounds that he already associated with Loretta and her many bangles and bracelets. No one was obeying Miss Hallie. Chairs scraped back; an ash tray clattered to the floor; Dr. Maybry uttered a disgusted "Damn!" that was drowned out by Bruce's violent laugh. Evelyn said:

"We should go home, anyway. I have a flashlight upstairs in my purse, and Dr. Carter and Freddie seem to be in difficulties."

"Any luck?" the old doctor was rumbling.

"Ouch! That's the third time I've burned my fingers with these matches. No, I can't find a fuse or candles.

Ian remembered an extra flashlight, besides the one they carried in the car, that Adela had put in his suitcase. He got up and felt his way toward the door into the hall. Others were doing the same thing; at least twice he felt that he narrowly escaped colliding with someone.

Once he located the stairway it was easy going. He reached the guest room before he remembered that Adela had already unpacked their suitcases. He lighted a match and looked into the bureau drawer that held his clothing, shrugged, and gave up the search. He knew that Adela's idea of where to put an object that might be urgently needed was never his. . . .

He realized suddenly as he groped his way back toward the stairs that Adela hadn't spoken after the lights went out. That was odd. Ordinarily she would have been prompt to issue orders and make efficient suggestions. Sulking, probably.

When he reached the lower hall again he guessed that several people must have joined Dr. Carter and Freddie in the dining room. Mr. Carter sounded thoroughly exasperated now.

"There are no candles in the sideboard, Aunt Hallie!" he bellowed. "And there are no fuses!"

From the living room Miss Hallie insisted tearfully that there must be fuses—unless she was mistaken or had forgotten to order them. And there certainly must be candles somewhere. . . .

Ian was no longer listening to her. Somewhere in the back part of the hall, around the corner of the stairway.

Adela was speaking. Her voice was very low; it was probably only because he was so familiar with it that he could make out her words.

"But you haven't changed, you see. And I've watched you very closely all evening. I never act hastily."

At that instant Dr. Carter let out a triumphant whoop that drowned out Adela's voice.

"Here's a fuse! Freddie, you go down and put it in. I might break my neck on those damned basement steps."

Miss Hallie's voice, calling plaintively: "I told you there was a fuse. Freddie dear, be careful," and then Adela again, from the blackness beyond the stairs:

"I hope I know my duty. You can't say I didn't take this opportunity to warn you. I have all the proof that's needed, so don't expect me to pity you."

A door banged in the basement beneath them, and Miss Hallie asked foolishly: "Freddie, you haven't fallen down the basement stairs?"

Ian thought that someone had answered Adela in an urgent whisper: man's or woman's voice, there was no telling which. It was still a full minute before the lights flashed on. When he rounded the stairway and looked down the hall Adela was just going through a door at the end of it.

Ian followed her. He discovered that the door led into the kitchen and that one of the kitchen doors opened into the dining room. Someone had had plenty of time to leave Adela and reach the dining room that way before the lights came on.

And everyone was there, everyone but Miss Hallie, Loretta, and Freddie. In an instant the two women came in together and Freddie was heard clattering up the basement steps. . . .

VI

Adela took off her dress, hung it carefully, wrong side out, on a padded hanger, and arranged a cellophane shoulder cover over it. She took off her shoes and put shoe trees in them, removed her stockings, went into the bathroom, and washed them and her face in tepid water.

Then she loosened the straps of her slip, put her nightgown over her head, turned her back to Ian, and wriggled out of girdle and underclothing. When she had arranged these neatly across a chair she put on a shapeless robe, sat down, and brushed her hair fifty strokes.

That was only half the nightly allowance, but by the time she had muttered "—and fifty," Ian was plumping up the pillow on his bed. Tonight he had resolved that it rested with Adela to cast the first stone. She held her brush poised over the unbrushed half of her hair and began:

"Ian, I cannot understand you calmly preparing to go to sleep after what happened tonight."

"It isn't my fault that the fuse blew out," Ian said significantly.

Adela glanced at him sharply. "Where were you when—? Well, that's beside the point. You and that girl! Even if you have no respect for yourself you might have some for me. Humiliating me when you were meeting my old friends for the first time!"

"That was unfortunate and I'm sorry that it turned out that way," Ian said truthfully.

"I should hope so. Oh," Adela said in a pitying tone that was more irritating than forthright reproach, "I know that the girl threw herself at you. I saw at once that she's no better than she should be."

She passed her tongue over her lips, and the hand holding the brush trembled slightly. "The bold way she looks at people and the clothes she wears—the flaunting way she wears them—"

"What nasty minds we good women have," Ian drawled.

Adela dropped her hairbrush. "Mother was right: you aren't well. If you were you wouldn't—"

"Come off it, Adela! I'm not even slightly potty. You remember that your mother didn't manage to hustle me off to a sanitarium. I told her that my health did not require a vacation but that I was willing to take one." He laughed. "Second honeymoon! As if our first hadn't been a painful enough affair."

"Oh! Oh," Adela whispered. "You know I've always—"

"I know you've always done your wifely duty and never failed at the same time to make me feel one of the lower orders of animal. But you can't help that. You're a married old maid, Adela, and as we are neither lovers nor friends I fail to see why two acquaintances should go on living together because they were once fools enough to marry."

"Fools! I married you because I loved you!"

"You married me because I was eligible and, to your way of thinking, to be unmarried stamps a woman as unsuccessful," Ian retorted. "You wanted a house and chest of linen and 'Mrs.' before your name. What a pity you had to marry a man to get those things."

"I've been a good wife to you."

"O God—yes! Routine and method and well-planned meals and self-improvement and systematic saving—"

"You talk like a crazy man," Adela said flatly. "What *do* you want?"

"I want a divorce. This trip was your idea and it's been fatal. You insisted on exposing me to more than a week of your unadulterated company, traveling all day long, cooped up in a car together. Evidently," Ian said, coming over behind her and staring at her face in the mirror, "you don't understand that I dislike you intensely. You bore and irritate me to the point of nausea. Women like you should be strangled at birth."

"Ian! You—you frighten me. And you're speaking very loudly."

Ian laughed. "I frighten you?" he said in a lower voice. "Nothing frightens you, Adela. And I want an answer!"

"An answer?" Ian gripped her shoulder roughly. "Very well," Adela said without wincing, "I won't give you a divorce. If you try to get one I'll enter countersuit, and Miss Antonia Jordan's name will be in it for alienation of affections."

"You—" Ian shook her. "You can't get away with a thing like that!"

"I think I can," Adela said coolly. "Everyone saw that disgusting exhibition tonight. If you merely desert me I'll still let it be known that you left me because of Miss Jordan. I've no pity for her, but Miss Hallie says her parents are very nice people, so— Ian, you're crushing my shoulder!"

Ian released her. If she was not frightened he was. For an instant there had been an actual red haze of rage before his eyes. He had wanted to put his hands about her throat and tighten them. . . . He stumbled over to his bed and sat down.

"All right," he said finally. "I know you'd do just what you threaten. It wouldn't occur to you that you may have made a dangerous decision: dangerous to your own life."

"You're talking too loudly again, Ian. Anyone in the bathroom could hear you. I should think you had caused me enough embarrassment to-night. And I'll risk the danger"—she smiled pity-ingly and picked up her hairbrush—"because I know this won't last, Ian. This is only a phase. Your better nature will reassert itself, and then you'll thank me—"

"I'll thank you to turn off the record," Ian said through set teeth.

He got into bed and turned his back to Adela. Presently the lights went out, but not until Adela had given her hair its other fifty strokes.

When he was quite certain that there was no chance of his sleeping and thought that Adela might be he got up very quietly and put on his clothes. He had no idea what time it was: whether ten minutes or an hour had passed since he got into bed.

But the house was as quiet as an old house that moved and groaned in its sleep could ever be. He reached the front door without mishap and then hesitated. As he had no latchkey there was nothing for it but to release the latch and leave the door unlocked. Perhaps he shouldn't do that.

Oh, the hell with it! he thought, turned the latch off, and stepped outside. Freddie had remarked this morning that the old doctor was very careless about "locking up. He hardly ever locks the garage doors because it takes time to unlock them when he's called out on an emergency case. He always goes, no matter how late it is. Maybe that's why he thinks no one around here would be ungrateful enough to steal his car."

Ian, remembering this, stopped halfway down the path that merged with the driveway. He looked toward the garage and said quickly: "Who's there?"

There was no answer. Far off, somewhere on San Francisco Bay, foghorns were mooing dismally. Where he stood it was perfectly dark, with the nearest street light several hundred yards away.

He took an irresolute step in the direction of the garage, stopped again, and shrugged. Certainly he had believed that he heard someone moving near the garage doors or in the trees and shrubbery at the corner of the house. But the wind had come up with the fog. Yes, it was only the wind after all.

He struck off down Vincentino Road. For a time that was later on calculated to have been nearly two hours he simply walked, as mechanically as a machine.

He went up winding streets and down winding streets, now and then stopping beneath a corner lamp to light a cigarette. The fog blew against his face and dampened his hair. When he rubbed a hand against his tweed sport coat it came away wet.

He paid no conscious attention to landmarks and did not bother to study street signs. When a street came to a dividing of ways, as these streets frequently did, he automatically bore to the left.

He walked until at last he became conscious of his own long strides and the effort that went into them. Then he turned, thinking, By the time I'm home I'll be tired enough to sleep.

Going back toward Vincentino Road, he took two wrong turnings, but his sense of direction kept him from going far astray. Weary as he was, he felt the usual surprise at discovering that a road once traveled never seems so long when you pass over it a second time.

He was sane now, he decided, smiling wryly. So perhaps he had better investigate those garage doors. Dr. Carter's car might be sacrosanct, but that didn't mean that Adela's and its new tires would be.

The garage doors were not locked. He pushed one of them open, lighted a match, and saw that Adela's car, the doctor's shabby sedan, and Freddie's ramshackle roadster were inside, still wearing their full quota of tires.

He lighted another match. Yes, there was a flight of steps at the far end of the garage. They must lead upstairs to the door he had noticed at one end of the living room. That door should certainly be locked. It would be best if he made certain that it was.

Afterward he realized that he had been concentrating on trivialities, as one in grief does, trying to delay realization. At the moment it seemed very important that he should see that the door at the top of the stairs into the garage was locked.

He felt his way past the three cars, stumbled on the first step, and then managed to grope his way up them. The door at their top was unlocked. He opened it, felt carpet underfoot, and struck a third match.

What he saw in that brief, uncertain flicker of light sent him plunging across the room to the light switch near the hall door. A chair teetered and crashed to the floor as he ran against it. He hunted for the switch, clawing at the wallpaper, his hands clammy with sweat. . . .

The lights flashed up. Adela lay on her side near the fireplace. There was a great red welt across one temple. Her thick hair was wet and sticky over the pulpy hole that had been the back of her head.

Ian knelt beside her. He spoke to her gently now, called her "dearest"—a term she had long ago pronounced foolish.

Her open eyes stared at him. He took one of her hands. It was limp, the possessive little fingers finally relaxed. That, more than anything, told him that Adela was dead. . . .

She was wearing the same blue robe in which she had brushed her hair. A heavy brass candlestick lay near her, several damp hairs curling across its base. Ian reached for it, dropped it, thought: I mustn't handle this. His fingers were stained, and he put them in his pocket, fumbling for a hand-kerchief.

Behind him someone uttered a sound that was half gasp, half gulp. He turned to see Freddie, his face pea green under his tousled pale hair.

"My God! I heard you threaten her, but I didn't think you—"

Ian was on his feet. He hit Mr. Carter on the point of the chin. Not, he realized as he stood looking down at Freddie, because he blamed him for his reaction, not even because Freddie endangered any plans of his, but simply because he had wanted to hit something. He'd had no plans a minute ago. But now . . . He echoed Freddie.

"My God! I haven't the chance of a snowball in hell! A stranger here with no friends. No, that's not quite right."

He picked Freddie up, slung him over one shoulder, and started upstairs. He had only to pound once on Dr. Carter's door before the old man opened it, wearing a flannel nightshirt piped with red.

"What—?" he began.

"He's all right," Ian said. "Let me put him on your bed. There. Now, as soon as I've gone, go down to the living room. You can't do anything but go down. I'll come back sometime tomorrow. . . ."

PART THREE

I

Mr. Dundas burrowed into his pillow as his wife shook him with premonitory gentleness and then forcefully.

"If that is our son, our heir, our pygmy counterpart, let him yell," he mumbled. "He might as well learn early in life that howling doesn't get you what you want."

"It isn't Ricky. Patton says there is a gentleman waiting to see you and that he says it is urgent."

Michael rolled over on his back and opened a reluctant eye in the direction of the clock.

"¡Maria santissima! It's only five—wartime. You're dreaming, love. Lie down and forget the nasty nightmare."

"I am not dreaming," Valerie said firmly.

"Then you've been hitting the bottle," Michael said and turned over on his side.

Valerie waited. Her husband made snuffling noises into his pillow to prove that he was sleeping soundly, finally sat up and cast the pillow on the floor.

"I will not entertain a Fuller Brush man at five. Did Patton say a 'gentleman' or a 'person'?"

"Definitely a gentleman."

Michael groaned, got out of bed, and reached for his dressing gown. "If any man is so gentlemanly that Patton will admit him at five o'clock in the morning I suppose I had better see this paragon."

He padded through the hall into the living room, opened the door, and stopped, peering in the dim light of the one table lamp that Patton had turned on at the man sitting on the chesterfield. Then:

"Why, damn you," he said, "you've grown a good three inches since you were twenty, Ian."

In his turn Ian stared and then laughed. "Now I feel I'm home again. You haven't changed, Michael. You almost look younger at thirty-four than you sometimes did at twenty."

"Oh," Michael admitted, grinning, "I very nearly died of old age at twenty." They shook hands, careful to be extremely casual about it. "Let me turn on a few more lights and get a better look at you, Ian."

He switched on the central lights, turned with one of his swift, catlike movements, and looked at Ian. Then he walked over to a table, poured a thick three fingers of whisky, and handed it to him.

"Drink it. Valerie! Will you make yourself decent and some black coffee and perhaps a sandwich or two as quickly as possible? What is it, Ian?"

"I married Adela Douglas because her people and mine wanted me to," Ian said. "I was married to her seven years and I wanted a divorce. She and her mother persuaded me to try a second honeymoon. We drove out here to visit old friends of hers in Berkeley. Tonight we quarreled. I could have killed her then but I didn't. I went walking because I couldn't sleep. When I came back someone had bashed her head in with a candlestick. That's all."

"I always admire economy, in narration as much as any other line," Michael said. "Have another drink. You can't fly on one wing. . . . Valerie, this is my cousin, Ian Maclean. I believe he is the only relative that I have ever mentioned to you—kindly."

"The one you were in college with? I remember."

Valerie put a glass coffee brewer on a table and plugged it into an outlet in the wall. "Patton had this all ready. I'm very glad to see you, Ian."

"You heard what I just said, didn't you?"

"Yes," Valerie said calmly, came over and kissed him lightly. "It's nice to acquire a cousin, even under these circumstances. Tell us all about it."

"Well, I don't know where to begin."

"With your marriage to Adela, I should think," Michael said. "Why the hell did you marry her?"

"Do you remember Adela at all?"

"I remember a schoolgirl whose expression, if you bothered to analyze it, was the essence of virtuous self-satisfaction."

"Even at twenty he knew all about women, Valerie," Ian remarked rather maliciously.

Michael reddened. "Why wouldn't I? While you were progressing through grade school and high school I was being towed from one European watering place to another by my mother and whoever her current lover happened to be. Don't digress."

"Well, you know how close our family and Adela's always were. I went into the family business later than most of us do. I had a graduate year at Wisconsin and then I was a Rhodes scholar—"

"You see, Valerie? He is brighter than he looks."

"I plugged along," Ian retorted. "Anyway, when I came home to stay Adela was practically a stranger to me.

"She'd been educated in a swank girls' school in Virginia. Then she came out here to visit a schoolmate named Rosalie Durdan. She was in Berkeley three months and then came home. I'd never even considered marrying before. But people threw Adela and me together, and everyone thought we should marry. So we did," Ian said bleakly.

"I thought it would turn out all right. Adela never admitted it hadn't. I'm not a complex person or foolishly romantic. I could get along with a little honest affection and some laughter. . . . Adela never laughed, except politely. The things that strike me irresistibly funny she considered frightfully 'vulgar' or merely 'childish.' She was virtuous and sensible and thrifty and efficient. And she was mean and stingy and narrow-minded and unbelievably smug. She even made a virtue of frigidity."

"Yes," Michael said warningly, "we get the general idea. Cigarette?" Then he laughed. "That sounds like a line from one of these smooth, bloodless drawing-room dramas."

"Still afraid you might be theatrical?" Ian said. "Well, I stuck it out for seven years."

"'Seven years with the wrong woman,'" Michael hummed. "Why?"

"I'm of an obliging nature," Ian said sardonically. "You should know that. You warned me once that the desire to have everyone like you may be dangerous. However, for the last several years I have been really needed at the mill. You haven't asked after Grandfather—"

"Is he still in the land of the living?"

Ian looked at his cousin with instinctive disapproval and reluctant admiration. "Don't you ever relinquish a grudge, Michael?"

"Not willingly," Valerie said, "or unless it can be marked 'paid in full.'"

"Well, it's a pity I haven't some of the inflexibility you and Grandfather seem to have divided between you. But Grandfather is seventy-nine, and my father is dead."

"I'm sorry," Michael said. "I liked him."

"I know. Well, except for you, I'm the oldest of the grandsons. The younger ones have been drafted or joined the army. We're shy on executives, so I am needed now. Nevertheless, I finally rebelled and told Adela I wanted at least a separation.

"I will draw a veil over the subsequent proceedings," Ian continued in a tone that made Valerie decide that he and Michael did resemble each other. "Adela confided in her mother, which meant she might as well have broadcast it. She also consulted various dear friends who've successfully subdued recalcitrant husbands already."

"The Housewives' Protective League," Valerie said. "An organization for the subjugation of unsatisfactory spouses. All methods thoroughly tested and stamped with the *Good Housekeeping* seal of approval before being put on the open market."

Ian stared at her. "Good lord—you're wonderful! You get the idea. The important point is, considering the situation in which I now find myself, that the whole town was talking. Important point number two: Adela's mother managed a cross-continent hookup."

"You mean that she also broadcast the facts to the people you were to stay with here?" Michael asked.

"Yes. I knew that as soon as I met our hostess, Miss Hallie. I'm also quite certain that Miss Hallie passed her information on to everyone who was at dinner last night. That, of course, will be the groundwork of the case against me. And last night I said a few things to Adela that I've saved up for seven years. Three hours later she was killed. That's all."

"All?" Michael said. "Amigo, you haven't even started. That coffee is ready to drink. Give him some, Valerie, and keep it hot. Now, Ian, begin with your arrival in Berkeley. Tell me all you know, think, or feel about the people you've met since you've been here.

"Make their relations with one another and with Adela as clear as you can. I want every scrap of conversation that impressed you enough that you've remembered it, whether or not you believe it's important. Yes, and how did you discover my whereabouts?"

II

At six-thirty Patton brought in fresh coffee, toast, and eggs. Ian ate the toast but shuddered away from the eggs. At seven-thirty Valerie protested;

"Michael, let him rest! He's exhausted."

"I can't help that," Michael said relentlessly.

It had been some time since he had sat down. He kept prowling about the living room, needing, Valerie thought, only a plumy black tail to swish.

"I know you're out on your feet, Ian," Michael added. "But your mind is still working independently of your body and it isn't fuzzy yet, though it takes a lot of prodding to make you remember."

"I'm not one of these females who can reproduce conversations down to the last 'I sez' and 'he sex,'" Ian retorted.

Nevertheless, Michael had squeezed driblets of information from him that he hadn't known he possessed. From Monday night's dinner on Vincentino Road he had worked his way doggedly through his own activities before Tuesday's breakfast, his exploration of the little ravine, his meeting with

Judith Maybry and her children, their nursemaid, and Bruce Ferrell.

That led him naturally to Freddie's remarks regarding the Ferrells and Maybrys following their luncheon in Oakland. He recalled those in outline easily enough and on any matter that touched Adela he was letter perfect.

"I tried to avoid friction, so I came to be able to calculate Adela's reactions beforehand," he explained. "Everything was black or white, right or wrong in her mind. I got to know her facial expressions and tones of voice, too, and to predict just what she would say—"

"You are giving us a damning and damnable portrait of the dear deceased," Michael said. "Let's go over this again. Adela spent yesterday reorganizing Miss Hallie's household, insulting servants, and listening to Miss Hallie's confidences?"

"And suggesting to her that Antonia would not make Freddie a good wife," Valerie remarked.

"I fancy Adela did. But how—?"

"Oh, I know Toni, Ian. I'm getting to know Adela. Adela wouldn't like Toni. Adela wouldn't have liked me."

"She would have hated your guts," Michael agreed. "Well, Adela had been in the house all day and hadn't gone to see any of her old friends."

"She would expect them to call on her first. Visiting lady, you know," Ian said.

"Then she hadn't been out of the house all day until she went out to take a stroll about the neighborhood. Because she believed in moderate and regular exercise, you thought. How long do you think she was out of the house?"

Ian frowned. "She left about four-ten. It was six when I woke and heard her talking to Loretta. She was still wearing her coat. Probably the maid, Maria, let her in."

"That's something we must find out as well as where she walked, if anyone noticed her."

"Perhaps she strolled down one side of Vincentino Road and back up the other," Ian said. "She told Judith Maybry last night that she had passed their house and that she saw a man she thought must have been Dr. Maybry get into his car there. The Maybry place is directly across from Dr. Carter's."

"Yes. Now as to this conversation that Adela had been having with Loretta van Horn—"

"I told you," Ian said irritably. "I gathered that Adela had asked Loretta for some sort of explanation and that Loretta had just given it. But she didn't expect Adela to understand and didn't care to continue the conversation."

"Did you think that Adela was threatening Loretta when she said: 'I think we must discuss it again'?"

"No, I didn't and I don't, in spite of what happened afterward. I— What are you thinking, Valerie?"

"Oh, I was wondering how I'd feel if I was around thirty, unmarried, a drudge and poor relation, and King Cophetua suddenly stooped and lifted me from the dust. Richard Prince, I mean. And what I'd do in case anything threatened that marriage."

"Let's not indulge in theories so soon," Michael said. "Loretta left Adela. Then Adela spent several minutes coming to some decision. Then you thought, Ian, that she went into someone's bedroom and talked for several more minutes.

"After that she came out into the hall again and stopped to look at something under the light. Something that was small enough to hold in the palm of her hand, which she put into the pocket of her coat."

"I think so. And then," Ian said, "she told me that she had been inquiring after Miss Hallie's health. I thought she was lying then, but now I feel that she may have been telling the truth— but with reservations. Everything is colored in my

mind because I *knew* she was pleased with herself.
I knew it then and I was even more certain of it
later, and I knew that it meant trouble for someone."

"I believe you," Michael said. "But will a jury?
Well, you went down to dinner. Judith Maybry
dropped a brick of immense magnitude—"

"And I said—and no one will forget that—that
it might be dangerous for Adela not to believe in
divorce. I've told you all that I remember about
the rest of the dinner and tried to describe everyone who was there. When they began playing
bridge there was Maybry's crack about playing
games with other people's husbands or wives.
And I suppose I've made it clear that Miss Hallie
patronized him.

"I'd rather not tell this next," Ian went on. "But
the great balcony scene can't be omitted. You see,
Antonia and I went out onto a little balcony to
get some fresh air—"

"¡Jesús, María, y José! What a time you chose
to sample another woman's wares," Michael said
when Ian had finished. "After that—"

"I haven't finished," Ian said grimly. "Though
the next thing that seems worth telling did take
the pressure off Antonia and me."

He described James Maybry's reaction to Bruce's
"It's a wise child that knows his own father."

"I don't believe that was premeditated," he said. "Bruce is given to uttering meaningless tags and filling in the space with that laugh of his. Personally, I think he's a nasty piece of work. I've told you that Judith Maybry poses for him. Well, though the oldest Maybry son is as dark as both his parents are, Little Brother—Bobby—is a towhead. That is the only explanation I could think of for Maybry's reaction to Bruce's remark."

"But what caused Bruce to come forth with that inanity?"

Ian rubbed his forehead. "I don't— No, Valerie dear! I can't drink any more coffee. You'd better give me another shot of whisky. . . . Oh. Judith said Bobby had come home with wet feet—"

"From an afternoon walk?" Michael asked.

"I suppose so. Youngsters are aired twice a day, aren't they? Judith said Lulu Mae brought them home late and that though she had forbidden Lulu Mae to take the boys up that canyon, she thought Lulu Mae might have, because Bobby's feet were wet.

"So what it worked around to was that Judith complained that their children never got any medical attention from Dr. Maybry. That was when Bruce dropped his little brick. Then Freddie saved the situation by offering to get Miss Hallie a drink of water. While he was in the dining room the lights went out."

"How very opportune," Michael commented.

"It was for Adela. That is, she must have been wanting to speak to someone privately, but of course she had nothing to do with the fuse's going out. There's no use my trying to say what people were doing while it was dark. I thought I heard Loretta moving about, jingling. Evelyn and Judith each spoke once. Bruce laughed, and Maybry said 'Damn,' but at that time I don't think anyone but Freddie and Dr. Carter had left the living room. I don't know, of course."

"You do know that Freddie had left the room?" Michael said. "What about Dr. Carter?"

"He said he'd help Freddie look for a fuse, and you could hear him talking to him. The living room is large, and there was enough noise that Adela could have whispered to someone without being overheard," Ian said. "Then people did wander out of the living room. I did. . . ."

He told them how he had gone upstairs, given up trying to find his flashlight, come down again, and heard Adela talking in the darkness at the end of the hall. When he had finished Valerie sighed.

"Oh, if you'd only seen whom she was talking to! Or if you had even heard that person—"

"That wouldn't have done any good unless the words in some way identified the speaker," Michael said: "A whisper lacks character. Now, Ian—"

He took Ian through the whole episode again: not so much Adela's words, but the shouted three-cornered conversation between Freddie, Dr. Carter, and Miss Hallie that had gone on while Ian was standing at the stairway, trying to hear what Adela was saying.

"Well," Michael said finally, "that seems to let those three out. None of them could have been talking to Adela. As to Loretta, though she joined you in company with Miss Hallie after the lights went on, you don't know that she was with Miss Hallie in the living room all during the black-out."

"No. But," Ian said, smiling, "I don't think it will do you, as my cousin, any good to ask Miss Hallie that—or anything."

"Oh, I don't know. He's had a long experience in the line of business in dealing with unreasonable old biddies like your Miss Hallie," Valerie said.

Michael ignored her. "Do you think Loretta had time to go from the hall into the kitchen, on into and through the dining room, and reach the living room again before the lights came on?"

"No. But if she was the one who was talking to Adela she could have come past me, I suppose. That would be the nearest way back into the living room. I stood on the stairs and I wasn't listening for anyone going past me. I was thinking about Adela and what she had said. The only thing is, considering all those dingle-dangles Loretta wears, I don't know how she could have managed to move quietly."

"Oh. Well, what happened then?"

"Everyone went home," Ian said, "and we went upstairs to bed. . . ."

III

He closed his eyes and told them exactly what he had said to Adela in their bedroom last night. As he had already remarked, he had been seven years rehearsing some of the speeches he had thrown at Adela. It was natural that he should have no trouble remembering his lines now.

There was a significant lack of comment from his audience when he had finished. He went on without opening his eyes, describing his walk, how he had reentered the house by the garage, his discovery of Adela's body, Freddie's discovery of him.

Then at last he looked at Michael and Valerie. "Well?" he said.

"'The jury brought the verdict—"Murder in the first degree." The judge said: "Take the prisoner To the penitentiary."'"

"Michael!"

"It's all right, Valerie," Ian said. "It's his way of saying that I haven't a Chinaman's chance."

"I didn't say that!" Michael snapped. "I do say the odds are a thousand to one that you'll be arrested as soon as you come within striking distance of the Berkeley police. Looking at it from their viewpoint, what else can they do? You know, *amigo,* I think you have been used."

"What? Oh, you mean someone wanted to kill Adela and dared to because he knew that I'd be blamed? Yes, that's reasonable. Only," Ian objected, "doesn't that point to someone in the house's having killed her?"

"Because only someone in the house could have overheard the great bedroom scene? I don't think that's conclusive," Michael said. "Everyone knew what the situation was between you and Adela. Those who saw you embracing Antonia Jordan—"

"Oh, shut up!"

"—undoubtedly passed on that tidbit to those who hadn't. One wouldn't need any terrific amount of brains to guess that Adela would haul you over the coals last night. Or that you were a trifle on the prod and wouldn't take it lying down.

"Well, Freddie evidently overheard that conversation—and offhand I can't think of anything that you said to Adela that wouldn't have been better left unsaid, if you'd known what was going to happen to her several hours later."

"I know," Ian said wearily. "I was weaving a rope for my own neck. Oh, pardon me. I believe California has renounced the noose for lethal gas. I suppose Freddie was in the bathroom next door to our room. Or if he'd wanted to listen from the hall perhaps he could have heard part of what I said."

"Did you speak very loudly?"

"I never shout. Telling me that I did was just one of Adela's little tricks," Ian said resentfully. "My voice carries, just as yours does, because we both have a peculiar habit of pronouncing words."

"I know. Would Adela have objected to witnesses?"

"Hmm? I suppose not," Ian said slowly, "since Adela realized that everyone was in the know, anyway, and she threatened, if necessary, to have them testify to that—that damn foolishness with Antonia. Adela only shushed me *after* I'd—well, I suppose the police would say I'd definitely threatened her."

"I'm sure that is exactly what they will say. So you think it is possible that Adela knew someone was in the bathroom but preferred to have that person hear you tell her that (1) she should have been strangled at birth and (2) that her determination not to give you a divorce might be dangerous to her own life?"

Ian winced. "It sounds very damning when someone else says it. Yes, I do think Adela might have done that. And," he added, "if she wasn't threatening Loretta before dinner she was threatening whomever she talked to during the blackout after dinner. Except that Adela never threatened. She handed down verdicts and there was no appeal.

"Her tone last night was the same I've heard when she dismissed a maid who'd been so indelicate and ungrateful as to become pregnant while in our service. That she was a youngster from an orphan asylum, inexperienced and starved for affection, was, as Adela was so fond of saying, beside the point. She always knew what was right, not just for herself but for everyone else."

"And you haven't the slightest idea," Michael said, "whom Adela was threatening with exposure or what sort of knowledge she could have acquired that made her dangerous to someone?"

"How can I guess? Though I've been thinking that so many roads seem to lead back to Miss Hallie's daughter Rosalie."

"I'd noticed that," Michael said.

"And what could Adela have found out in that short time unless it was something that tied in with something else she already knew—had known for eight years? And if you have to dig back to eight years ago—"

"Perhaps I won't. I've found, in other affairs of this sort, that it is sometimes a mistake to insist on doing things the hard way. However, we can't ignore the fact that if Adela hadn't visited Rosalie eight years ago she wouldn't have known any of these people.

"I can't delve into their pasts. The police could, but I don't expect any co-operation from them. There are no strings I can pull in Berkeley. So I'll hire a private detective to look into the backgrounds of these people. You will pay the bill, Ian," Michael added thriftily. "His services will come high because he is good and more or less retired now. His name is Dana Clyde; he was born in Berkeley and he has connections. There is just one point in your favor."

"Really? I hadn't been able to think of one."

"Why would you kill Adela in the living room?"

"Oh. I did wonder what the devil she was doing down there," Ian said. "But then it occurred to me that perhaps when I was gone for so long she got up and came down to wait for me."

Michael frowned. "And *that* should have occurred to me. No doubt it will to the police. However, if you were right and there was someone hanging about the house, that person certainly saw you start off on your walk. That was another thing I had in mind when I said I thought you had been used."

"Well—yes. It's possible I heard nothing but the wind. But if someone else couldn't sleep and happened to be looking out as I left the house— Well, I certainly could have been seen walking away by someone in the Maybry house. And I rather imagine you must be able to see the Carter house from some of the Ferrells' upstairs windows. I see that knowing I wasn't with Adela would make a difference. The front door and the garage doors weren't locked. But if someone from outside entered the house Adela had to be persuaded to come downstairs."

"You've already told us that Adela didn't frighten easily."

"My God, no! She might have thought she heard someone downstairs, gone down, found it was someone she knew, and been persuaded to grant another interview. Well, for that matter, if she'd thought she heard someone downstairs she probably would have thought it was I and come down to keep me out of mischief."

"That's the simplest and most sensible explanation yet." Michael had been sitting still for several minutes, but now he began walking restlessly about the room again. "Would you like to run for it, Ian?" he said abruptly.

"Run for—? No. They'd catch up with me."

"I really meant: will you hide out here?"

"In this house?"

"No. There are other places."

"Forget them if there are," Ian said decidedly. "I'll go back and give myself up. Perhaps it will be a point in my favor if I appear at police headquarters of my own accord before they take me up."

"If *we* appear at police headquarters," Michael amended. "You didn't mention our relationship to anyone but Antonia, did you? Do you think she will tell Dr. Carter that you may have come here?"

"I'm quite sure she won't. Why?"

"Oh, it will be much better for you to walk into the police station yourself than for them to track you down here and drag you back to Berkeley," Michael said so glibly that Valerie glanced at him sharply. "I'll get dressed. Valerie, where have you hidden those new shirts of mine?"

Mr. Dundas is, in some respects, a little on the finicky side. His bureau drawers his kingdom are, and he arranges their contents himself. Nevertheless, Valerie rose, trying to appear the harassed housewife, and followed him into the bedroom.

"Be entertaining," he whispered. "Keep Ian talking or talk yourself so that he won't hear me chatting over the telephone."

"Oh. Well—"

Valerie went into another room off the hall and in a few minutes rejoined Ian with a nursing bottle in one hand and what appeared to be a collection of blue-and-white blankets in the other.

"Want to see something funny?" she asked, peeling down the blankets. "There! Second edition Dundas. Have you ever seen an uglier infant in your life?"

"Uh," said Ian, uncertain whether to acknowledge the obvious truth of this statement or hastily to deny it. Valerie laughed.

"He's going to look exactly like Michael."

"And that's the important thing—to you?"

"Of course. I'm not awfully maternal, you know. And so—here!"

She hastily popped the nipple of the nursing bottle into the baby's mouth. "Chew on that. Nature did not provide, you see. He doesn't even cry like most babies. He snarls. And he doesn't like me much. Unfair to organized motherhood, I call it."

Ian laughed. "Don't you care?"

"He will like me when he is old enough to appreciate my peculiar charm. Now, I don't blame him. I stick pins in him when I try to change a diaper, and when it comes to bathing him—well, I have never known anything with so many angles to be so slippery!"

"Again like Michael," Ian said dryly. "Name?"

"Ricky to me: Roderick to Michael. You may have noticed that our maid is a superior English person. Patton copes beautifully, but if she didn't Michael could. Don't tell him I told you. Years ago when he first came to San Francisco he took care of a baby for his dinners. The mother was a taxi dancer and the father drove one—at night, that is."

"I suppose," Ian said slowly, "that he had a fairly tough time of it at first. He couldn't have left Wisconsin with much money in his pockets."

"He landed here with two dollars. And," Valerie proudly, "the income tax we paid this year is a very nice contribution toward winning this war. Yes, he had a hard time of it. So if you ever think he is a shade unscrupulous or too harsh with fools and weaklings— Oh, dear! You know I didn't mean—"

"Didn't you?" Ian said, still smiling. "I thought I'd indicated that I realized my own shortcomings and—"

Michael came back into the living room. "Ian, what did you—? *¡Por Dios, niña!* You can't hold a child like that!"

"But I am holding him like this."

"Well, put your hand under his back if you don't want him to grow up curved. A child this age hasn't an adult backbone, you know. Ian, what did you do after you left Dr. Carter last night? You didn't get here until five o'clock."

"It was really this morning that I left him, you know. When I got over your Bay Bridge it was nearly three. I abandoned my car—"

"Not downtown, I hope!"

"No, somewhere a long ways out. I was in no state of mind to take note of streets. I walked until I found an open-all-night drugstore. I looked up your number and found there was a map in the telephone directory. I tore it out, and since I'm good at maps I got here without having to make inquiries."

"Good. Well, you had better come into the bathroom and shave. Just now you rather look the part of a murderer. This way."

Michael opened the door from the living room into a square hall and stood aside for Ian to pass him. He closed the door. Valerie investigated her son's most intimate garments and murmured absently: "You little drip."

There was a sound rather like that a smallish tree would make crashing to earth. She plopped the baby into a chair and ran to the hall.

Ian was lying full length on the floor with his head just touching the bathroom door.

"D-did he faint?" Valerie asked.

Michael looked lovingly at the limber black object he held in his left hand. "No. The hand has not lost its cunning and is still quicker than the eye."

"A blackjack!"

"Yes. Ian was a collegiate boxing champion. And if he hadn't been it is unlikely that I could hit him hard enough to knock him out for the necessary period of time," Michael said reasonably. "*If* I wanted to risk breaking my hand on his jaw."

"What a rat you are, darling," Mrs. Dundas said admiringly. "What are you going to do with him?"

Michael lifted one of Ian's eyelids and then investigated the lump behind one ear. "Very good. Oh, I'm sending him to Saul Hirsh's sanitarium. I haven't time to tell you about that establishment now, but the police won't find Ian there, and Saul won't allow him to leave. So . . ."

The dining-room door opened, and Patton looked in on them. Patton never listened behind doors and always knew precisely what was happening. But only the most proper shade of concern crossed her well-bred servant's countenance.

"Has Mr. Maclean been taken ill, sir?"

"Mr. Maclean has never been here, Patton. This that you see on the floor is only a figment of your imagination."

"I understand, sir," Patton said and withdrew.

"But, Michael, are you sure you are doing the right thing?" Valerie said.

"Honestly, I don't know, my dear. If Adela had been killed in San Francisco I would have handed Ian over to the police. Nick Prevost wouldn't try to keep me from carrying on an investigation: he'd even help me.

"But though Berkeley has a very fine police force, I'll get nothing but polite regret from them. However, if they cannot prove that I have seen Ian or talked to him they can't deny that it's natural for me to ask questions while waiting for them to find Ian."

"Yes, you'd be entitled to know what the case against Ian is," Valerie admitted. "And while people are accusing him you can slip in questions that they mightn't answer if he were safely in jail, charged with murder. But how are you supposed to know what has happened if you are supposed not to have talked to him? Did you read about it in the newspapers?"

Michael grinned. "My story will be that Antonia told me. I called Toni just now. Freddie Carter had let her know what had happened, but she hasn't been interviewed by the police yet. Toni is to call me back any minute now.

"That's in case they check on us. She will tell me that my cousin Ian is in California and believed to have murdered his wife, and I will be very much surprised and concerned. Then I'll go over to Berkeley, pick up Toni, and go with her to the Carters' to express my regrets and my belief in Ian's innocence."

"I see. After seeing your private detective and putting him to work, I suppose. What about Ian?"

"In a few minutes now two very discreet gentlemen will drive their car into our garage and take Ian away via the basement route so that no one in the neighborhood will see him go. They—

"That will be Toni now," Michael said as the telephone rang. "As soon as she and I have finished our little act I'll be leaving. Hello. . . . Yes, Toni, this is Michael. . . ."

PART FOUR

I

"Well," Michael said, stopping his car before Dr. Carter's house, "this is not what I would call a congested residential district."

"I told you that all sorts of people could go wandering around here at night without anyone's noticing it," Antonia said wearily. "But then I've told you so much."

"But your account of your conversations with Miss Hallie, Loretta, Freddie, and the old doctor on the afternoon that Ian and Adela arrived has made me understand all of them better. Miss Hallie's attitude toward Loretta and her engagement to Richard Prince is interesting."

"It's disgusting. But what roused my curiosity was Dr. Carter's saying there isn't a mean bone in Loretta's body because if there was 'she could have—' Could have done what, I wonder, if she'd wanted to be mean?"

"Well," Michael said, "if we must dig back eight years about all we have is that Adela was expected to marry Bruce Ferrell, that she didn't, and that she returned to Wisconsin rather suddenly."

"And that Rosalie died very suddenly soon after Adela left," Antonia remarked. "Not that that could have anything to do with this."

"What was the cause of Rosalie's death?"

"Whatever they call it when your appendix bursts."

Michael raised his eyebrows. "Appendicitis covers a multitude of sins. Did you witness the meeting between Adela and Mr. Ferrell last night? Ian didn't, you know."

"Yes. I'd say Bruce tried to achieve an 'Adela-after-all-these-years' attitude. And to look wistful and decently regretful for the old love. He thinks that sort of thing is expected of him. He is not a wolf; he's an old-fashioned masher. But Adela wouldn't play up."

Antonia giggled. "She said: 'How nice to see you again, Bruce. How well you are looking. You have gained weight, haven't you?'"

"Deflating," Michael said.

"Yes. I thought Evelyn Ferrell was amused. She and Adela greeted each other politely but not enthusiastically. But neither of them is given to gushing. Adela said that Evelyn had been Mrs.

Blake when she last saw her. Evelyn only nodded. Then Bruce congratulated Loretta on her engagement, and Adela looked amused. Taking her cue from Miss Hallie, I suppose. Adela said she had met Richard Prince and then talked about the weather."

"And you think that the detective who questioned you later this morning did so merely as 'a matter of routine'?"

"Well, no one's told him about what you say Ian calls the balcony scene. And that was all my fault! As I told Ian, any pretty girl would have done—"

"Oh, I don't know, my child. The Macleans are choosy."

"But then I kissed him, and naturally—well, it doesn't matter whose fault it was. Someone will tell the police about it. I can take it, but it's going to make things that much worse for Ian. Freddie didn't tell, but he wouldn't. I think he was more embarrassed than anything else last night. But don't underestimate Freddie."

"I won't." Michael got out to open the car door for her. "But if he is twenty-six and able-bodied why isn't he in the army?"

"They rejected him last year because his eyes aren't too good. They'll probably take him now. I don't say Freddie is bursting with a desire to die for his country," Antonia said, "but he certainly expects to be inducted into some branch of the armed forces even though Miss Hallie weeps at the notion. She considers the war a personal inconvenience and is fretful about it."

"Well, go and prepare the way for me. Call me if Dr. Carter will talk to me but be certain first that there are no cops in the house. They should have finished here since it's past eleven and they've had since about two o'clock this morning. They are probably concentrating on finding Ian now."

He had walked with her along the driveway to where it met the path that led to the front steps. When Antonia went on he saw the other path that led around the left side of the house. He thought: I'll have time to look around before Toni gets back.

Like Ian, he followed the path down the steep bank to the stream. It was still foggy at eleven o'clock, and trees, shrubbery, and the ground underfoot were as damp as Ian had found them yesterday.

The path was moist enough that in several places parts of the outline of a man's shoe showed plainly. A heel print in one place; a toe print farther on. But in other spots, in between these, were long smudges as if someone had smoothed down the earth with the sole of his shoe.

"That's queer," Michael muttered and then looked up quickly as someone cleared his throat.

A man Michael identified from Ian's description as Bruce Ferrell was sitting on the crude bench Ian had spoken of. He said:

"Pardon me, but are you a policeman?"

"No, I am Ian Maclean's cousin, Michael Dundas."

"Dundas? Oh. I mean to say, I've heard of you," Bruce said with his abrupt laugh. "But I had no idea you and Ian were related. You don't look at all alike."

"Would you like to see my birth certificate?"

"Oh lord, no. I mean to say, of course you're his cousin if you say you are. But how did you find out about this mess he's in? Or did he—?"

"He didn't get in touch with me," Michael said mechanically. He was staring at the knees of Mr. Ferrell's slacks which were soiled and damp: newly damp as if he might have just knelt down in the path. "Ian had mentioned me to Antonia Jordan, whom I know very well, and she telephoned me this morning."

"Yes, Toni would," Mr. Ferrell said with an unpleasant grin. "But about all you can do for Ian is to get him a good lawyer. I mean to say, the police consider it an open-and-shut case."

"Did they tell you so?"

"They don't need to. I mean to say, besides what I heard and saw with my own eyes, there's the threats Freddie heard Ian make last night. Of course," Bruce said hastily, "this has been a great shock to all of us."

"So great a shock that you sought the solace of nature?" Michael suggested, looking about at the dripping trees and shivering in the wind that knifed down the little canyon.

"Uh," said Mr. Ferrell doubtfully. "I mean to say, I wanted a walk."

"You weren't walking," Michael pointed out, looking at the bench and the paired initials carved on it. "And if you wanted to walk, why choose to walk here?"

"Because we used to— What the devil business is it of yours?" Mr. Ferrell said, his light eyes suddenly wary. Then he laughed again. "I'm afraid we're both a little on edge. I don't blame you," he said nobly.

Michael did not deny the charge, and Bruce sighed gustily. "Poor little Adela! The last person in the world you'd have expected would die a violent death."

"She wouldn't have considered it quite ladylike, would she?"

Bruce looked startled. "How did you guess that? Did you know Adela?"

"I met her once or twice years ago. Isn't it true that you two thought of marrying eight years ago?"

"I suppose we did," Mr. Ferrell said cautiously. "It was one of these summer romances. But Adela had a good deal of the reformer in her even at that age."

Michael thought that had the ring of candor, but in an instant Bruce assumed the role of connoisseur and interpreter of women.

"Only I've found it's not wise to knuckle under to any female. I mean to say, they don't really want you to, though they'll do their damnedest to make you. Adela wanted me to go into business. She considered art a 'little immoral,'" Bruce said with a brief flash of humor.

"And at that time I thought sculpture was my field, and it wasn't a paying proposition. I wouldn't give in, but Adela thought I would—if she just went home. She thought I'd follow her there, but no woman can give me the run-around," he finished complacently.

"But when you met again last night you were not averse to a mild flirtation? After all . . ." Michael shrugged encouragingly and Bruce agreed.

"Yes, after all, your old flames expect something like that. I'd expected to be decently attentive: complimentary, that sort of thing, perfectly harmless. But Adela was worried and quiet. You can see why she was. I mean to say, I'm devoted to my wife. She is a fine woman."

Oh lord, I knew that line would pop up some-time, Michael thought. If I were a woman he would add: but my wife doesn't understand me.

"But your wife does not act as the model for your drawings—which I have often admired," he said suggestively.

"Well, no. She— Say, what are you driving at? What the hell has Toni Jordan been saying to you about me?"

"Doesn't Antonia like you?" Michael inquired blandly. "I mean to say, why shouldn't she?"

"Well—Toni wanted to model for me. I thought she might do for some drawings I was making to advertise ski clothes. But she wouldn't do and she's never forgiven me for telling her so. So I can imagine what she may have said to you about Judith Maybry and me. But I can't see what that has to do with Adela's death. I mean to say—"

"I don't believe that Ian killed Adela and I can't be satisfied with merely a routine investigation," Michael said. "That is—uh—blood is thicker than water, and he is my cousin."

"Oh, I understand you grabbing at straws. I mean to say, family feeling . . . But if you like Toni give her a word of advice. Tell her she can't dish out the dirt without getting dirty herself. Toni knows that we all understand each other: Judith, my wife, and I."

"*And* Dr. Maybry?" Michael said.

Bruce hesitated. It wasn't difficult to guess that he was wondering just how much Antonia had told Michael and that, rather than be proved a liar later, he decided not to risk a flat denial.

"Jim Maybry is one of these thin-skinned, nervy fellows who fire up when you least expect it," he said tolerantly. "He takes his work seriously and last night he was on edge because he'd only been able to save a mother but not the baby. He doesn't want Judy to pose for me any more: that's true.

"But Judy likes to because sometimes she wants a little money of her own. I've made my name using her as a model, and no one else does as well. My wife understands that. Are you married, Dundas? Then I'll give you some advice about Toni. That little girl can be had, as your cousin Ian would tell you."

My cousin Ian would knock those tooth-paste-ad teeth down your throat, Michael reflected. He said respectfully:

"You know a great deal about women."

He didn't hope that even Bruce would rise to that blatant hunk of bait, but Bruce smiled complacently.

"I've devoted a great deal of time to their study. I mean to say, the little dears aren't really so mysterious. The main thing is to play hard to get."

"Yes, I fancy it *is* just as well to keep your stud fee pretty high," Michael drawled.

Mr. Ferrell's mouth fell open. Then he rose and launched himself toward Mr. Dundas. Michael backpedaled, seeking solid footing. Mr. Ferrell did not seek or find it. His feet went out from under him, and he sat down in a prickly-leaved bush.

"Good. I haven't the time nor the inclination to paste you one," Michael said, "though when I consider some remarks of yours that I have let pass unprotested— What did you say?"

Mr. Ferrell said that if Mr. Dundas would help him to his feet he would make mincemeat of him.

"Thank you, no, another time. I'm sure Toni must be wondering what has become of me."

Now what, Michael thought, walking away, inspired me to begin proceedings by making an enemy? Oh well, Bruce would soon have described Toni's and Ian's misbehavior on the balcony to the police in any case. I wonder that he hasn't already done so.

And why the devil did he walk up here this morning? Did he want to gaze regretfully at his and Adela's initials carved on that bench? Perhaps he would make that sort of gesture.

But Adela bruised his vanity last night, and I think he does know enough about women to realize how lucky he was to escape her eight years ago. Besides, what had he been doing to get damp earth on the knees of his slacks?

II

Dr. Carter squinted thoughtfully through his glasses and for perhaps the tenth time settled them on his nose again.

"And I'm afraid, my boy, that's all that I can tell you," he said.

Michael had listened as attentively to the old man's story as if every fact in it were new to him. Actually Dr. Carter had told him very little that he hadn't already learned from Ian and Antonia.

However, Ian had been vague about times, and the old doctor was not. It had been eleven o'clock when he had wound his watch before getting into bed last night. No one had heard Ian leave the house. The servants—Maria and the cook—were in bed on the third floor by nine o'clock, and both were sound sleepers.

It had been ten minutes of two when Ian woke him and laid Freddie on his bed, Dr. Carter said. It was his opinion that Adela had been dead about a quarter of an hour then. The police surgeon agreed with him but added that she might have been killed as early as twelve forty-five.

"He was fair," Dr. Carter added. "You might ask, as I did, why Ian would stick around for perhaps as long as twenty-five or thirty minutes after he killed Adela. But that doesn't carry much weight against the fact that Freddie found him with the weapon in his hand, apparently just removing his fingerprints from it."

"I only said," Freddie protested, "that Ian dropped the candlestick and put his hand in his pocket."

"But that one set of Ian's prints were the only ones on the candlestick. So the police argue that he had already removed all others and that Freddie surprised him before he had quite finished the job," Dr. Carter said. "The first blow just stunned her; then her head was bashed in.

"And that follows a pattern. The first blow is apt to be the fatal one so far as the murderer himself is concerned. He strikes that and it releases something in him and he finishes the job in a red rage. But then he may be stunned by what he has done. I was called in once on a case where a man beat his wife to death. For half an hour he sat there, rocking her back and forth in his arms, crying. The police remember cases like that and judge this one by them."

As the police reconstructed events, Ian had left the house for some reason. One officer had remarked that he usually took a turn around the block after he'd had a row with his wife. And

Freddie and the doctor could testify that Ian was wearing sport clothes and heavy shoes at one-fifty. Also, the latch was off the front door.

"So they argue that Adela missed Ian and came downstairs to wait for him. Or heard him downstairs and came down to urge him to come back to bed. They'd quarreled once, as Freddie could testify. The police argue that they took up where they'd left off when Ian came back and that this time he did kill her."

As to Freddie's account of the conversation he'd overheard between Ian and Adela in their bedroom, Michael had noticed the gaps in it, though he could not comment on them. Growing more pink by the minute, Freddie had managed to summarize Ian's summary of his own and Adela's marriage. He had heard Ian say: "Women like you should be strangled at birth" and Adela's "You frighten me."

"Though I don't think she was frightened," Mr. Carter said shrewdly. "It was damned embarrassing. I've told Aunt Hallie that when the guest room is occupied I don't know whether to gargle loudly so everyone will know I'm performing the nightly ablutions or try to be so quiet they won't know I'm in the bathroom."

"Apparently you were quiet last night," Michael said.

"Not especially, and I think Adela may have known I was there. Ian had his mind on what he was saying. After she said he frightened her he did talk more softly for a while. For quite a while," Freddie added hastily.

This, Michael knew, would cover Adela's refusal to give Ian a divorce and her threat to involve Antonia if he tried to obtain one.

"I left the bathroom," Freddie went on, "but from the hall I heard Ian tell Adela that she might have made a decision that might be dangerous to her life. I shouldn't have stayed in the bathroom and gone on listening, though the way Ian told her off was something to hear. But it's more embarrassing to let people know you've been listening than just to keep quiet and listen.

"I don't know what woke me up around one-thirty. Some noise downstairs, I thought, when I first woke. I got up and the light was on downstairs, so I went down. You know what I saw, but I've been wondering all morning if I can trust my own eyes. Because I like Ian and," Freddie finished candidly, "to my way of thinking, Adela was a perfect specimen of zombie. . . ."

Neither he nor Dr. Carter had mentioned Loretta. Now Michael asked:

"Is Miss van Horn at home? You asked Antonia to go up and talk to your aunt."

"Loretta offered to stay home though she has music lessons to give. But Aunt Hallie threw a bedroom slipper at her, so she went on."

"My sister had hysterics when I told her what had happened," Dr. Carter said. "She's been in bed all day. We wired Adela's mother. We've had an answer saying that she is prostrated and can't travel. The wire ended: 'George will come.' Have you any idea who George is?"

Michael frowned. "I believe there was a vague person named George who was a poor relation in Adela's family and employed by them as a glorified errand boy, I hope that he travels by train. Did your sister immediately accuse Ian?"

"Violently. So did Adela's mother by Western Union. You'll never get a word out of Hallie, boy."

"I was afraid of that. Well, I'd like to talk about that private black-out you had last night."

"Toni told you about that? But why should that interest you?" Freddie asked.

"I won't tell you that—if you don't mind."

It was Mr. Carter's first experience of the peculiar inflection Mr. Dundas manages to give those four words. He stared and then grinned.

"And the hell with it if I do mind?" he suggested. "Well, shoot."

"Who was in the dining room with you and Dr. Carter just before you finally found a fuse?"

"I don't know. I was so busy trying to find that damned fuse or some candles—"

Dr. Carter removed his glasses, held them off, and squinted through them at his nephew. "Were you, Freddie?" he said gently.

Freddie eyed his uncle speculatively, sleeked down his hair, and grinned. "Well, Mr. Dundas, I blew that fuse myself. These parties get me down, and you'd know why if you had to play cards with Aunt Hallie, as I always do. Besides, there had been several embarrassing episodes. Did Toni tell you—?"

"She told me everything," Michael said.

"Well, when Bruce made that crack about 'it's a wise child that knows his own father' and Jimmy Maybry got white around the gills I thought it was time the party broke up. I came out in the dining room and stuck a fork in a socket and wham!—out went the fuse."

"You pulled that trick another time when we'd been playing cards too long and Hallie wasn't ready to stop," Dr. Carter said. "But you were right, Freddie: it was time people went home. There was a definite sense of strain all evening."

"I thought I put on a good act," Freddie said modestly. "I finally pretended I was out of matches and stopped lighting them. But don't expect me to remember who came out to help. Uncle Doc first."

The old man chuckled. "I didn't try very hard, my boy. Toni was in the dining room with us for quite a while, though, because I spoke to her several times."

"I remember that. And Judy was there. I know because I'm allergic to perfumes."

"That must make life rather difficult unless you are also allergic to women," Michael remarked.

Freddie grimaced. "Many a promising romance has been blighted because the gal would soak herself in Christmas Night. I'm not as bad as I was when I was a kid. Then perfumes gave me a swell dose of hay fever."

"They still have that effect on Loretta," Dr. Carter said. "It's a family idiosyncrasy. My niece, Rosalie, was just like Loretta."

"Well, Toni doesn't wear scent, just to oblige me, and Adela, Loretta, and Evelyn just don't. But Judy reeked of some heavy, expensive stuff, so I know she was in the dining room for a while at least. But once having smelled that perfume, I suppose I might think I still smelled it even if Judy left the dining room for a few minutes."

"Are you interested principally in the few minutes just before I found a fuse and decided I might as well produce it because people were ready to go home?" Dr. Carter said.

"I think those few minutes are the most important," Michael said cautiously.

"I'm afraid I can't help you either. Bruce was in the room sometime. I heard him laugh."

"If Jimmy Maybry was in the dining room at any time during the black-out I never saw him while I was still lighting matches or heard him speak," Freddie said. "Or Evelyn either."

"I can't say that Jimmy was there," Dr. Carter said reluctantly. "But Evelyn was because I stepped on her foot. Loretta stayed with Hallie all through the blackout, I think. But it's no use, my boy. If you start questioning the others on this subject I dare say no two of them will agree."

"And if you can spare me I think I'd better rescue Toni from Aunt Hallie—or Aunt Hallie from Toni," Freddie said. "I don't know just how long Toni can manage to be polite and tactful. . . ."

III

They had been talking in the doctor's little study. When Freddie went out the old man swiveled about abruptly in his ancient desk chair and barked:

"Do you know where Ian is?"

"If I did do you think I'd tell you?"

"Certainly not. Wouldn't want you to."

"Oh?" Michael said. "Then perhaps we understand each other. That would simplify matters. I do not ask you to help me to conceal a fugitive from justice: only that if you guess that I know certain things that only Ian could have told me you will not comment on that fact."

Dr. Carter chuckled. "Yes, we understand each other. But this whole thing is baffling."

"I wouldna say it's no," Michael said absently.

"Eh?"

"What? Oh." Michael laughed. "Our grandfather, mine and Ian's, has never cared to lose his Scotch burr. He also is not given to committing himself. If I held up this cigarette and said: 'Isn't this a cigarette, Grandfather?' he would probably answer: 'I wouldna say it's no.' In my youth I was given to mimicking him. I haven't for years.

"But," he added unwillingly, "any number of things I haven't thought of for years have come back to me today. I don't believe that blood is thicker than water or that you owe your relatives anything simply because they are your relatives. It doesn't matter that Ian is my first cousin. It does matter that he was the first, and for many years the only, friend of my own age that I'd ever had. What the hell are you grinning about?"

"At you," the old doctor said, "and your glib assertion that blood ties don't matter."

"But I— Oh well, have it your own way. You make me feel very young, and that's an unusual

sensation. As to this thing's being baffling, I agree
with you. I feel as if I were trying to scale a per-
pendicular cliff, hunting for hand- or toe-holds
and not finding any. However . . .

"You know that Adela went for a walk yesterday
afternoon? We do know she went by the Maybry
house while she was out, but of course it is directly
opposite this one. I've been wondering if she might
have had any reason to walk up the little canyon
at the side of this house. It isn't the most pleasant
place in the world at this time of year, but—"

"But Adela might have," Dr. Carter said. "Most
of us do like to revisit familiar places, and that
canyon is a pleasant spot in summer and fall. It
was a great place for young people to go to—well,
I dare say they called it necking eight years ago.
Or was it still 'petting'?

"Rosalie, Judith, Loretta, Adela, Bruce, and
whatever young men were on hand spent a lot of
time up there when Adela was here before. Yes,
she might have gone up there to see if the bench
we put up was still standing."

"Will you try to find out if anyone saw her go
up there?" Michael said.

"Do you think that's important?"

"I do think it may be important to know where
Adela went and whom she saw late yesterday afternoon. She went out for her walk around four-
fifteen. I don't know what time she returned."

"Just before six. I was in this room and heard her come in and say something to Maria, who'd let her in."

"Then she must have gone straight upstairs and either met Miss van Horn or insisted on speaking to her. They talked together in the hall. Ian heard the last part of their conversation. . . ."

Michael told Dr. Carter what Ian had heard Loretta say to Adela. The old man frowned; involuntarily, Michael thought, since in an instant it was an inscrutable physician's countenance that he faced.

"I'll ask Loretta about that," Dr. Carter said easily. "But I dare say Adela considered Loretta had been unfriendly and wanted an explanation."

"Would Adela have been right?"

"I suppose so. Loretta is usually anxious to please, but she and Adela were never friends. A little jealousy there, I dare say, because Loretta was extremely fond of Rosalie. Eight years ago I'm speaking of now.

"Rosalie was a sweet girl, not much sillier than many girls are at twenty-one, but easily influenced by anyone she admired who had any force of character. So she was pretty well under Adela's thumb, and I dare say Loretta resented that."

"Rosalie died very suddenly, didn't she?"

"Yes."

It was one of those monosyllables that have the same sound as that made by a cork being pounded

into a bottle—and the same effect. Michael had
wanted to ask the old man why Adela had had
such great influence over Miss Hallie, but he decided not to risk the question. He asked, instead:

"You didn't care for Adela, did you?"

"No," Dr. Carter said promptly. "Adela was a
good woman, a righteous woman. And no one can
make more trouble than a self-righteous woman if
she is also self-willed, self-satisfied, and has time
on her hands to oversee others' behavior too.

"I suspected Adela would be like that at twenty-
nine. At twenty-one she was a smug little prude,
but young people wouldn't notice that. She was
inexperienced in the way girls who are carefully
raised and sheltered are sometimes. She could still
giggle like a schoolgirl, though she had no sense
of humor; she was attractive and well-bred and
was normally interested in men, though even then
she intended to make over the man she married
according to her own specifications."

"So Mr. Ferrell told me, in different words. I
strolled up your little canyon and met him there,"
Michael said.

"You did? What the devil was Bruce doing there?
He's a lazy beggar and never willingly walks."

"Perhaps he went there to pray. At any rate,
he'd recently knelt down on damp ground. Have
you any idea why he would do that?"

"I'll be damned if I have!"

"Neither have I. He wouldn't need to kneel to smudge out footprints. The path is damp enough to take them rather well, and Ferrell's were plain enough in some places. If Adela walked up there yesterday afternoon she should have left tracks. The path is distinct enough, but there's obviously no great amount of traffic over it. But in several places there were smudges as if someone had obliterated footprints."

"Well, I'll be damned!" the doctor said.

"That's what I thought and one reason why I'm interested in Adela's little constitutional yesterday afternoon. Also, after she returned to the house and talked to Loretta in the upstairs hall Ian is certain she spent several minutes more talking to someone in one of the other bedrooms. You were in here when Adela returned from her walk. Did you go upstairs before dinner?"

"About six-fifteen I decided I'd better put on a fresh shirt. Adela wasn't in the hall then. But my bedroom is next to Hallie's, and I thought I heard her in there talking to Hallie."

"Oh—did you?" Michael said.

"You sound disappointed, son."

"I shouldn't be, I suppose. Adela told Ian that she had gone in to ask how Miss Hallie was. He had an idea that she wasn't quite telling the truth."

"But that would be the natural thing for Adela to do. Hallie was all a-dither because Adela had discovered the cook is given to drinking rum in her tea. I recommended rest and quiet for Hallie until dinnertime. However, that's not important."

"I don't suppose it is," Michael agreed—and they were both wrong. "However, will you, at some propitious moment, ask your sister what Adela said to her yesterday afternoon?"

"Certainly, if you want me to. I don't see—"

"Oh, neither do I," Michael said irritably. "But I do know that Adela was out of this house for several hours yesterday afternoon and that when she returned Ian believed that she was very well pleased with herself. I think Ian knows."

"I thought myself that she was looking around the dinner table once with a cat-that-swallowed-the-canary smile," the old man said. "And you're guessing that Adela had found out something— well, at least unpleasant—about someone who was here last night and was prepared to spill the beans when the right moment had arrived?"

"I am not really guessing about that, Doctor. Ian overheard Adela talking to someone while the lights were off. What he heard her say makes it quite clear that she was going to spill the beans, though she preferred to call it 'doing her duty.'"

"That's Adela. But I can't see how she could stumble on any dangerous information in a walk of less than two hours or during any walk."

"Is there anyone in this neighborhood she might have called on? Ian says she would not have dropped in on any of the old friends who were here last night since she was visiting lady here. But perhaps some quite elderly person in the neighborhood—"

Dr. Carter shook his head quickly. "I don't know of anyone like that."

"Well, Adela did pass the Maybry house. And," Michael said casually, "saw a man that she argued must be Dr. Maybry get into his car. One thing Ian heard her say into the darkness was: 'But you haven't changed, you see. And I've watched you very closely all evening. I never act hastily.'"

"Oh, fiddlesticks! Adela never met Jimmy Maybry until tonight. I didn't know him myself eight years ago."

"Did your niece Rosalie?"

"Rosalie? If Rosalie had known him socially I'd have met him here at the house. And she never had any doctor in her life but me," Dr. Carter said angrily.

Michael's eyebrows went up. "I didn't mean to offend you," he said.

Mr. Dundas' apologies often merely underline the fact that he considers that he has said nothing to which a reasonable person could object. The old doctor scowled, made a growling noise in his throat, and then laughed.

"I'm fond of Jimmy Maybry, though he's a damned fool about his wife. Suppose that youngest boy of his is a towhead. But Adela wasn't necessarily talking about appearance, you know. She might have been speaking of character, not looks."

"But whether Adela meant character or physical appearance she did say: 'You haven't changed.' And that is why I keep asking you to go back eight years, Doctor, even when I suspect that you don't want to."

"Where did you get that idea, son?" Dr. Carter was bland and inscrutable again. "I see your point now. But I can't remember any juicy bit of scandal or even hint of scandal from eight years back. All that happened while Adela was here was that she didn't marry Bruce. I thought it was as well she didn't. I've never liked Bruce, but Hallie has always been fond of him, so I put up with him."

Michael sighed. "Well, there is just one thing more. Did the police search Ian's and Adela's belongings thoroughly?"

"They didn't miss anything. They tore the guest room apart, and I saw them even examining shoes and turning pockets inside out and looking inside suitcase linings. Why?"

Michael hesitated briefly and then repeated Ian's description of Adela standing under one of the upstairs hall lights, studying the palm of her hand or something she held in it. For good measure he added the fact that Adela had assured someone later that night, during the blackout, that she had "all the proof" that would be needed.

It was Dr. Carter's turn to sigh. "Well, if she put something in her coat pocket, then, the police wouldn't have missed it if it had been there this morning. I don't think they would have missed anything she hid, either. They told me there were no signs anyone but Ian and Adela had been in the guest room, and it was plain enough that she was killed in the living room. Have a drink?"

"Oh"—Michael grinned—"I wouldna say no."

IV

When he came out into the hall again, somewhat fortified, Antonia and Freddie were sitting on the stairs. He was in time to hear Freddie say:

"I don't think anyone will tell, beautiful. Loretta, Judy, and Evelyn are good scouts, and Jimmy Maybry's no talker. Neither is Uncle Doc, and thank God Aunt Hallie's back was to the balcony and she was playing a tough hand at the time."

"You're leaving Bruce Ferrell out of it," Michael said. "If you are speaking of Toni's and Ian's little indiscretion I am afraid that Mr. Ferrell will not keep that to himself much longer. And that will be partly my fault."

"He'd tell even if you hadn't antagonized him," Antonia said. "He doesn't like me."

"So I gathered. According to the great lover, you have never forgiven him because you wanted to model for him and he had to tell you that you wouldn't do. He implied that one reason you wouldn't do was because you could not resist his charms."

"Why, the fatheaded so-and-so," Mr. Carter said amiably.

Antonia grinned. "You put it so nicely, Michael."

"I think so. But what is the truth of that story? Did he simply distort it slightly?"

"Yes. Bruce wanted me to pose for him in ski clothes. And I wouldn't mind posing in the nude for a real artist. The first thing was that Evelyn wasn't there, as I'd taken for granted she would be. Then Bruce wanted me to take off a few clothes, and somehow I got the idea that it wasn't in the interests of art, though he did have a lingerie ad to do."

Antonia laughed. "Actually, Freddie, he'd done himself up in a pink smock with a cute little round collar. He had incense and soft music going. And I simply shrieked—with laughter—and told him that his technique was overgrown with moss."

"I don't think that Mr. Ferrell would forgive you that," Michael said.

"The Great Panjandrum never forgives anyone who steps on his vanity," Freddie agreed. "Though he's self-satisfied enough that he doesn't always realize when people are laughing at him."

"But is it possible that he is now only coasting along on a reputation he acquired deservedly some years ago but has done nothing to deserve since?"

"You know," Freddie said, "I think you've got something there. He goes through all the motions when he meets a pretty woman, but—well, what do you think, Toni?"

"Oh, Bruce merely wanted to paint me in my lingerie. At first I thought: Why on earth should a working artist get a bang out of that? Then I realized it would make Bruce feel devilish because he knows me socially. But I don't think he would ever risk an affair with anyone in his own social circle."

"Why? Does Mrs. Ferrell have the money?" Michael asked.

"There's no money but what Bruce makes. Evelyn drove him into commercial art, and he does fairly well. But Bruce is crazy about their little girl," Freddie said. "She is an awfully cute kid, and he wouldn't want to lose her—by divorce."

"Of course that works two ways," Antonia pointed out. "Bruce would never give the little girl up to Evelyn if she was in the wrong. However, I do not think there's anything between Bruce and Judy. He's painted her for so long that she must be an old story to him. I have a notion that he might like to shop around."

"I think he does," Freddie said. "He lets things drop when he's with a bunch of men. I've gathered he knows a lot of good-looking waitresses, and so on, and that though they may give him their right names he doesn't tell them his. But that's not the sort of thing Dundas means, is it?"

"No."

"Bruce and Evelyn have been married about six years, and except for Judy I don't think there's ever been any definite gossip. He was mixed up with a couple of women before he married Evelyn. But I guess since then everyone has just gone on assuming that Bruce must be a—well—"

"Chaser is still a good word," Antonia said. "I think Evelyn knows he cheats and just doesn't care. Bruce takes vague business trips without her, doesn't he?"

"He went to New York without her last autumn," Freddie said. "And he goes off on week ends, hunting, fishing, and skiing. Those are supposed to be stag parties."

"Well, Evelyn's only maid is elderly and plain. I just remembered that it was Evelyn that Lulu Mae worked for first. Well, Lulu Mae is a pretty little thing." Antonia shrugged. "So Lulu Mae went to work for Judy before very long."

"Yes? And Lulu Mae is the next person I want to talk to," Michael said. "Will you take me over to the Maybrys', Toni? I know it's one o'clock," he added when they were outside, "and I'll see that you are fed before long."

"Oh, I'm not hungry. Michael, Miss Hallie is positively venomous. Nothing but the death sentence for Ian will satisfy her. If she had seen us on the balcony last night— You aren't listening to me."

"I heard you," Michael said, still frowning down at the street they were crossing.

"With one ear, maybe. What's the matter?"

"Have you ever studied chemistry, Toni?"

"No. Why?"

"If you don't know anything about chemical reactions—"

"What reaction? Whose? When?"

"No reaction," Michael said provokingly. "That is the trouble. There should have been one and there wasn't. Ring the doorbell, my child, and prepare to explain me to Mrs. Maybry."

They heard Mrs. Maybry before they saw her. "Billy, you come here to Mamma! I mean it! Someone's at the door."

A series of bumping sounds followed, as if some fairly soft object was rolling downstairs.

"Oh, good heavens! Billy, are you hurt? Precious, did you hurt yourself? Mamma's coming. Billy, don't open the door!"

Nevertheless, the door opened and Antonia and Michael found themselves confronting the black-browed child Ian had christened Sitting Bull. He was tastefully attired in a pair of socks and a very brief undervest. Antonia giggled, and Judith, coming down the stairway, shrugged resignedly.

"I guess he's young enough that it don't matter. I've been trying to put them down for their naps, but— Who is this with you, Toni?"

"This is Michael Dundas. He's Ian's cousin. Naturally, when I telephoned him and told him what had happened he came over here to see what he can do for Ian."

"Not much, can you?" Judith said placidly. "I'm sorry for Ian. I always thought Adela was a stinker. Are you the man that makes the dresses?"

"I'm a couturier, if that's what you mean," Mr. Dundas said coldly.

"That means you make dresses, don't it? I'm crazy about the ones Toni gets from you, but gosh, I can't keep the boys in shoes and pay much for my own clothes. Billy, if you'll go upstairs and take your nap Mamma will give you ten cents."

"I don't wanna take no nap," Billy whined.

"Well, if you'll put your clothes on you don't have to. Will you do that for Mamma?"

"And ten cents?" Sitting Bull specified.

"Well—yes. And don't wake Bobby. He's sound asleep like a good boy." Sitting Bull slouched up the stairs.

"Isn't he awfully big and bright for five years?" Judith said fondly. "Come in the living room. . . . I thought Ian was a swell guy, Mr. Dundas. I wondered how on earth Adela managed to land him and I'll bet she led him a dog's life. They didn't even have any children to make up for it. Have they caught him yet?"

Michael eyed her thoughtfully for a minute more before he answered. She wore shabby lounging pajamas, a kitchen apron, and no make-up. There was a smudge of grease on her forehead, and she was devastatingly beautiful.

"So far as I know, the police haven't found Ian yet," he said finally. "And naturally I feel that in this case their investigation isn't going to be as thorough as it would be if they weren't so certain that Ian is their man."

"You mean you're going to investigate yourself? Well, I'd do what I could to help Ian. I didn't tell the police about him kissing you, Toni."

"That was awfully nice of you."

"Jimmy said I mustn't tell. I didn't see you two, but he did and told me when we got home and— Oh, my goodness! Little Brother!"

She swooped down on the towhead who had just entered the cold, disordered living room and bore him, wriggling, over to the windows where the light was strongest.

His mouth was smeared with lipstick; there were splashes of rouge on his cheeks, a thick coating of powder over the rest of his face, and he reeked of some heavy, exotic scent. His attire was even more simple than that of his older brother. He wore nothing but cosmetics.

"Oh, Bobby, you've been into my make-up again! And that perfume I told you never, never to touch because Mamma couldn't afford to buy it herself. You're a bad boy, and Mamma is going to spank you."

Judith administered four light love taps, and Little Brother howled dismally. She sat down with

him in her arms and made cooing noises. Michael
ran his fingers through his hair.

I never saw him do that before, Antonia
thought. His hair always looks as if it had been
freshly combed into three deep waves. I believe
Judy is getting him down. She grinned at him, and
after an instant he shrugged and smiled wryly.

"Mrs. Maybry," he said, "if you will forget your
son's misdemeanors for just an instant I would
like to talk to your nursemaid."

"Oh," Judith said, "Lulu Mae isn't here. She
went off after lunch and she hasn't come back yet. I
mean she said she wouldn't be coming back today."

V

"She said she wouldn't— Well, where the hell does
she live, then?" Michael demanded, springing to
his feet.

Judith's lovely, slanted eyes widened reprovingly. "You don't need to swear, do you? I don't know
where she lives."

"*¡Jesús mil veces!* Oh, I'm sorry. Why should you
know? I suppose she comes by the day?"

"Yes, and she has no phone, so I've never looked
her up in the phone book."

"But you might," Michael said very politely,
"just happen to know her last name?"

"Yes, I know that. It's Brown."

"Brown! Well, I suppose it might have been Jones or Smith. Why did she go home today? She usually is with you all day, isn't she—and even looks after the children in the evening if you are not here?"

"Yes, she stayed with them last night. I guess she is about nineteen," Judith said reflectively. "She quit school about sixteen when her father died, and her mother works out by the day too. And she had a brother—well, she still has him, but he's in jail. And that's why Lulu Mae is scared of policemen, and I guess that's why she went home today after lunch."

"Did the police talk to her before lunch?"

"No, why would they? They came over and asked us questions about Ian and Adela. Miss Hallie had told us before they got here that Ian wanted a divorce and Adela wouldn't give him one. We had to say we knew that. And Bruce had already told the police about Ian saying at dinner last night that it might be dangerous for Adela *not* to believe in divorce.

"The police talked to us before Jimmy had gone to his office or Lulu Mae took the kids out for their morning walk," Judith went on. "She stayed upstairs till the policeman left. When she brought the boys back for lunch she kept asking me if I thought the police would come back. Jimmy had said they probably will. I told Lulu Mae so, and then she told me she hated policemen because once her brother just borrowed someone's car—"

"But the police, I presume, accused him of stealing it?" Michael said.

"Yes. They sent him to jail for it. Lulu Mae said they hit him until he confessed. I doubt if that's true, don't you? But all of a sudden she said she wasn't feeling good and was going home."

"But surely you have at least a vague notion where she lives?"

Judith considered, still cuddling Little Brother. "I'll tell you: it's somewhere near Alcatraz Avenue and the K line. Lulu Mae takes that car and gets off at College Avenue, and her boy friend that drives the grocery truck picks her up there and brings her up here. Bobby's asleep. I'll put him in his bed and be right back. . . ."

Sitting Bull sidled into the living room as his mother left it and began kicking the furniture. Antonia looked at Michael again.

"I have heard that you have 'a way with children,'" she said. "Let's see how far you get with Billy."

Michael met Sitting Bull's round, unwinking black stare and flinched.

"Is there a snake charmer in the house?" he muttered. "Oh well. Did Bobby fall into the water when Lulu Mae took you up the canyon yesterday afternoon, Billy?"

Billy eyed him scornfully. "Lulie Mae didn't take us up the canyon. Mamma said not to."

"Do you think," Michael murmured to Antonia, "that the little dear could be bribed?"

"I doubt it. I think Lulu Mae has them trained never to tell tales on her."

"Well. . . . Your mother does let you go up into the canyon when it is warm, doesn't she? What do you do then?"

Maybry Major considered this for several minutes, chinning himself on the bookcases. "Lulie Mae and Little Brother hide in the forest, and I shoot 'em with my gun," he said finally. "Bang-bang-bang! And sometimes we get poison oak."

"That must be simply delightful," Michael said. "And what—?"

"About Lulu Mae's boy friend," Judith said, coming back into the living room. "His name— Don't kick the piano, Billy. It wears out your shoes. His name is Jerry Something-or-other."

"That," Michael said, "will undoubtedly be a great help."

"You're sarcastic, aren't you? But he certainly knows where she lives. I don't remember what grocery he works for because I don't trade with them, but I think Evelyn Ferrell does. Anyway, Lulu Mae worked for Evelyn first, so she might know where Lulu Mae lives."

"Thank you. I think we'd better go over to the Ferrells' at once, Toni."

"All right. But—do you know why Lulu Mae didn't stay with Evelyn, Judy?"

"Oh, I guess Bruce was always trying to kiss her. He's kind of old-fashioned."

"Old-fashioned?" Antonia echoed.

"Isn't it, for men to make passes at the servants? I always think of that as going with sidewhiskers. Englishmen in the '90s, you know," Judith said lucidly.

Michael looked a trifle less morose. "Yes, I can see Mr. Ferrell done up in fancy waistcoats and several yards of watch chain chucking a pretty servant maid under the chin. Come along, Toni."

The Ferrells' maid was, as Antonia had said, an elderly, plain woman who had not even the distinction of being definitely ugly. She conducted them upstairs to a little sitting room where Evelyn was knitting in front of a wood fire. She thrust the knitting into a cretonne bag with a gesture of restrained impatience.

"I hope my patriotism will stand any test it's put to, but I'm not sure my knitting will. I'm afraid this sweater is going to turn into a sleeping bag. Come up to the fire. You both look a little blue."

"We've been at Judy's, and you know how she keeps her living room," Antonia said. "Evelyn, this is Mr. Dundas. He—"

"Bruce came home and told me he had met Mr. Dundas. I'm glad that Ian Maclean has someone to stand by him."

"Then you don't think that the only thing I can do for Ian is to get him a good lawyer?" Michael asked.

"I'm afraid that's what I do think, Mr. Dundas. I liked Ian. But he did strike me as a normally very self-controlled man whose nerves were so raw that his self-control might snap at any time. I'm sorry, but—"

"But that is probably what I would think myself if I were a disinterested party."

"Disinterested? But we aren't, are we? How can we be? We'll have to give evidence if Ian is tried for murder. So far the police haven't asked us many questions, but later on I'm sure they will question us more thoroughly."

"Just now they assume that Ian's flight is equivalent to confession," Michael said. "Without having heard his story they can't even set about disproving it. Ordinarily they'd begin at once to trace Adela's movements yesterday in detail. Well, Dr. Carter did tell me that Adela didn't go out at all yesterday until around four-fifteen, when she went for a walk. If the police know that it apparently doesn't interest them."

"But it does interest you?" Evelyn said.

"She was out of the house for nearly two hours, and you can do a tremendous amount of walking in two hours. So I doubt if she was walking all the time."

"I wonder. . . . Toni, you know old Mrs. Twelvetrees? She lives on the other side of this vacant lot that's next to us, Mr. Dundas. I got home from shopping yesterday between four-thirty and a quarter of five. And when I drove by Mrs. Twelvetrees' house I noticed there was a woman standing on her porch.

"Her back was to me, but you get to know everyone in the immediate neighborhood, and I didn't recognize this woman. I remember thinking: If that's a solicitor Mrs. Twelvetrees will make short work of her."

"She would," Antonia said. "She has been old as long as I remember, Michael. She never goes anywhere, but her tongue is still vigorous. She's known Dr. Carter and Miss Hallie for years. So she must have met Adela eight years ago, because from what Mrs. Twelvetrees has said to me Rosalie was a favorite of hers."

"Yet when I asked Dr. Carter if Adela might not have spent part of those two hours visiting someone like Mrs. Twelvetrees he didn't mention Mrs. Twelvetrees," Michael remarked.

Evelyn frowned slightly but said nothing. Antonia was not so discreet. "Damn funny, if you ask me," she said.

"Perhaps. But though I'm glad now that I did mention Adela's afternoon walk to you, Mrs. Ferrell, I really came to ask you if you can help me locate Lulu Mae Brown."

"Isn't she looking after Judy's boys this afternoon?"

"The sight of the police unnerved her. She left the Maybry house after lunch and said she wouldn't be coming back today."

"Oh, that foolish child," Evelyn said. "She has a worthless brother who, if he hadn't been arrested for stealing a car, would probably have tried to hold up a store sometime. But Lulu Mae and her mother are devoted to him and still think he was innocent. Lulu Mae is a sweet child and only stupid in spots, but it's that terrible, stubborn stupidity that won't yield even to facts."

"Something like Miss Hallie," Antonia suggested.

Evelyn laughed. "Something like a lot of people in the world. But I don't know Lulu Mae's home address, and they have no telephone. But I can tell you the name of the young man she's been going around with and the grocery store where he works. In fact—"

She glanced at the clock on the mantelpiece. "Yes, he should be here in a little while with some things I ordered. It's after two now, and he usually gets here before three. I'll tell Elsa to call us when Jerry gets here, shall I?"

VI

Jerry Flanigan was a muscular, wedge-shaped person permanently decorated with freckles and temporarily with the marks of someone's knuckles on his chin and nose. He spilled the Ferrell groceries out onto the kitchen table.

"Sure I can tell you where Lulie Mae lives, Mrs. Ferrell," he said with a reluctant sort of civility. "But you know she hasn't got no phone and, anyway, she ain't home."

"Oh. But her mother would know where she is, wouldn't she?" Evelyn asked.

"Did you want to see Lulie Mae for something, Mrs. Ferrell?" Mr. Flanigan inquired pointedly.

"No, this gentleman, Mr. Dundas, wants to talk to her."

Mr. Flanigan gave Mr. Dundas an unfriendly look. "Well, Lulie Mae's mother isn't home either. Is there anything more you want me to bring you, Mrs. Ferrell?"

"But, Jerry—" Evelyn began. Michael, standing behind Mr. Flanigan, shook his head. "No, Jerry, that's all today."

Mr. Flanigan shouldered the box that had held Evelyn's groceries and tramped out the back door. Michael left the two women in the kitchen, quit the house by the front door, and met Mr. Flanigan at his truck.

"I think," he said, "that we may do better without Mrs. Ferrell, since you may be as impolite to me as you choose. I have never seen your Lulu Mae and I have no designs on her virtue. I am a married man and a father."

"Them's the worst kind," Mr. Flanigan observed, glaring at the Ferrell residence.

Michael grinned. "Yes, that was a singularly fatuous remark, but I had hoped it might reassure you. Well, do you know what happened over there last night?"

He gestured toward Dr. Carter's house. Jerry Flanigan nodded.

"I read about it in the papers at lunch. But the dame's husband killed her, didn't he?"

"I don't think so, because the husband in question happens to be my cousin."

"Oh well, then you got to stand by him. Only where does Lulie Mae come in? I don't guess she ever saw those Macleans at all."

"I know. I only want to ask her if she took the Maybry children up that canyon yesterday afternoon. And if she did I want to know if she saw Mrs. Maclean walking up there."

"Well, there's no harm in that," Jerry admitted. "But won't the kids tell you?"

"Mrs. Maybry had forbidden Lulu Mae to take them up there, and if she did disobey Mrs. Maybry the boys won't admit that she did. Besides, even the oldest is a little young to be a reliable witness."

"I guess Lulie Mae has them young hellions right under her thumb, all right," Jerry said absently. He kicked the truck's front tires, rubbing one large ear. "Look, Mr. Dundas, do you suppose that there's anything wrong? Oh, I know Lulie Mae hasn't *done* anything wrong. But it's kinda funny—"

"What is it that you think is 'kinda funny'?" Michael asked quickly.

"Well, she called me up about one when she knew I'd be in the grocery loading the truck for the afternoon deliveries. She'd stopped at some phone—she didn't say where—and she broke a date she had with me tonight."

"Then she isn't given to doing that?"

"No. We'd get married if I didn't have a mother and kid sister to support. I'll swear she wasn't standing me up for some other guy. But first she said she wasn't working this afternoon because she didn't feel good. So I said I'd come over and see how she was when I got off work about six-thirty."

Mr. Flanigan dug his scarred knuckles into his forehead, frowning.

"But then, quick, she said she wouldn't be home then. So I says: 'But I thought you don't feel good.' And she said: oh well, as long as she had the afternoon off, she'd like to go down to Oakland to a show."

"Alone?"

"I asked her that," Jerry said. "In fact, I said: 'Are you going somewheres with Bill Madigan?' That's a guy we know and I don't like. Lulie Mae said she guessed if she was going out with Bill or anyone else she wouldn't be scared to tell me. And that's the truth. She kinda likes to see me get hot under the collar."

"Don't the best of them? Was that all?"

"No, she told me not to fuss. Then she said if I could stay awake till nine o'clock I could come round to say good night. That's another reason I don't think she's just two-timing me. If she was going out with Bill Madigan, f'instance, he'd never get her home by nine."

"And you say her mother isn't at home either?"

"Mrs. Brown won't be till nine. She's kind of a practical nurse and she stays with some woman who's sick from one to nine. Mrs. Brown wouldn't know any more than I do."

"You brought Lulu Mae up here this morning?" Michael said. "Did either of you know then that Mrs. Maclean had been killed?"

"I didn't know. I didn't see a paper till lunch. And I didn't bring Lulie Mae to work this morning on account of she stayed at the Maybrys' last night."

"She— Oh. Mrs. Maybry neglected to tell me that, you see."

"Did she? Well, Lulie Mae often stays all night if the Maybrys get home so late that Dr. Maybry don't want to take her home or to the nearest bus or car line. She don't like to walk down these hills alone late at night. Lulie Mae told me yesterday Mrs. Maybry said she'd better just plan to go to bed in the boys' room."

"I see. Well . . ." Michael wrote his telephone number on a page from a notebook, gave it and a handful of small change to Jerry.

"If you find out anything call me. My wife will take the message if I'm not home."

"And would I call you after I've talked to Lulie Mae—after nine tonight?"

"I hope you will," Michael said with a peculiar emphasis that fortunately escaped Mr. Flanigan. He drove away down the street. Michael watched him go, then:

"Damn, damn, damn!" he muttered. "What—?"

"Yes?" Antonia said, coming up behind him.

"What can I do? Lost in the haystack of Oakland or Berkeley one nineteen-year-old girl who, according to Ian, must look very much like hundreds of other girls. Well, I can't just let this slide. But I'll have to approach my objective from the rear. There is a drugstore near the Claremont Hotel, isn't there? Do you want to come along and have something to eat while I'm telephoning?"

PART FIVE

I

Michael retired into a telephone booth with another handful of change and finally managed to locate Inspector Nicholas Prevost of the San Francisco homicide detail.

"Oh, it's you," Prevost said. "I've been wanting to talk to you."

"Can't that wait?"

"No, it can't wait! We're asked to scour the city for an Ian Maclean who killed his wife in Berkeley last night and who happens to be your cousin."

"Who told you that, Nicholas? That is, who told the Berkeley police?"

"A fellow named Ferrell let them know that you are in the neighborhood. 'Poking your nose into things' is the way he put it. We were on the lookout for Maclean or his car long before that. We found the car before noon where he'd left it, way out in the Mission.

"Then," Prevost continued, "we turned up a drugstore clerk who remembered that a fellow answering Maclean's description looked at the telephone directory in the early hours of the morning. And tore out the city map, the clerk found out later. Then when we were told that this Maclean is your cousin—"

"Don't you think Valerie is looking well today?" Mr. Dundas inquired blandly.

"Someone had to make certain Maclean isn't hiding at your house! I could have sent someone else; I don't have to do routine jobs like that. But—"

"But you thought it would be a nice gesture if you went yourself. It was, Nicholas," Michael said grudgingly. "I hope you searched the place thoroughly—and I'm sure you did."

"And you know damned well that we have to cooperate with the Berkeley police. If I can guess where your cousin is hiding—where you've hidden him—"

"If you can guess that the joke will be on me, *amigo*. I know: you're warning me. Well, reserve me a comfortable steam-heated cell with southern exposure if you are afraid you may have to book me for conspiring to conceal a fugitive from justice. Don't worry about it, because I am certain that Ian did not kill his wife, and before too long he will surrender himself to the authorities."

"Well, that's a load off my mind," Prevost said. It was typical of their relationship that he did not even hint that Michael should tell him where Ian was. "And what's on your mind?"

"Do you have any friends on the Berkeley homicide detail?"

"I know Sanders pretty well. He's an interesting specimen. He has a Ph.D. in history from California. He was what they used to call a campus cop, paid his way through college working on the Berkeley police force. He meant to teach, but no good jobs came along, and Vollmer was sure he'd make a good detective. Obie decided to give it a try, and he's been giving it a try for fifteen years now. Obie still speaks of the job as being only temporary."

"Obie?" Michael said.

Prevost laughed. "Oswald Bartholomew—but he'll never tell. He's in charge of your case. I've talked to him several times this morning."

"Is he broad-minded?"

"Well, you know, Michael, when you ask if a copper is broad-minded you're too apt to mean: will he let me do as I damn please and to hell with regulations?" Prevost said dryly. "But Obie is not

what you would call stuffy or too much wedded to
rules and regulations. And he would like to talk to
you more or less unofficially."

"Would anything you told him have something
to do with that?" Michael asked astutely.

"I told him that even if he seems to have an
open-and-shut case against Maclean he'll be wise
to talk to you. I also told him that if you have
hidden Maclean he might as well not waste breath
asking you where. After all, the necessary official inquiries have been made at your home. And,"
Prevost said without animosity, "no one saw your
cousin come to your home or leave it."

"If he did either," Michael said.

Prevost's answer was one short censorable word.
"But Sanders won't try to grill you. You are known
by reputation, at least, even in Berkeley. Do you
want to talk to him?"

"I do and I would rather keep it strictly unofficial. But I think he had better talk to me, Nick.
I have something to tell him that, if he is a good
detective, he can't afford to ignore."

"All right. Are you in a pay station? Then give
me fifteen minutes and call me back."

Michael joined Antonia at the soda fountain,
ordered coffee and a sandwich, and then did not
eat the sandwich.

"Aren't you ever hungry?" Antonia said. "If you don't want it I do." She ate half the sandwich and sighed. "I go on poking food down my throat yet I'm really very unhappy. Had you noticed?"

She laughed as she said it, but when Michael answered gravely: "Yes, I had noticed, Antonia," her lips trembled.

"He didn't do it, Michael! He couldn't! And you have to prove that he didn't."

Michael's strong, slim fingers tightened about the handle of the thick coffee cup. "And I'm not at all certain that I can. You might as well know that. This morning I was very cocksure. But after more than four hours of battering my head against stone walls the head is beginning to ache and the walls are still intact.

"¡Por Dios! Don't look like that, child! You've known Ian perhaps forty-eight hours, seen him twice. Now he's in trouble, and that makes him a romantic figure to you."

"That is a lot of malarkey and you know it! I'm not a child and I'm not romantic, so don't be paternal."

"My feeling for you has never been at all fatherly, Antonia," Michael said coolly. "And I'm not your keeper, but it does occur to me that your father and mother are going to have a few things to say to me if I allow you to become more involved with Ian than you already are. I've always gotten the impression that you and your parents are very good friends: that they do not allow you to annoy them but are also careful not to annoy you."

"That's so. We are good friends. But they're still so much in love with each other that sometimes I feel a little lonely. I mean: I wouldn't go to Sun Valley with them last week because I knew they'd like to go alone. I suppose it's because their marriage is an extra-special one that I haven't married. I won't put up with substitutes."

"Don't," Michael said briefly. "If you are ever tempted to just consider Ian's case. Nevertheless, I wish that your parents were here now or that you would wire them to come back. You won't? I was afraid of that. Well, I haven't time to be paternal. I must call Nick Prevost again. . . ."

"Michael?" Prevost said. "Well, it's three-thirty now. If you'd like to go to a restaurant called the H. & M. Grill on University Avenue near Shattuck and the U.C. Theater and get yourself a cup of coffee Obie Sanders will be wandering in there for coffee himself in about fifteen minutes. I've described you to him—and good luck."

Michael went back to Antonia. "I have to go down to University Avenue and I can't take you. Can you get home by yourself or could you kill an hour or so at Dr. Carter's? I want to talk to Mrs. Twelvetrees and I'll need you to introduce me."

"I can kill time at Dr. Carter's. Loretta might be home by now."

"And you might pick up some useful crumbs in just casual conversation with her," Michael said. "I'll have time to take you back there. . . ."

Twenty minutes later he entered a small and rather dingy grill and fish grotto on University Avenue. A meager, grayish, pedantic-looking person was sitting halfway up the lunch counter.

"That's Sanders," Michael thought, but he did not introduce himself. He sat down at one of the two tables in front of a row of curtained booths and ordered coffee.

The door opened and a male animal, too large for a man but not large enough for a horse, entered the restaurant. He had a scrubbed pink, lopsided moonface, the type of sandy mustache once known as a soup strainer, and mild, bovine eyes. He looked about the place and came over to Michael.

"You're Dundas, aren't you? I'm O. B. Sanders. Glad to know you."

"And what will you have, Mr. Sanders?" the waitress asked, arriving with Michael's coffee.

"Well, I should drink milk, but I like tea so much better that I'll take coffee," Sanders said seriously.

He had a high-pitched, faintly plaintive voice that made every statement seem a mild complaint. He tested a chair for durability and settled himself in it with an air of fearing the worst.

"Nick Prevost says you have something important to tell me. I hadn't expected that."

"Neither had I expected to hand out information to the Berkeley police," Michael said candidly. "But I don't dare not to. You didn't interview the Maybrys' nursemaid, Lulu Mae Brown."

Sanders waited until the waitress had brought his coffee. Then: "Well, this Lulu Mae doesn't live with the Maybrys, you know," he said.

"But did you know that, since the Maybrys were to be out late, Lulu Mae spent the night in their home last night?"

"She did? Nobody mentioned that."

"Mrs. Maybry certainly did not to me," Michael said. "Even before that I wanted to talk to Lulu Mae. Now that I know she spent the night across from the Carter house I'm even more anxious to locate her. But I can't."

"Can't, hey? Why not?" Sanders said, fingering the Phi Bete key that was a tiny, lonesome bright spot on his vast front.

Michael told him what Judith and Evelyn had said about Lulu Mae and, in detail, his conversation with Jerry Flanigan.

"I may be getting the wind up for nothing," he concluded. "But I'm afraid that someone has advised the girl to stay away from home today in case you might try to question her there. She told Jerry Flanigan he could see her at home after nine o'clock. So I'm wondering if she has an appointment with someone sometime before nine."

"I was wondering too," Sanders said complainingly. "I'll try to pick the girl up. Can't afford not to, though in spite of what her boy friend says, the girl may just have another man on the string. So you're interested in Mrs. Maclean's movements yesterday?"

"Don't you think you should be too?"

"Just now we are more interested in Mr. Maclean's movements," Sanders remarked pointedly. "If he has a story to tell and he told it we might know what lines of inquiry we should follow."

"But would you explore them very thoroughly since you have an open-and-shut case against Ian?"

Sanders regarded him sadly. "I guess you could go on like this for hours. Well, let's say that everyone else on the force is satisfied with the case against your cousin. On the surface it looks airtight to me. But I'm really a historian. I distrust surfaces.

"If you ever do any historical research you find yourself going perpetually backward in time. You find yourself studying the French Revolution to account for Hitler."

"Then you don't think that it is unimportant that Adela Maclean visited here eight years ago and met all the people concerned then?" Michael asked.

"No historian worth his salt can ignore that fact. Neither am I ignoring the history of Adela and Ian Maclean's marriage, as I've pieced it together. Probably he did finally just see red and bash her head in. Just the same," Sanders said placidly, "before I'm through I'll know a lot more about these people than they mostly want me to. You've hired Dana Clyde to look into their backgrounds, haven't you?"

"Yes. Did he tell you?"

"He's one private dick that's always played ball with me. He told me and he's the man for that job. Well, is there anything more you'd like to tell me—or ask me?"

"Did any of Adela's shoes have damp earth on them?"

"N-no. No, there was a pair of walking shoes, but they were clean and dry."

Michael sighed. "Oh, of course Adela would clean her shoes very carefully before entering the house again. Have any of these people alibis for the time when Adela was killed?"

"Not to speak of. Everyone says they were sleeping, of course. The Maybrys do occupy the same room. Twin beds. The Ferrells don't share a bedroom. His is a front room, and hers is a back one. We do find out these things," Sanders said reproachfully. "Anything else?"

"No, I think that's all."

II

Dr. Carter's tired old car was parked in front of the house when Michael left Antonia there. She found the front door open, thought: Oh well, I won't bother Maria. The doctor won't care if I just walk in. He's probably in his study.

She stepped into the hall and started toward the study. Its door was evidently open too. At any rate, she heard Loretta's voice clearly.

"Adela and I did talk a few minutes in the upstairs hall yesterday evening when she'd just come back from her walk. But I don't see why I needed to tell the police that, Cousin Doc."

"I dare say you didn't. But you might tell me about it, Loretta."

"Well—we just—just talked. Adela didn't say where she'd been. She said she'd been taking her constitutional and didn't I think regular exercise did wonders for one? She'd noticed people who didn't exercise were apt to get very stoop-shoul-dered and even hollow-chested. She meant me. Then she commented on my engagement ring. I won't say she admired it. What she meant, if you knew Adela, was: 'Isn't it just a little too ostenta-tious, my dear?'

"Perhapth it is a little ostentatious," Loretta said, "but Richard chose it and I love it. And I told Adela that I thought that even if a man can't really afford to be extravagant you should always act as if any gift he gives you is just exactly what you wanted."

Dr. Carter chuckled. "Yes, I dare say poor Ian never gave Adela an extravagant, worthless trifle that she didn't exchange it for 'something she re-ally needed.'"

"That's what I was thinking. But of course Adela reminded me, so politely, that she'd been married seven years, and I'm an old maid at nearly thirty. She gave the impression that it was all so amusing, the idea that I was going to marry Rich-ard. Then she said—well, she said she thought I owed her an explanation."

"An explanation?" the old man repeated.

"She said I'd made her feel she wasn't wanted here. She reminded me that this is Cousin Hallie's home, not mine."

"It's my house," Dr. Carter snorted. "Though I'll admit that to all practical purposes it's Hallie's. Then what?"

"Adela said that it distressed Cousin Hallie to feel that I hadn't been very cordial to her and Ian." Loretta laughed briefly. "As if Cousin Hallie would have thought much about it if Adela hadn't pointed it out to her. Then Adela said she would like to know in what way she offended *me,* in a tone that meant I'd offended *her.*"

There was a minute of silence. Antonia's nose twitched. She fumbled for a handkerchief, pressed her finger firmly over her upper lip, and managed to keep from sneezing.

"Did you answer her?" Dr. Carter asked.

"I told her I'd despised her for years," Loretta lisped. "I'd never liked her, and after what she did to poor Rosalie—"

"Eh? What do you mean?"

"Oh, Cousin Doc, you must have guessed that Adela was the very first person Rosalie would have confided in. We never talked about it, but I supposed you knew—"

"I should have," the old man said slowly. "That's why Adela— Loretta! Child, did Rosalie go to you then? Before—"

"Yes." Antonia thought that Loretta was crying. "I've wanted to tell you for so many years. Adela

could always insist that *she* did nothing wrong.
But I—"

Antonia sneezed so shatteringly that the sound
could not be muffled in her handkerchief. She
backed hastily toward the front door, switched
around it, and was standing outside, ringing the
doorbell and blowing her nose, when Dr. Carter
came to let her in.

"I think I'm getting a cold," she remarked and
sneezed again.

"And I thought you were in the hall when you
sneezed the first time, Toni."

"Me?" Antonia shook her head. "You've always
said I have a very unladylike sneeze, you know.
Michael just brought me by. Can I stay here until
he comes back for me?"

"You know you can," the doctor said more gra-
ciously. "Until he comes back for you, eh? That
young man has more energy—"

"I never think of Michael as being energetic,
ordinarily."

"I should have called it driving force. He has
an unfair amount of charm too."

"But I never thought of Michael as being charming either," Antonia objected.

"I didn't say he *is* charming. God forbid," Dr.
Carter grunted. "I do say that if he didn't have
personal magnetism and force enough to impose

his will on others he couldn't get away with this kind of thing. Loretta's in the living room. . . ."

Loretta was at the piano playing "The Bedouin Love Song" which Antonia knew, from having heard him sing it at least ten times, to be one of Richard Prince's favorites.

"Sit down, Toni," Dr. Carter went on. "I have to go out again. The little Harlan girl is very low. I want to see her again, so I won't be home when Dundas comes back."

"There's something you want me to tell him?"

"Yes, tell him that Loretta talked to Adela yesterday afternoon, but Adela didn't say where she'd walked to. The rest of their conversation isn't worth repeating. Is that right, do you think, Loretta?"

"That'th wight," Loretta agreed. She struck two false chords, left the sands of the desert to grow cold, and began to play "Asleep in the Deep."

"Oh, Adela was a little stuffy because she thought Loretta hadn't been too cordial," Dr. Carter said easily. "She wanted Loretta to explain that. Adela always wanted explanations."

"I told her I wath afwaid I hadn't quite come down to earth yet." Loretta was disastrously girlish. "Wichard only went away day before yesterday, and I just wathn't in the mood for company."

"Yes. Well, tell Dundas that Adela went into Hallie's room after she talked to Loretta. Hallie doesn't remember that Adela did anything more than ask her how she was feeling and if she wanted any help dressing. Adela said she'd been 'walking around the neighborhood.' That's all I had time for and I must be on my way."

In the doorway the old man paused. "Oh, you might ask Loretta where she was when the lights were out last night, Toni. Dundas wanted to know."

"Well?" Antonia said when the front door had banged and the doctor's car wheezed away from the house.

"Well, what? Oh." Loretta nibbled at a finger and appeared to consider. "Oh, when the lights first went out I did get up and try to find some matches. But Cousin Hallie fussed so and wanted people to sit still, so I jus' sat down again, that'th all. I like to sit in the dark, don't you?"

"Not for that long," Antonia said. "I wandered into the dining room myself. I never heard you soothing Miss Hallie."

"I didn't." Loretta abandoned her sprightly manner as if she realized that Antonia had found it unconvincing. "Cousin Hallie was very well occupied shouting to Freddie and Cousin Doc. I didn't speak to her until an instant before the lights came on. She was startled, of course.

"And I thought it was time people were going home," Loretta added with a look that brought the color to Antonia's cheeks. "I thought the longer the black-out lasted the less likely people were to come back to the card tables. So I didn't try to find candles or fuses myself. I knew Freddie had fused the lights—"

"He—what?"

"Freddie deliberately fused the lights. I suspected he had last night, and he admitted he had this morning. I suppose I shouldn't have told you."

"Why not? More power to Freddie, I say."

Loretta smiled. "He'd done it once before or I wouldn't have been suspicious. I knew he'd take as much time as he could before he found any kind of light, so Cousin Hallie would forget she wanted to go on playing cards."

"I suppose Adela would have been mortally insulted if she'd known what Freddie had done, even though the evening had had its little embarrassments and everyone wanted to go home."

"Oh, but Adela knew that her own behavior had been beyond criticism," Loretta said with unexpected dryness. "Of course she wouldn't have thought it funny. Freddie's always been a tease. Rosalie and I never minded, but Adela said he spied on her."

"When Adela was here before, you mean?"

Loretta nodded. "I suppose she meant he spied on her and Bruce. Freddie wasn't eighteen, and he

must have thought Adela and Bruce took themselves very seriously. He—oh, I know. Adela gave
Bruce a lock of her hair."

She laughed as Antonia grimaced. "I remember
that even I thought that was pretty Victorian. And
Freddie saw her do it at the bench in the canyon
and never stopped teasing her and Bruce about
it. There was some old poem he used to throw
at them. And he teased them about playing post
office—kissing games, you know."

Well, we've gone pretty far afield, Antonia
thought. But Michael said just casual conversation, and I don't want to antagonize Loretta by
asking her pointed questions. . . .

"Have you done any shopping yet?" she asked.

"No, but"—Loretta's thin tired face lighted
up—"Cousin Doc just gave me a check for a hundred dollars. He is so good, Toni. He can't afford
that, I know. But I hate to go to Richard with
nothing. Did I tell you Richard insisted Monday
that I use his roadster while he's away and until
we're married? I'm keeping it down the street in
half the Kelseys' garage. There wasn't room for it
and Ian's car both in the garage here.

"It's wonderful not having to walk or take
busses and streetcars from one lesson to another.
Wichard wanted me to give my pupils notice at
once. But I want those few extra dollars, and it

isn't fair to my advanced piano students to just abandon them before I can arrange for someone else to take them over. . . ."

III

When, after half an hour of this sort of conversation, the doorbell rang Loretta rose to answer it.

"Maria is sulky," she remarked. "And besides, Cousin Hallie is keeping her busy wringing out cold cloths for the head and filling hot-water bottles for the feet. And the cook is still here only because the police told her that she must stay."

She opened the door. "It's all right," Antonia said. "Loretta van Horn, Michael."

"I'm very glad to meet you, Mr. Dundas," Loretta said unenthusiastically. "And now, if you'll excuse me, I really must look in on Cousin Hallie."

Michael watched her willowy form out of sight up the stairway. "Do I smell?" he inquired.

Antonia laughed. "You are not popular. It isn't because she doesn't like Ian."

"I suppose not. Very much the startled fawn, I'd say. Well, shall we call on Mrs. Twelvetrees?"

"Drive down to her house and park," Antonia said, following him to the car. "I have a message for you from Dr. Carter. He wanted me to tell you . . ."

She repeated the old doctor's statements regarding Loretta's conversation with Adela and Adela's

with Miss Hallie between six and seven o'clock of
the previous evening.

"That's not helpful," Michael commented.

"He lied in his teeth," Miss Jordan said succinctly. "Listen! The front door was open and I
just walked in. Loretta and the doctor were talking
in his study. He was asking her about talking to
Adela in the upstairs hall last night. This is what
Loretta really said. . . ."

"You choose the damnedest times to sneeze,
Toni," Michael said when she had finished.

"I know. But what did Adela do to Miss Hallie's Rosalie? Loretta said that Adela could claim
that *she'd* done nothing wrong. What did Loretta
do? What has she wanted to tell Dr. Carter for so
long?"

"I don't know. Neither do I know why the doctor decided that conversation had better not be
repeated. I wonder if he is also lying about Miss
Hallie's conversation with Adela before dinner
yesterday."

"I doubt it. For one thing, I don't think Miss
Hallie would remember much in her present state
of mind."

"Well—anything more?"

"Loretta insists she never left the living room
during the black-out. I didn't think there was any
use heckling her on that subject. I couldn't, really,

because I was in the dining room and I don't think she ever was. She jingles, you know."

"So I've been told. I didn't think it wise to question anyone else on that subject. If people want to know why I'm interested in what happened during the black-out I can't tell Ian's story since I'm supposed not to have seen him yet. It might have been better if I had let him surrender to the police."

"No!" Antonia said. "At least he isn't locked into a cell, charged with murder."

"Well, what else did Miss van Horn have to say?" Michael asked.

"She'd guessed, even before Freddie told her so this morning, that he had deliberately fused the lights last night."

"Oh, did she?"

"Do you think that could matter? Then she told me how Freddie used to tease Bruce and Adela eight years ago. He said they played post office. And he saw Adela give Bruce a lock of her hair at the love seat up in the canyon."

"No!" Michael said.

"Yes." Antonia laughed. "I'll bet Adela had never read anything stronger than Sir Walter Scott at twenty-one or the *Little Colonel* series. Of course Freddie thought it was all very funny, and he used to throw some poem at them. Loretta didn't say what."

Michael chuckled. "I'll wager I can guess." He spoke in a dreadful falsetto. "'O Ringlet, O Ringlet, She blushed a rosy red, When Ringlet, O Ringlet, She clipt you from her head.'"

"Gee whillikers! Is there any more?"

"'And Ringlet, O Ringlet, She gave you me, and said, "Come, kiss it, love, and put it by, If this can change, why so can I."' A. Tennyson. Your education has been sadly neglected, Toni. Come along and introduce me to your Mrs. Twelvetrees."

Mrs. Twelvetrees was not one of these women who, we are assured, retain traces of former beauty even in extreme old age. For one thing, she had never been beautiful. Also, she was eighty and looked it.

She wore a preposterous wig "for warmth" and with no intention to deceive. Indeed, since the color of her wigs varied from red to black, according to her mood, deception was out of the question.

Her profile rather resembled that of an elderly goose, and her habit of honking "Hey?" intensified the resemblance. A few of the usual stage properties were present, however: a cane, a footstool, the shawl that draped the shoulders of the quilted black robe that covered her gaunt bony frame.

"Maclean's cousin, hey? Step around where I can see you, young man. Humph! Is Maclean anything like this one, Antonia?"

"Not much, or he probably *would* have killed his wife. Either that or dealt with her adequately some other way."

"You flatter me," Michael said. "I have only one rule for women like Adela, and that is to run like hell when I encounter one."

"Good rule," Mrs. Twelvetrees grunted. "I've seen you coming and going with Antonia today and I guess that you want to know if Adela came to see me yesterday."

Mrs. Twelvetrees' chair stood in a large bay window from which she could look up and down and across the street, see the front of Dr. Carter's house, the back end of the Ferrells', and one side of the Maybrys'. The window drapes were not only pulled back but also firmly thumbtacked away from the panes.

"You needn't laugh," Mrs. Twelvetrees said tartly, seeing Michael grin. "I never liked to read, and I can't sleep more than six hours. Heaven knows there's little enough happens in this neighborhood to amuse me. And as a lookout this is just tolerable: no more. Well, Adela did drop in on me about four-thirty yesterday, but if the fool police haven't gumption enough to ask me why should I tell 'em?"

"Why, indeed? Did you see her coming?" Michael asked. "She left Dr. Carter's around four-ten or -fifteen."

"I was upstairs changing my wig then in case I had visitors around four-thirty. The doorbell rang just as I came downstairs. Well, butter wouldn't melt in her mouth."

Mrs. Twelvetrees mimicked Adela crudely. "She just had to see Mrs. Twelvetrees at once and she'd bring her husband in to meet me the next day. So good to see everyone again, especially dear Mrs. Twelvetrees."

"And what do you think was her real reason for coming?"

"You're sharp, aren't you? So am I," the old woman said complacently. "Why, Adela wanted to pick up a little dirt, as you young people say, before dinner last night. Lord, why did she come to me when she'd had all one evening and most of the day with Hallie Durdan?"

"Well, Miss Hallie's accounts are apt to be a little disjointed," Antonia pointed out. "And you know that you learn or guess at things that no one else ever knows—unless you tell them."

She also knew that if Mrs. Twelvetrees liked you impertinence rather pleased her. If she didn't like you not all your charm or any amount of courtesy would win Mrs. Twelvetrees over.

"Maybe. Adela was particularly interested in Judith," Mrs. Twelvetrees recalled. "Wanted to know what Jimmy Maybry's like. Thought she had seen him getting into his car. I guess she had; he'd driven up in it just before I went upstairs, and the car was gone again when Adela got here. She knew about Judith's posing for Bruce Ferrell—"

"And didn't approve?" Michael said.

"No. Neither do I. Maybe Judy does pose with all her clothes on, but Bruce's drawings show he has a good idea how she'd look in the altogether, as they say. I saw Judith scurrying over to the house yesterday afternoon when Evelyn had gone shopping. To pose for Bruce, I suppose. But I didn't tell Adela that."

"It's only fair to say that Evelyn is usually home when Judy is posing," Antonia remarked.

"We-ll, yes. Evelyn's a fool. Oh, not to take steps to stop that gossip, I mean. Nothing more than that. Evelyn acts as we used to do—"

"In the 'age of innocence'?" Michael said blandly.

"That's all right, young man. It worked out very well. We got along tolerably, and if our husbands had their little diversions it simply didn't touch us—as long as they didn't divert themselves with any woman we knew socially. We were as happy as these girls who dash to Reno as soon as they find out their husbands are men and not gods. This is Evelyn's second marriage. She married a young

fellow who was under his mother's thumb. Bruce's
mother isn't living, and I'd guess he's easy enough
to live with.

"Not that I said any of this to Adela. I enlarged
on how ideally happy Bruce and Evelyn are," Mrs.
Twelvetrees said with a wicked grin. "Praised
Judith to the skies, too, and Jimmy Maybry. In
fact, I said a good word for everyone, Freddie
included."

"Why 'Freddie included'?" Antonia said combatively. "I like Freddie."

"Not enough to marry him, do you? Oh, I don't
dislike Freddie, and they tell me he's a smart lawyer, but he does sponge off Hallie and Breck Carter. I don't care how much money he gets from
Hallie; she might as well spend it on someone as
hoard it. And I didn't take it kindly, Adela's wanting to know if 'Freddie had improved' or 'made
anything of himself after all Miss Hallie has done
for him.' I gave a glowing account of Loretta's
affairs, too, and sent Adela off with a flea in her
ear. Nearly six, that was. Since she came to talk, I
kept talking longer than she really wanted me to."

"And of course you talked about Rosalie
Durdan?" Michael said. "I believe she died soon
after Adela ended her visit here eight years ago?"

"We didn't talk about Rosalie," Mrs. Twelvetrees said brusquely.

"But why not? Adela and Rosalie were very close friends and—"

"Oh, Adela said how sad it was that Rosalie was not here to welcome her. That was all. I'm tired," Mrs. Twelvetrees declared vigorously. "You children had better run along."

"Of course." Michael got up. "Have you seen Dr. Carter today?"

"Oh, he dropped by for— What business is it of yours, young man?"

Michael grinned at her. "You said I'm sharp— and so are you. Thank you, Mrs. Twelvetrees. . . . But she has spoken her mind too many years to be a good dissembler," he added to Antonia outside.

"You think Dr. Carter didn't mention her to you this morning so he could have time to warn her what not to say if you did call on her?"

"What else? I'd hoped this thing could be solved without going back eight years." Michael got into the car. "But in some quarters there is a definite touchiness on the subject of Rosalie's death."

He started the car. "So perhaps it isn't so important that Adela walked up that canyon yesterday afternoon—if she did go there. Of course it didn't take her fifteen minutes to walk from Dr. Carter's house down to Mrs. Twelvetrees'. And Bruce Ferrell did hike up to that canyon this morning, and someone had smudged out footprints on the path."

"Aren't you trying to locate Lulu Mae?"

"The Berkeley police have taken over that job. But even if Lulu Mae was up the canyon yesterday afternoon and did see Adela there that may not be important. Because Lulu Mae stayed at the Maybry house all last night. . . . Since your parents are away, I think I'll take you home with me, Antonia. And, much later on, to see Ian."

"Why take me with you?"

"Well, I hope that your presence may restrain him slightly, both in speech and action."

"But why should Ian—? Michael, how did you persuade him to hide out?"

"With a 'persuader.' A blackjack, to you."

"A blackjack? You hit him with a— Oh, I hate you!"

"*¡Qué estás tonta!*" Mr. Dundas was not impressed. "I was fresh out of brass knuckles or knockout drops. Besides, 'at least he isn't locked in a cell, charged with murder.' Remember who said that, Antonia?"

IV

Mr. Franklin Parkman was finally homeward bound. Mr. Parkman was nicely, thank you, and, leaving Oakland, inclined to sing all four parts of "Sweet Adeline."

But the glow within Mr. Parkman was mild and the way home long and cold. Mr. Parkman thought of logs blazing in the fireplace, of his smoking jacket and old slippers. Then Mr. Parkman looked at his windshield wiper, wagging steadily back and forth, and thought of Mrs. Parkman.

Mr. Parkman sold furniture, and he had never been able to make his wife understand that there were times when it would be bad business not to drink with a buyer. But Mrs. Parkman would understand that it was nearly ten o'clock, that dinner had been ready at six-thirty, that the telephone is here to stay, and the cost of a call from Oakland to Berkeley just one nickel.

Mr. Parkman sighed. When he remembered that his wife had wanted to use the car tonight to visit her sister in Thousand Oaks he groaned and stepped on the gas.

In another ten years the Parkmans would own their own home. They lived on Avenida Drive, a down-curling offshoot of Grizzly Peak Boulevard. This was a section where most homes were new, where bus stops were few and far between, where houses and groups of houses were interspersed with hillsides not yet cleared of trees and brush.

Mr. Parkman had worked his way up from downtown Berkeley and was nearly home. Rehearsing a speech that began: "Well, dear, you see it was like this—" he had to slam on his brakes to avoid collision with a car that came spinning up Avenida into the boulevard.

His tires failed to grip the highway, slippery with rain. Mr. Parkman's car skidded across the highway. The other car cleared him by six inches while its driver shouted: "What the blankety—?"

"Blankety-blank yourself," Mr. Parkman responded automatically. Then he sat still, shaking a little. His front bumper touched a telephone pole, and his headlights illumined an untenanted hillside.

Finally he muttered: "Boy, that was close!" and got out to look at his bumper. A hundred yards from the road an irregular file of eucalyptus trees marched across the grassy hillside Behind one tree and the real-estate- agency sign nailed to it something that looked like an old coat was stirring in the wind.

Mr. Parkman was a kindhearted man and a thoughtful man except in the matter of notifying his wife that he would be late to dinner. He thought: Maybe some kid's coat blew out of a rumble seat. I'd better pick it up.

He climbed toward the coat. His body was between it and his headlights. He had stooped over and was yanking at the sleeve before he realized that there was something in the coat. An arm and a shoulder and a girl's face above that, with damp curly hair straggling over wide-open, protruding eyes. . . .

Mr. Parkman stood still and screeched until he roused the small excitable dog named Ezra who was attached to 191 Avenida Drive. The couple who belonged to Ezra came out and supported Mr. Parkman into their house. Mr. Parkman telephoned the police and took another drink.

At nine-thirty that night Jerry Flanigan had telephoned Michael Dundas to say that Lulu Mae had not come home.

PART SIX

I

Valerie sat back and settled her hat, which had been skidding down the back of her head for the last ten minutes.

"Was this entirely necessary?" she inquired acidly.

They were in the Richmond district now, but they had come there via Mission Street through Daly City; then over to the Skyline Boulevard, past Lake Merced and Fleishhacker; along the ocean, around Land's End, and through Seacliff; then over to California Street and back toward the beach again until they struck Twenty-ninth Avenue.

For the first half-hour or so Michael had driven as if tire rationing did not exist and new cars were to be had for the asking. They had not even gone straight out Mission but had used it only as a base for sorties into narrow alleys, brief but jolting excursions into side streets, and an expedition around Balboa Park.

If during the journey his passengers' hats had been shaken off, so had much of the restlessness that had possessed Michael since he had talked to Jerry Flanigan over the telephone. He said amiably:

"We were being tailed, my love."

"What? Oh, I don't believe it."

"But we were. When we leave home in a car we have to exit onto Jones at Vallejo, you know. There was a police car waiting to pick us up there. I think I lost them before we went around Balboa Park, but I wanted to be sure."

"Well, then, I'll forgive you. But you still haven't explained Saul Hirsh's sanitarium to us."

"Have you never heard of it? He is an extremely clever surgeon and a very wealthy man. I suppose the police have viewed his establishment with suspicion for many years. Unfortunately, from their point of view, the names of a great many of Saul's patients are in the social register."

"Oh," Valerie said in a tone of enlightenment. "Abortions a specialty, cure guaranteed—if you can pay the price."

"And silence guaranteed too, I suppose," Antonia said. "Silence on both sides. I read an article about abortions the other day that said in some establishments where cures aren't guaranteed the patient never sees the doctor. It can't always be that way, of course. If it was they'd never convict doctors of that kind of malpractice—unless a patient died during the operation. But go on."

Michael did not answer. Valerie leaned forward and tapped him on the shoulder.

"Michael, don't tell me Toni's little dissertation has shocked you into silence."

"What? Don't be foolish. I was—thinking. Well, Saul has other lines of work. His place is a good one to send a half-witted relative or one who is afflicted with paresis if you'd rather have 'angina' on the death certificate.

"I don't think he extracts many bullets nowadays except for very old friends," Michael went on, "but before Prohibition was repealed and if you had the right connections Saul would treat your bullet wounds and forget to report them to the police."

He stopped the car. "I don't see anything that looks like a sanitarium," Antonia objected.

Michael grinned. "You're going to walk about ten blocks now. You don't suppose I'd risk parking my car in front of the place, do you? It isn't raining—much. Come along."

"I suppose," Valerie said, "that while you were driving a taxi in your early days here you brought some sort of crook with a bullet in him to Dr. Hirsh, and that's your hold over him."

Michael looked at her disapprovingly. "Say that Saul owes me a favor and he is the sort of Jew who pays his debts. His staff is entirely trustworthy. Also, he always has some quite ordinary patients. He only supplies a demand that will still exist when Saul no longer does. If they couldn't come to him people would patronize less discreet and less competent doctors. . . ."

"Is that it?" Valerie asked when another ten minutes and some seven or eight blocks had gone past. "That big house that's a relic of the '90s?"

"That's it. It was an old family mansion of twenty very large rooms. It's been done over inside and an addition built on in back. Saul lives here, so he should be around."

Michael opened the front door. They walked into a hall where the usual starched white nurse presided over the usual desk and switchboard.

"Hopelessly ordinary," Antonia murmured to Valerie. "I'm disappointed."

Michael was inquiring discreetly after his "friend." The inquiries were as discreetly answered; the receptionist plugged in a number on her switchboard and Dr. Hirsh appeared.

He looked like the Lord Beaconsfield of the '70s minus the velvet coat. He had beautiful hands, an incisive, slightly amused voice, and unhappy black eyes.

"Your friend is dying nicely," he said, leading the way to an elevator. "I think he may have visitors. . . .

"But you'll have to talk fast, Mr. Dundas," he added when the elevator door was closed. "Once he was over the worst of his headache I had to threaten to put him in a strait jacket. I finally persuaded him to promise to stay here until you appeared. This is his room."

He indicated a door at the end of the long upstairs hall. Michael eyed it gloomily. He removed his hat, opened the door, and sent the hat skimming into the room.

"Is it safe for me to follow it?" he said after a minute.

"Oh—come ahead," Ian's voice said grudgingly.

They entered a regulation hospital room. Ian sat in a chair by the window with a goose egg behind one ear and a most ominous expression on his face.

"I know," Michael said. "It was a 'dirty dago trick'—quoting Grandfather."

Ian scowled. "Don't you try to lead me up the garden just because you know I don't approve of grandfather's habit of labeling anyone who isn't pure Anglo-Saxon a 'dago: Besides—"

"Besides, if I had not employed a blackjack you would admire me more. But I know that you haven't a glass jaw, Mr. Maclean, and you may remember that I have brittle hands. Also, you may take it out of my hide later on, if it will make you feel better. Not now, please. I need my strength for the work at hand."

Ian smiled reluctantly. "You know damned well that I won't."

"May I count on that?" Michael asked hopefully.

"He has no shame," Valerie said. "But I should warn you that he doesn't fight the way you were taught to in college, Ian. He—"

"You talk too much," her husband said. "And Ian served time in a lumber camp. He knows a few tricks himself. But I will admit that I may have taken too much on myself, Ian."

"You mean that you haven't made any head-way?"

"Well, what do you expect him to do in one day?" Valerie demanded. "He's put in a full day, certainly."

Michael looked at his watch. "And it's eleven o'clock. I don't want to stay here too long. It would take too much time to give you a complete résumé, Ian. I've tried to follow up the leads you gave me."

"Anything on whom Adela may have been talking to during the black-out last night?"

"I'm sorry, no. That was the best lead, but it's the hardest to follow up. Well, tell me this. Was it Adela's idea, originally, that you should visit Miss Hallie during your trip?"

"Hmm? No, I think it was her mother's idea. I can't remember that Adela ever really opposed the plan, but it seems—"

Ian stopped and trailed his fingers, slowly and hard, across his forehead. If I went to him now, Antonia thought, and drew him back against me he'd close his eyes and relax. Then I'd— I'm maundering, the way girls do in books. I should feel silly and I don't, though everyone here knows how I feel. Everyone but Ian.

"It seems now that I thought Adela wasn't too enthusiastic about visiting Miss Hallie," Ian went on. "But perhaps I only imagine that I thought that—"

"Loretta thought it was Adela's mother who engineered the visit," Antonia said. "Loretta said Monday that she hadn't thought Adela would come back."

"Yes, you told me that," Michael said. "But hadn't Adela talked a good deal about the people she met out here eight years ago, Ian?"

"Miss Hallie's name came up often, but usually when we were with Adela's mother, I think. They had never stopped writing to each other. Adela wrote Miss Hallie now and then. But she didn't really begin to talk about Loretta, Freddie, Judith, and Dr. Carter until we were on our way here."

"But she had talked of Bruce Ferrell?"

"To do her justice, not as much as some women would talk about a man they might have married. It was Adela's mother who first mentioned Bruce to me, just to let me know that—well—"

"That you were not the only man that Adela might have married," Valerie finished.

"Yes. Adela didn't deny her mother's statements. She'd mention Bruce when it was natural that she should. She never seemed to avoid mentioning him. One time when I was going through her desk looking for a receipted bill we couldn't locate—"

Ian stopped and smiled wryly. "Adela always kept receipts and canceled checks. In this case it turned out that I'd mislaid the receipt. Anyway, I came across a drawerful of letters tied up with pink and blue ribbons."

"Sentiment or possessiveness?" Michael asked.

"Possessiveness. Adela never parted with anything that was hers. I noticed one bundle because it was very small and the notes—that's all they were—weren't in envelopes. I made some comment, and Adela said that Bruce Ferrell had written them to her."

"Didn't she have a photograph of Bruce?"

"N-no. Yet she kept photographs too. I had to work my way through a stack of them when we were first engaged. There must have been two dozen of girls she'd gone to school with."

"Was Miss Hallie's Rosalie a pretty girl?"

"Why—why, Adela didn't have one of Rosalie! Yes, that's odd," Ian said as Michael raised his eyebrows. "I should have thought of that too."

"'Too?' What else did you think of, *amigo?*"

"I've done nothing but think since my head stopped aching. And it occurred to me that though I was always told that Rosalie was Adela's dearest friend, Adela never talked about Rosalie. Except for one time when I found Adela crying and she said it was because she was thinking about Rosalie. To comfort her I kissed her. Then," Ian said grimly, "somehow it seemed that we were engaged."

"Can you remember at all how long Adela had been home then?"

"Two or three weeks, maybe a month. I wasn't used to her being grown up yet, when I'd remembered her as a schoolgirl with braces on her teeth. But it does seem to me that Adela hadn't been home more than a few days before Rosalie died."

"I see. Why did Adela have such great influence over Miss Hallie? I'm handicapped by not having met Miss Hallie, but—"

"But you'd think she'd believe Adela was too young to know much," Antonia said. "She always seems to pity my youth and ignorance. And Loretta's. But neither of us is married; therefore, we are failures. I think the answer is that Miss Hallie and Adela are—were—very much alike."

Ian nodded. "I thought they had the same sort of hands. Tight, possessive little hands, you know. Of course there are differences."

"Yes," Antonia agreed. "Fighting Miss Hallie would be like hitting a feather pillow."

"While fighting Adela was as foolish as hoping to dent a granite cliff by throwing pebbles at it. And I imagine Miss Hallie is inclined to be lazy—physically."

"That's it," Antonia said. "She is and Adela wasn't, I suppose. But I'll bet on all important subjects—what they'd call important—they were in perfect accord. But does that matter?"

"I don't know," Michael said. "I don't know that any of it is going to matter." Yet he now had most of the essential facts that would lead him to Adela's murderer. "However, I have to go on asking—"

Dr. Hirsh entered the room unceremoniously. "There's a police officer downstairs," he said. "They just flashed the warning signal. . . ."

II

At eleven-thirty that Wednesday night O. B.
Sanders was driving up Vincentino Road in an
ancient car, as productive among his friends of
as many jokes as Jack Benny's Maxwell. But Obie
loved his car because it was roomy; it had wide
running boards and was in no way streamlined or
low-slung. Indeed, in the opinion of one of his
subordinates, it looked like "part of a boxcar on
wheels."

Mr. Sanders had left it to others to go on questioning Jerry Flanigan. He believed he had wrung
Lulu Mae's mother dry and that the only item
Mrs. Brown had to contribute was the fact that
her daughter had been alive at seven o'clock.

Mrs. Brown had recently suffered from "dizzy
spells," but, as she said, "poor folks can't afford
to be sick." A few minutes before seven Lulu Mae
had called her mother at the house where she was
working and wanted to know how Ma was feeling.

She was phoning from a drugstore, Lulu Mae
had added. Yes, she'd had something to eat but
not at the drugstore. She'd eaten in Oakland after
she went to see *Roxie Hart* at the Fox-Oakland.
Mrs. Maybry had given her the afternoon off, but
she was going home pretty soon now. . . .

"And then I heard this sick lady I look after
calling to me," Mrs. Brown said. "They don't like

I should get phone calls there, so I said to Lulu Mae I'd better not talk no more."

Obie Sanders sighed. Men were already making inquiries at all drugstores that were still open. Tomorrow they would take up where they had to leave off tonight. That was routine, and he didn't expect anything would come of it.

Obie sighed again: a vast sigh that made the Phi Bete key on his vest quiver. He liked to be on good terms with everyone, and his superiors were irritated with him, the irritation being in direct proportion to the number of times that Obie had said: "I told you so."

He thought he would like to talk to someone sympathetic. Then he grinned slowly at the notion of calling Michael Dundas "sympathetic." Nevertheless, he had telephoned Michael's home and been told by a wooden English voice that Mr. Dundas was not at home.

"Probably out seeing Maclean, wherever he has him hidden," Obie thought and stopped his car in front of the Maybry house.

It was not his intention to drag the Maybrys, Carters, or Ferrells from their beds. For one thing, it had been rather forcibly suggested to him that he wait until morning to question them. Obie merely wished to "ponder and brood a spell," and he pondered best in his car in quiet secluded spots.

But when he saw that there was a light burning downstairs in the Carter house he heaved himself out of the car. Dr. Carter answered the doorbell promptly, Dr. Maybry just behind him.

"You'd better stick around awhile, Dr. Maybry," Obie said. "We found that nursemaid of yours."

"Lulu Mae? I didn't know she was missing."

"Didn't you? Mind if I come in?"

"Of course not. Excuse my bad manners," Dr. Carter said. "In here."

In the living room Sanders settled like a small landslide into a large wing chair. "I didn't mean to get you folks up, but since you are up—we found Lulu Mae. A little ways off Grizzly Peak Boulevard. You know that section. She might have laid there all night if a guy hadn't skidded around so his headlights were pointed right at her."

"You mean she's dead?" Dr. Carter barked.

"Yes. Somebody stunned her, probably with a monkey wrench, and then put a thin wire around her neck and strangled her," Obie said placidly. "A woman could do that as easy as a man, but a car is indicated. She was alive at seven and dead by nine, the doctor says. Well, you two have cars."

The old doctor and the young looked at each other. Then Dr. Carter shrugged.

"Seven to nine, eh? I was out in my car shortly after seven. We had an early dinner. My nephew didn't eat with us. Miss van Horn and I were alone, as my sister is still in bed. I called on a patient— the little Harlan girl, Jimmy. I'm afraid I'm going to lose her. Say I left the Harlans' about a quarter to eight. Then," the old doctor finished with a take-it-or-leave-it air, "I drove around for about twenty minutes. Just drove, thinking."

"Well, it doesn't really matter if anyone saw you come home if— What time did you get to these Harlans' place?" Obie asked.

"I don't know exactly. I just went there when we'd finished dinner. I dare say it was seven-fifteen or so. You were out, too, weren't you, Jimmy?"

"What? Oh—oh yes, I made a call at Alta Bates just after seven," Maybry said. "I was telling you about that, Doctor. Then I went to my office, Mr. Sanders. It's in the Acheson Building on University Avenue. I don't know if anyone saw me go in."

"Why'd you go there, Doctor?" Sanders said.

"To go over some accounts. We're breaking in a green girl just now."

"Our office nurse volunteered for service with the armed forces," Dr. Carter said. "I've never been any good at sending out bills or doing any kind of paper work."

"Well, I worked there until after nine," Maybry said. "Then Freddie Carter came in. He has an office in the same building. I might as well tell you that he said he'd had dinner with a client and had been working on his own, Dr. Carter's, and Miss Hallie's income-tax reports."

"He always does that for us," Dr. Carter said. "And today is March eleventh, you know."

"Freddie got some figures from me," Maybry went on. "Then he said he thought he'd knock off work for the night. We left the building together."

"He had his car too?" Sanders asked.

"Yes. We'd both parked just around the corner on Walnut."

"Would you like to talk to Freddie?" Dr. Carter said. "He's in bed, but I can wake him."

"Oh, tomorrow will do for that. How did it happen that your wife gave Lulu Mae the afternoon off, Dr. Maybry?"

"What?"

Maybry bit at his small mustache. He's an awfully nervous fellow, Sanders thought. But I've seen doctors that are, outside a sickroom or operating room.

"I don't believe Judith did give her the afternoon off. I understood that Lulu Mae said she didn't feel well and simply walked out. You may remember that you didn't see Lulu Mae when you talked to my wife and me this morning."

"No, I didn't," Obie said sadly. "I didn't know she was there and I didn't know she had stayed all night at your place. Where did she sleep?"

"In the boys' room: the nursery."

"Of course a healthy youngster never wakes up all night long," Obie remarked. "And Lulu Mae was young and healthy enough to sleep the whole night through too. Wouldn't you think so? Does your wife drive a car, Doctor?"

"Yes," Maybry said stiffly, "but we have only the one car, and I use it pretty constantly myself."

"I guess you do. The Ferrells have a car and they both drive it?"

"Of course," Dr. Carter said impatiently. "And I suppose I might as well tell you that Miss van Horn has had the use of a car since Tuesday morning: yesterday morning, that is. It's a roadster that belongs to her fiancé, Richard Prince."

"So Richard Prince is finally getting married? Is this car in your garage, Doctor?"

"No, it's in half the Kelseys' garage, though with Maclean's car gone, Loretta could get it in ours now. The Kelseys' is the fifth house down from here on the right. But I'm sure Loretta didn't go out tonight. She was here when I left and just going to bed when I got home."

"But why," Maybry broke in abruptly, "would Maclean kill Lulu Mae?"

Sanders regarded him mournfully. "That's what some other die-hards are trying to figure out,

Doctor. I'm sure he didn't kill her. How could he arrange to meet her, get a car to pick her up in—"

"He's right: it won't wash," the old doctor said. "But suppose Lulu Mae's death had nothing at all to do with Adela's?"

"That's another school of thought that has its stanch adherents. I'm not one of them." Obie got to his feet. "Well, I'll say good night."

He turned his car, ran five houses down Vincentino Road, and parked again. The Kelsey house was one of the older ones on the street. It had a large front and side lawn, the driveway into the garage bordering on the latter.

Sanders surged quietly toward the garage. He examined its lock under the light from his torch and sniffed disparagingly. In five minutes he had the garage open and was gazing at a roadster's splattered fenders.

"Tsk, tsk!" he muttered. "I'll bet Mr. Richard Prince turned this car over to Miss van Horn all bright and shining. And we haven't had any real rain for ten days—until tonight."

III

Valerie and Michael spoke almost together.

"Is he alone?" Valerie asked.

"Has he a search warrant?" said Mr. Dundas.

"He has no search warrant and he has entered this building alone," Dr. Hirsh said precisely. "It's Nicholas Prevost and he is asking, very politely, if he can be shown over the establishment. The receptionist was assuring him, just as politely, that of course he can be as soon as I have time to put on some clothes, since I have retired for the night."

"We'd better get out of here," Michael said. "Damn Nick's soul! Why must he have brain storms at nearly midnight and—"

"This way," Dr. Hirsh said. "This is the service elevator. . . . I think," he added as the elevator bore them downward, "that we could manage to keep Prevost from seeing Mr. Maclean if you—"

"No!" Ian said. "I'm not going to get you into trouble."

"And if Nick is not satisfied he may come back tomorrow and not alone," Michael observed. "Also, he might have the place watched. So I think Ian had better go while he can."

Dr. Hirsh pulled back the elevator door. They stepped into a basement and furnace room. He led them toward the door at its far end, opened it, and looked out.

"No one here. Follow this alley over to the next street while I delay Prevost. Good luck."

When they emerged from the narrow alley into the street Antonia broke into a half trot. "If we hurry we can get to the car before—"

Michael caught her arm in a grip that made her wince. "Saunter," he said curtly. "Take Ian's arm and talk to him if we meet anyone. Laugh if you can."

"Michael will demonstrate laughing—but out of the other side of his mouth," Valerie said sweetly. "Didn't you assure me this morning that Ian would be perfectly safe at Dr. Hirsh's?"

Antonia waited for the explosion. When Michael only grinned ruefully and answered: "Yes, love, and if you care to drop one pace behind you may kick me," she thought: Well, at least sulking when he's been made to look foolish isn't one of his faults.

Valerie promptly descended to the other side of the fence. "However, I think Nick might find better ways to spend his time than in trying to locate Ian: a job that's hardly in his department. It's almost as if it were a personal matter."

"It is," Michael said without rancor. "I virtually dared him to pick Ian up. I'd do the same thing if our positions were reversed."

"But I thought you and Mr. Prevost were friends!" Antonia said. Ian laughed.

"Women don't understand these things."

"No," Michael agreed, "and I don't understand how Nick came to think of the Hirsh Sanitarium. I'm not given to mentioning connections that might be useful sometime. I'd never mentioned

Saul Hirsh to Valerie. When did I ever take down my hair to the extent of telling Nick that I even know Saul?"

"You are not usually what I'd call expansive," his wife said. Then she giggled suddenly. "Darling, have you forgotten the stag dinner you gave Nick before he married Marcia Bondurant?"

"What? Good lord, I believe you're right. I was fairly fiddled that night. I took Nick home, poured him into a chair, and we talked for hours. He certainly told me a good many things about himself that he has never referred to since. I must have done likewise."

"Well, I confess I don't know where to take Ian now. Nick knows the more disreputable parts of this city too well. And he knows how my mind works or I'd risk stowing Ian away in the store-room at Gisele's."

"Don't stow me away anywhere. Take me over to Berkeley police headquarters."

"Get in the car!" Michael snapped, unlocking it. "Your ingratitude—"

"My— Well, my hat! I've been slugged from behind, spent the day recovering, the evening waiting for you—only to be smuggled out the back door one step ahead of the police, and now I'm—"

Michael grinned. "Feeling very sorry for yourself, no doubt," he finished.

"Well, why shouldn't he!" Antonia flared. "Any-one would—"

"Never mind, Antonia," Ian said and got into the car. Valerie and Antonia looked at each other without speaking, but their eyebrows shrieked: "Men!"

"Well," Antonia said with exaggerated meekness when the car was under way, "if I may speak, I've been thinking. We own a house on Spruce Street in Berkeley. It's so large we have a hard time keeping it rented. Dad gave me the keys when he left. Wouldn't it do? The only danger would be that a real-estate agent might show someone through it tomorrow, but it's an even chance that he won't."

"I doubt if we can do better," Michael said. "The police aren't apt to nose around trying to discover if your father owns any vacant houses—for a while, at least. But I think we'd better go a roundabout way."

"To avoid the bridges?" Valerie said. "Do you think Nick might have told them to watch for you?"

"I don't think Nick would—but Nick might. There's a short cut from San Mateo over to Hayward that will take us into Oakland in not more than two hours—probably less."

Michael settled down behind the wheel. Valerie curled up beside him and seemed to go to sleep.

Antonia sat in one corner of the back seat, Ian in the other. But when they struck San Mateo she saw him shiver. In an instant she had slid out of her polo coat.

"It's overcoat weather and you aren't warmly dressed. Sit close to me—put your arm around me—and this will go crosswise over our shoulders with material to spare."

Well, she thought, suppose I do practically cast myself into his arms? He thinks I'm just being kind. If he didn't he wouldn't consider it right not to be decently depressed about Adela for at least a year. But—she settled her head against his shoulder—for this little while he's mine. . . .

It was two o'clock when Michael parked the car on Spruce Street. They had stopped once at an open-all-night lunch counter to buy hamburgers, milk, and a flat, pallid apple pie. When Antonia had remarked that they would have to go to her home first so that she could get the keys to the house Michael had said:

"I put my pet picklocks in my pocket this morning in case I might have use for them. I can unlock your house, Toni."

He opened the front door now, and they stepped into a large square hall. The air was the cold dead air of an untenanted house. Valerie put the bags of food on the floor, and Antonia threw her coat over Ian's arm.

"Keep this. I'll be all right without it from here to Piedmont. The couch I told you the last tenants left here is in the kitchen: down this hall and through that door."

Michael took off his overcoat and gave it and his flashlight to Ian. "Cigarettes and matches in the pockets," he said. "Don't set the place on fire."

But he put his hand briefly on his cousin's shoulder. Ian remembered how much Michael disliked patting or being patted on the back and smiled.

"I'll be all right. The place will be less like a tomb in the morning."

"And you'll stay under cover until I get in touch with you again? I'll come up here as soon after dark in the evening as I can and, whether disguised or as myself, knock five times on the back door. . . ."

IV

"So after I took a look at the car Richard Prince loaned Miss van Horn there wasn't anything more I could do last night," O. B. Sanders said apologetically. "That's all the information I have now, and I know that six-thirty is pretty early to call you."

"It's all right," Michael said, yawning. "But did I gather that you are the only member of the homicide detail who is convinced that Lulu Mae's death is the direct result of Adela Maclean's?"

"You know how it is. They're sure Maclean killed his wife and they can't fit Lulu Mae's death into that picture. They aren't," Obie said in a grieved voice, "good historians. If a competent historian turns up a lot of inconvenient facts during his research—inconvenient because they don't fit in with his working theory—he doesn't discard them. He alters his theory.

"Of course Jerry Flanigan and Lulu Mae had quarreled now and then. They couldn't get married, and I've noticed that's hard on the temper. But Flanigan has an old car, and he says he was just driving around in it between eight and nine, passing Lulu Mae's house, hoping she'd come home."

"They're still questioning him?" Michael said.

"Yes, and I'm sorry for the boy. Then there's another young fellow that liked Lulu Mae. He's got a car and can't account for his movements between seven and eight too well. He's supposed to resent the fact that Lulu Mae threw him over for young Flanigan. They keep questioning him too."

"And where does that leave you?"

"I'm still looking after the Maclean case—in my own way," Sanders said placidly. "They give me plenty of rope. I told them that if they'd kept an eye on the folks up around Dr. Carter's place the way I wanted yesterday afternoon when I started them looking for Lulu Mae we might know more.

"They might have tried a little harder to find her too. We're shorthanded and overworked, doing our part in civilian defense and helping to round up enemy aliens, but that's not enough excuse. Uh— off the record, could your cousin alibi himself for the time of Lulu Mae's death, do you think?"

"Well," Michael said, "in the interests of sound historical research—"

"I guess maybe you're laughing at me."

"Not at all. You needn't alter your working theory. Ian can be alibied for the time of Lulu Mae's death if it is vitally necessary. I hope it won't be, because that would embarrass and inconvenience the people who can alibi him. Ian wouldn't want that—"

"I understand. Well, would you like to plod around with me this morning? I'll be having breakfast in the H. & M. where you met me yesterday."

"Wait for me," Michael said.

He broke the connection and dialed a San Francisco number. "Marcia?" he said when a woman's voice answered. "Is Nick home?"

"He's shaving," Marcia Prevost said, "and unusually cross about it too. He's whistling 'Durant

Jail' and he wanted to know if I'd been using his razors to trim linoleum."

"The honeymoon is over. Well, when he has had breakfast and several cups of your superlative coffee and has finished kissing you good-by, you tell the Iron Czar that I said: 'Better luck next time,'" Michael said and hung up.

Valerie wandered into the hall clad in a trifle of silk and lace and sat down on his knees. "That is not really fair since Ian is in Berkeley now and out of Nick's jurisdiction."

"Never mind. Nick caused me great inconvenience last night. My love, this telephone stool is a fragile piece of furniture."

"Pooh. My weight's back to what it was before I had Ricky. Of course there have been certain developments, but they are rather becoming than otherwise. Michael, do you think I look best with my clothes on or off?"

"¡*Madre santíssima!* What—?"

"I was remembering what Ian said about Evelyn Ferrell when he described her. What did you think when you saw her?"

"I did not give the matter any thought," Mr. Dundas said austerely.

"You wouldn't kid me, would you, mister?"

Michael chuckled. "Well, you know that my main interest from a business standpoint is how women look *in* their clothes. I did think that, dressed correctly—"

"By Gisele's."

"Certainly. Correctly dressed, Mrs. Ferrell could hold her own with any woman. If, that is, she would pull her hair back from her face. For that matter, I could make Loretta a bride to be remembered if she would also do something about her hair."

"Could she?"

"Not being a hairdresser, I don't know. I would recommend, though, that she comb it."

"Umm," Valerie said absently. "Well, I suspect Mrs. Ferrell. Everyone speaks too well of her. I think she killed Adela and Lulu Mae Brown."

"Why?"

"I don't know. I just think she did."

"I'm certainly not counting her out. I am usually suspicious myself of anyone of whom everyone speaks well. But I have a notion that Mrs. Ferrell is only a self-controlled woman, not an insufferably virtuous one. I—but I must get started, *querida*."

"Oh, do you have to go?" Valerie tightened her arms about his neck. "You were away all day yesterday and—"

Michael slid an arm under her knees, stood up, and started for the bedroom. There, having kissed

her very thoroughly in transit, he dumped her
unceremoniously onto the bed and grinned down
at her.

"'Oh woman, thou wert fashioned to beguile—'"

Valerie promptly finished the quotation they
had come across on one of the printed slips that
are tucked inside Chinese teacakes.

"'So sages say and poets sang erstwhile.' I know.
You and your will power. Brute." She snuggled
down into bed. "You have no idea how comfortable this is."

Michael groaned. "But I have: that's the sad
thing. However, I must go. I don't suppose it takes
even O. B. Sanders more than an hour to consume
enough breakfast to sustain life. . . ."

However, Sanders had only progressed to his
third cup of coffee and the stage of mopping up
his plate with bits of toast when Michael entered
the grill-and-fish grotto on University Avenue.

"Have something to eat," he invited. "The ham
and eggs are best, but the steaks are so much better that if I were you I'd take wheat cakes."

"Well, I should order toast, but I prefer coffee-
cake, so I think I'll have doughnuts," Michael responded gravely.

"I guess you're making fun of me," Obie said
mournfully.

"Do you mind?"

"Not if you keep it friendly. Just coffee? Well, that won't take long. Have you any special line you want to follow up?"

"I have an idea, put into my head by something my wife and a friend of hers said last night."

"Miss Jordan? We have our eye on her. This fellow Ferrell thought it was his duty to tell us about Maclean and Miss Jordan yesterday afternoon. Now, wait! I know it's no life-or-death matter, a man kissing a pretty girl.

"But that would give another reason why Maclean quarreled with his wife, according to the prevailing school of thought at headquarters. Anyway, we know what time you dropped Miss Jordan at her home this morning. She'll be questioned today—but tactfully."

"Why tactfully?"

"Because her father is a prominent, architect. Then a lot of fellows are out combing drugstores where Lulu Mae might have made that telephone call to her mother and looking over people's cars, though Lulu Mae didn't bleed. The blow that stunned her didn't break the flesh. Still, there could be some of her hair on whatever she was hit with—say a monkey wrench.

"And there are fellows checking at the Acheson Building where the two doctors and young Carter have offices. But I know already that you can

come and go in that place at night without being
noticed. Carter and Dr. Maybry are only on the
second floor. And someone is checking on Maybry's movements before he went to his office and
on the old doctor's—"

"What does that leave you to do?" Michael asked.

Sanders extracted himself from his chair. "Oh,
I guess I'll find things. . . . You want to ride in
my car?"

Mr. Dundas looked at Mr. Sanders' car and
murmured: "My God!" but with the reverence due
old age.

"I think I'll stick to my own, if you don't mind.
I'll wait for you in front of the Maybrys' house."

V

But when Sanders had maneuvered his vehicle
into a parking space behind Michael's car Freddie
Carter was just opening the doors of the doctor's
garage. Sanders produced a gentle shout.

"Wait a minute, son! I want to see you."

Freddie crossed the street promptly, eyed Mr.
Sanders' car, whistled briefly, and grinned. "If it's
about last night—"

"I have all that. Though you might tell me the
name of the client you had dinner with." Obie
wrote the name Freddie gave him in a tiny notebook. "And what time did you get through dinner?"

"I'm not sure. About seven, I think. You ask my client. I left him at Drake's since he had his own car. I went on to my office and—"

"I know. Would you have said that Lulu Mae was a pretty girl, Mr. Carter?"

"What? Why—why, I guess she was. I— Hey!" Mr. Carter protested. "Are you by any chance asking me if I ever—uh—dallied with Lulu Mae?"

"That was the idea," Sanders admitted.

"Heaven does not need to protect the woiking goil from me," Freddie said with some dignity. "I made no passes at Lulu Mae. That kind of thing is Bruce Ferrell's line, not mine. Why pick on me?"

"It occurred to me that maybe when Lulu Mae decided yesterday that she didn't want to talk to the police she might have thought, or someone might have advised her, to talk to a lawyer first."

Mr. Carter said: "Jeepers!" It was Michael's turn to whistle. "One up to you, Mr. Sanders," he remarked.

"But if she wanted to talk to a lawyer she didn't have to wait until evening to do that," Freddie objected. "She could have seen me in my office in the afternoon."

"And I'll be fair with you and admit that Lulu Mae and her mother didn't like lawyers either. They paid a smart shyster a lot to defend this no-good brother of Lulu Mae's when there wasn't any

defense, and a reputable lawyer would have told
them so. But I did think Lulu Mac might have
been willing to go to a lawyer she knew, like you."

"Would she have taken me seriously? I always
got the idea, when I'd meet her out with Judy's
brats, that she considered us all three of an age.
However"—Freddie shrugged resignedly—"there's
no use my protesting when I can't prove anything.
But neither can you, you know."

He waited politely but, as Sanders merely
sighed, went on: "I want to help you, but if that's
all you have to ask me I'd like to get to the office
early today."

"Go right ahead," Sanders said and, when Freddie had driven away in his old roadster: "That's
a smart young fellow in spite of the way he talks
at times. And though we know anyone could have
gotten into the house from the outside and killed
Mrs. Maclean—"

"How do you know that?" Michael said.

"The garage doors weren't locked. Neither was
the door from the garage up into the living room.
We may not be inspired, but we're thorough, you
know. We presume Maclean went out for a while,
or why was he dressed as young Carter said? Maclean would have to leave the front door off the
latch, and the old doctor found it that way after

Maclean skedaddled. But it still would have been easiest for someone inside the house to have killed Mrs. Maclean."

"Yes. However," Michael said, "the murder was not premeditated to the extent of the murderer's providing himself with a weapon."

Sanders sighed again. "That's so. And though people around here would know there was a chance Dr. Carter hadn't locked the garage or the door from it up into the house, I do think that if someone outside the house killed Mrs. Maclean that person must have seen Maclean go off for his walk. Anyone but Mrs. Ferrell could have seen him from a bedroom window. Her bedroom windows face the vacant lot and the back of that Mrs. Twelve-trees' house. But let's go see the Ferrells. . . ."

The elderly maid told them that Mr. Ferrell was not home and that Mrs. Ferrell was engaged, but Evelyn called from somewhere upstairs:

"I can be with you in ten minutes if you want to wait. Show them into my sitting room."

They entered the same upstairs sitting room where Antonia and Michael had talked to Evelyn yesterday. This morning its only occupant was a yellow-haired doll of a child with a large book across her pink knees. She smiled at them self-confidently.

"Mamma is washing her hair," she remarked.

She eyed O. B. Sanders with wide-eyed wonder but politely made no comment on his size. Then after studying Michael for several minutes she asked:

"Would you like to look at my picture book?"

"Why not? Shouldn't we be introduced? My name is Michael, and you may call this gentleman Obie."

"I'm Ev'lyn for Mamma, but they call me Lynn. I guess I'd better get on your lap. Then we can both see. There! Daddy made this for me."

The book was a collection of fairy tales and poems, the text hand-printed in large letters, the facing illustrations beautifully drawn and colored.

"They're my fav'rite stories people tell me," Lynn said. "Daddy printed them and drew the pictures. Here's the Lady of Shalott."

Michael looked at Bruce's drawing of a woman in medieval costume; face, figure, and loom and the distant towers of Camelot reflected in an oval mirror.

"That's Loretta van Horn's face," he said. "But isn't *The Lady of Shalott* rather strong fare for you, *niña?*"

"It makes my back feel nice and cold when the lady says, 'The curse has come upon me.' I don't know what all of it means when Loretta says it to me, but it has nice whispery sounds."

"'Willows whiten, aspens quiver, Little breezes dusk and shiver,'" Michael repeated reflectively. "You're right. Is this Cinderella?"

"Lulu Mae liked Cinderella," Miss Ferrell said tolerantly. "She just knew old stories. I like the picture Daddy made though. See? There's the proud sisters all ready to go to the ball, telling Cinderella to stay home and clean house."

"Hmm," Michael said. Adela's picture had been splashed over the newspapers this morning, and even he could detect the resemblance between Adela and the proud sisters in Bruce's drawing.

"And Little Miss Muffet is me," Lynn said, pointing to another drawing, "and so is Goldilocks. And this is Mamma, so I like it best of all."

Michael looked at the very charming sketch illustrating the story of Rapunzel, showing a woman at a casement window with her long hair cascading over its sill.

"It isn't your mother's face," he objected. "It's Mrs. Maybry's."

"It's Mamma's hair. Judy's wouldn't be long enough to let down to the ground so the prince could climb up on it. Well, neither would Mamma's," the child added practically. "Do you think

Judy's much prettier than Mamma? I don't. But see—"

She turned several pages quickly, one after another. "Judy's most of the princesses: the Sleeping Beauty and the Princess Who Could Not Laugh. And the lady in the *Mistletoe Bough*. And here's Fweddie in the Pied Piper. See? He's the piper with all the little rats following him."

"For so young a lady you have a very catholic taste in literature," Michael said. Sanders muttered protestingly:

"She can't understand you."

"If she wants to she'll ask questions. Who else is in your book, Lynn?"

"Hansel and Gretel. See? Miss Hallie is the old witch. But Daddy says I mustn't show this to Miss Hallie. She wouldn't like it, and we mustn't make her mad. And here's Dr. Carter in *The Night Before Christmas*. He's Santa Claus, you see. I think he's just like—"

Bruce Ferrell entered the living room, paused for an instant in the doorway, then crossed the room to snatch his daughter and her book away from Michael. The child looked a little surprised but promptly kissed her father's ear and wound her arms about his neck. Mr. Dundas raised an eyebrow.

"I give you my word I have no contagious disease. She was showing me her book. Those are charming sketches, Mr. Ferrell."

"Oh, they're nothing." But Mr. Ferrell promptly unbent. "I can draw," he admitted. "And I like to fool around with water colors sometimes. I suppose I'll have to make allowances for you, Dundas."

O. B. Sanders grinned sleepily. He had an idea that Mr. Dundas set his teeth for an instant before he achieved a smile.

"You had a shock yesterday morning," Bruce said magnanimously. "As to what you said to me— well, I suppose you know my reputation. I mean to say, give a dog a bad name, you know."

He smiled complacently, then settled his daughter more comfortably in the crook of his arm and turned to Sanders.

"It's not the kind of thing one likes to bring up, but Tuesday morning I accepted an engagement for this coming week end. My host is valuable to me in a business way and a rather touchy person. Do you think I'll have to call it off?"

"Oh, this is only Thursday. You wait and see. Is Mrs. Ferrell going with you?"

"No. Evelyn won't leave Lynn—well, neither would I—and she doesn't believe in taking youngsters on week ends or even long trips."

"I want down, Daddy," Lynn decided suddenly.
"I want to look at my book some more."

"All right, doll baby." Bruce established her on
a low stool and put the book across her knees.

"Pity," he said rather morosely, "that women
aren't as easily pleased as children when it comes
to gifts. I mean to say, you get gray hairs trying
to bring one of them something that will please
her and pay a fancy price for it. Then she says:
'Oh, didn't you know? I don't use it any more.' I
mean to say, for years they plaster themselves with
rouge. Then all of a sudden rouge is out or—"

"Or what, Mr. Ferrell?" Michael said quickly.

"Hmm? Oh—yes, I thought I heard her. Here's
Evelyn."

VI

Evelyn came in with her hair in a thick, loosely
plaited braid that nearly reached her waist.

"It isn't quite dry yet, and I should have guessed
someone would come to see us this morning, but—
well, washing my hair is my favorite safety valve. I
needed one after I heard about Lulu Mae."

"She worked for you a little while, didn't she?"
Sanders asked. "So are you sure she didn't come to
you for advice yesterday?"

"She did not. My maid can tell you—"

"I should have said 'asked' you for advice. She could have telephoned you."

"Yes. I answer the telephone very often myself. But if she wanted advice there was Judy. No, I don't suppose Lulu Mae would have gone to Judy for advice," Evelyn admitted. "Judy can't control her own children and Lulu Mae could, so Lulu Mae rather patronized Judy."

"She'd have been more apt to consult Jimmy Maybry," Bruce said. "She had a very respectful attitude toward doctors. Judy said once she thought Lulu Mae had a slight crush on Jimmy. Not that Judy minded, I mean to say," he added hastily.

"But might Lulu Mae have been willing to consult a lawyer if she knew something she didn't really want to tell the police but was afraid she'd get into trouble if she didn't tell?" Sanders asked.

Evelyn frowned. "She and her mother didn't 'hold with' lawyers, Mr. Sanders."

"I know that. But a lawyer she knew?"

"Freddie Carter?" Evelyn smiled. "I suppose you can say that Lulu Mae knew him, but would she have taken him seriously as a lawyer?"

"Do any of us?" Bruce said. "And what makes you think Lulu Mae consulted anybody? I mean to say—"

"Oh, somehow it doesn't seem in character to me that of her own accord she kept away from her

home all day after she left the Maybrys' place.
That is, she must have had definite plans. She
could tell her boy friend she wouldn't be home
at six-thirty but would be home after nine—she
thought then.

"Perhaps she thought out her plans herself, but
it's clear that someone else knew what she knew—I
know!" Sanders held up a large weary hand. "That's
only if her death was connected with Mrs. Maclean's. I know the newspapers hint this morning
that one of the girl's boy friends killed her. Just
the same, I'll ask you where you were between
seven and nine last night."

"We were here."

"Don't be silly, Bruce," Evelyn said sharply.
"People around here must have seen me go out in
our car. That was about seven-thirty. I took some
books back to the Public library: the main library
at Kittredge and Shattuck."

"They know you there, Mrs. Ferrell?"

"By sight, I suppose. They could tell you that
I returned books and that I took more out. But
I was in the library, browsing, for more than an
hour. It takes quite a while to choose books at
times."

"It's Sanders' problem to turn up someone who
noticed you there," Bruce said aggressively. "I was

here, but the baby was in bed and the maid down-stairs. No one can prove I stayed in, I mean to say."

"But if you did go out someone may have seen you," Sanders remarked. He hauled himself to his feet and to end the session on an unofficial note added: "That's a nice little girl you've got."

"We think so," Bruce said fondly. Evelyn's glance at her child was remarkably impersonal.

"I'm afraid she talks and acts like a little old woman, but what can you expect when she never plays with other children?"

"What other children would she play with?" Bruce asked combatively and so quickly that Sanders guessed the difference of opinion was an old one.

He was also aware that Michael had made his way noiselessly over to Lynn and bent over so that his lips were close to her ear. I'd like to know what he's saying to her, Obie thought. Something Ferrell said certainly sent Dundas off into a brown study. He didn't seem to be listening while I was questioning the Ferrells.

He tried to hear what the little girl said to Michael or catch a glimpse of the illustration in her storybook she was pointing to. But Lynn had evidently been trained not to speak loudly when her parents were talking, and Bruce was still speaking.

"I won't have my child playing with every Tom, Dick, and Mary——"

"Our child," Evelyn corrected him pleasantly. "I don't believe there's any doubt about that, is there? At least, it seems to me it wasn't you in the maternity ward at Alta Bates."

Bruce's smile was quick and conciliatory. "No, but there's no one in the immediate neighborhood near enough Lynn's age except Judy's oldest. That wild Indian. I mean to say, he'd probably kick Lynn's teeth out."

"She could play with Little Brother. You wouldn't object to that, would you?"

Bruce's florid face reddened. He did not answer for an instant while Obie watched them interestedly.

Little Brother: that's the Maybry boy that's a towhead, he thought. It would be funny if he's Ferrell's child, not Maybry's. That would make him really this little girl's little brother. I wonder if Mrs. Ferrell. . . . No, I don't believe she intended to be malicious. But she might be cracking the whip over Ferrell, at that. You can't always tell with these quiet women. Ferrell isn't too sure himself. . . .

"Since Bobby and Billy are inseparable, Lynn would have to take both of them on," Bruce said. "And that assignment's always been too much for even a grownup."

Sanders saw that Michael had unobtrusively joined them again and said: "Well, good morning, folks. I suppose," he went on when they were walking back toward the Maybry house, "that you wouldn't like to tell me what you asked that little girl?"

Michael shook his head. "Not just yet. You see, I don't like to be laughed at even when you keep it friendly."

"All right," Obie said placidly and rang the Maybrys' doorbell.

They waited several minutes before Judith opened the door. She wore the same lounging pajamas with the same apron, a day dirtier than it had been yesterday. This morning her face was smudged both with grease and a peculiar white substance that filled the bowl she held in one hand.

"You'll have to sit down and wait. This is seven-minute frosting, and I've got to keep on beating it for five minutes more. But sometimes it takes fourteen minutes or even twenty-eight. I never know. You know where the living room is."

Little Brother was at one end of the living room behind a barricade of chairs. A similar barricade had been erected around the piano, and Sitting Bull was tied to one of its legs. Michael surveyed the scene thoughtfully.

"It's a little hard to believe that Mrs. Maybry ever willingly told Lulu Mae that she might have an afternoon off."

"It certainly looks like she needs someone to turn these two over to," Sanders agreed, sitting down. "Well, sonny, are you playing you're a big dog?"

Sitting Bull made a vulgar noise. "Not the right approach," Michael said. "This specimen of care-free childhood baffles me."

Sitting Bull, having deftly untied the rope about the piano leg, scaled the breastworks in front of him and advanced on the enemy. Michael retreated hastily.

"If you kick me I'll warm your bottom for you," he promised. "Do you understand that? I thought you would, you're such a big bright boy for your age. Annoy the other gentleman."

Sitting Bull transferred his attention to Sanders. Apparently Obie's size made him decide against a frontal assault. He began circling him slowly.

Michael strolled over to Little Brother to whom an exotic fragrance still clung. Not only was his mother's favorite perfume remarkable for its enduring quality, but it was doubtful that Little Brother had been washed overnight. He was very dirty and tear-stained and would soon, unless aid was forthcoming, be also very damp. He made known his wants.

Michael grinned and scooped him up. "This," he remarked, cryptically so far as Sanders was concerned, "is very convenient. Come on; we will go upstairs and locate the necessary facilities."

Upstairs he deposited Little Brother on the essential utensil and went looking for the Maybrys' bedroom and bureau. Its scarf was covered with a fine film of powder, stray hairs, crumpled pieces of Kleenex, dabs of cold cream and lipstick. Still there were very few cosmetics on it—an inexpensive brand of cold cream, an equally low-priced box of powder, a shrunken lipstick.

These rubbed elbows with Dr. Maybry's very military brushes and a bottle of tonic guaranteed to prevent falling hair. There was a flask of cologne labeled "violet," but it resembled Prohibition liquor in that any other label, carnation, rose, or lily, would have done as well. Beside it was a slim flagon bearing the label of a New York perfumer.

Michael removed the stopper and sniffed. Then he began, sure sign that he was pleased, to whistle "La Golondrina." He collected Little Brother, buttoned what buttons remained on his rompers, tucked him under an arm, and went back downstairs.

Sitting Bull had scaled the fortress. His feet were planted firmly on one of Obie Sanders' massive thighs, and he was looting the Sanders' pockets.

As Michael entered the living room Obie was saying in a soothing rumble:

"So then Lulie Mae told you to duck back along
the path so the lady wouldn't see you and maybe
tell your mamma? And you did?"

"Lulie Mae shoved me behind her," Sitting Bull
said abstractedly, investigating the mechanism of
Sanders' fountain pen. Fortunately for all concerned there was no ink in it. "But I peeked out.
The lady just sat down on the bench for a while."

He found a lopsided gumdrop in Obie's vest
pocket and became enmeshed in it. Obie sighed,
reached into another pocket, and laid his pet cigarette lighter on the altar of historical research.

When Sitting Bull was well occupied again,
snapping on the lighter's flame and trying to blow
it out, to the imminent danger of his own and Mr.
Sanders' eyebrows, Obie said thoughtfully:

"I guess you got pretty tired just waiting while
the lady sat on the bench."

"She didn't sit long. She got up and begun to
dig around."

"Dig? In the dirt? With her hands?"

"Not in the dirt. In the bushes round the bench.
I saw her feeling under them with her hands. Then
Lulie Mae slapped me and shoved me back. Then
she said the lady was gone and we come home.
Mamma says Lulie Mae ain't coming back. Why

ain't she? Mamma says you found her. Why don't you bring her back?"

Sanders cleared his throat loudly and reclaimed his cigarette lighter. "You know how to work my fountain pen? How's about finding some ink and putting it in for me, hmm? You know where some is?"

"Dad's office." Sitting Bull chugged out of the room.

Michael stood aside mechanically to let him pass. He was still standing in the doorway and seemed to have forgotten he held Little Brother under his arm.

"Lulu Mae did take them up the canyon. I got that out of him," Obie said. "They went up past that bench quite a way and then started back. Just before they got back to the bench they heard this 'lady' he speaks of. It must have been Mrs. Maclean. Then—well, you heard the rest of what he said. Does it makes sense to you? What's the matter?"

"I was remembering what Loretta told Antonia about Freddie teasing Bruce and Adela eight years ago," Michael said slowly.

He put Little Brother back behind the barricade. "I think I'm beginning to see a pattern. Where is there a Western Union office in Berkeley?"

"There's one on Shattuck near Addison. But— Are you leaving?"

"For as long," Michael said, "as it will take me to go down there and back. . . ."

In the telegraph office he sat down at one of the writing tables and drew a telegram blank toward him. He took out his own pencil, wrote "Mr. Douglas Maclean" and an address in Wisconsin. Then he frowned and threw the pencil down almost violently. He sat scowling at the blank before he addressed himself severely.

"You poor damned fool, you're thirty-four and it's high time you stopped being childish. Do you prefer to have Ian arrested for murder or be the first to break the silence?"

He grimaced, picked up the pencil, and wrote:

GRANDFATHER:

If you would like to save your favorite grandson from being tried for murdering his wife go to Adela's mother at once and force her to let you go through Adela's desk. You'll find many old letters there. The important ones will be a small bundle of notes without envelopes. They should be signed by "Bruce" if not some nauseating pet name. Read them and let me know your impression of them.

He stopped. Certainly his grandfather could not be called suggestible, but he was anxious that the old man should not read those notes with any preconceived theory in mind. At last he wrote:

> *Also, and this is important, let me know if you find anything in those notes that indicates where they were mailed. Wire me at once at 75 Russian Hill Place, San Francisco.*

He read over what he had written, grinned suddenly, put a dash after the last word, and added "*collect*" before he signed his name.

PART SEVEN

I

When Michael reached the end of Vincentino Road again he found Sanders leaning disconsolately against his car.

"Just taking a deep breath," he said. "I couldn't get anything out of Mrs. Maybry. She says she certainly did not give Lulu Mae the afternoon off, that the girl just left. She had to look after the boys then, but they're in bed by seven and sleep soundly. Dr. Maybry was out by seven, so there's no one to say whether she did stay home with the children from seven to nine.

"Mrs. Maybry claims she did. Of course she didn't have the use of their car, and whoever killed Lulu Mae had to have a car." Obie scrubbed at a blotch of ink on his chin. "And that oldest boy filled my fountain pen all right. He— Hey, are you in a hurry to see somebody at the Carters'?"

"I'm going to talk to Miss Hallie," Michael announced.

He went on across the street. Obie ambled after him and caught his arm as he reached the driveway.

"Why is it the old lady you want to talk to?"

"Because after she came back from her walk and before dinner on Tuesday, Adela stopped to talk a few minutes to Miss Hallie in her bedroom. If you want to know how I know that you can put it on the record that Dr. Carter told me."

Michael removed his coat sleeve politely but pointedly from Sanders' bearlike paw. Obie grinned.

"All right, but I talked to Miss Hallie yesterday and I think her animosity for your cousin is large enough to embrace you too. Probably she'll refuse to see you."

"I shan't ask her if she will see me," Michael said and went on toward the front door.

Sanders was about to follow when he saw one of the plain-clothes men who was making inquiries in the neighborhood. The man was hurrying past the Ferrell house, signaling to Obie. Sanders stopped and waited, listening to Maria telling Michael that "Miss van Horn's home, but the doctor's out and Miss Hallie's still in bed."

Michael stepped into the hall and closed the front door. "Good," he said. "You needn't bother to announce me. I'll go right up."

He brushed past Maria and was halfway up the stairs before she could squawk: "But, mister, if you're that Mr. Maclean's cousin Miss Hallie won't want to—"

Michael threw a soothing "Don't worry; I'll tell her you tried to protect her," over his shoulder and went on to the upper hall.

He guessed that Miss Hallie's bedroom would be one of the two desirable front ones. He opened a door to his right, found that room empty, and crossed the hall. A fretful voice inquired:

"Is that you, Maria? I want another hot-water bottle and—"

"It's not Maria. May I come in?" Michael said and opened the door.

Miss Hallie's bedroom was "feminine." There were ruffles on every article of furniture to which a ruffle can be attached. The dressing table wore a frilled peplum and pale blue pantalets, and all the chairs were garbed in prim pink petticoats.

The lamp shades were tucked and shirred georgettes, decorated with artificial flowers and coy bowknots. The pink wallpaper crawled with blue roses, but very little of it showed since the walls were infested with pictures and photographs, framed and unframed.

The pictures were heavy oils in elaborate gilt frames. At least twelve of the photographs were of Miss Hallie herself and another half dozen of a child and girl who strongly resembled her.

There were photographs of Miss Hallie's husband, of Dr. Carter as a young man, one of a woman in a feathered hat. The face was vaguely familiar to Michael. That, he guessed, was Adela's mother, and beneath it was an enlarged snapshot of two girls standing with their arms about each other—Adela and Miss Hallie's Rosalie.

An overposed study of her daughter held the place of honor in a silver frame on Miss Hallie's dressing table. A pretty, characterless face framed in fine blonde hair; an inscription in delicate, characterless handwriting: "To dearest Mother from Rosalie."

Other photographs, framed in lesser metals than silver, fought with Miss Hallie's numerous toilet articles and a collection of small china boxes for a toe hold on the dressing table. There was an apologetic likeness of Loretta inscribed in an unexpectedly firm, strong hand to "Dear Cousin Hallie."

This was at the back of the dressing table, nearly hidden by Freddie in cap and gown, looking as complacently foolish as one usually does in that costume. Near Freddie was Bruce, carefully unposed, lounging against a table, shirt open at the neck. Freddie had endorsed his picture to "Aunt

Hallie from her grateful nephew," but Bruce's was inscribed to "Miss Hallie, the queen of all our hearts."

Michael snorted. Actually his quick glance about the room had taken only an instant during which Miss Hallie had time to hitch herself up in bed and clutch the covers about her neck.

"I'm Ian's cousin, Michael Dundas," Michael said. "I want—"

Miss Hallie uttered the sort of noise one who does not like spiders is apt to make on being confronted with an unusually large black specimen.

"His cousin! Go away! Maria! Doctor! Freddie! Help!"

Michael looked at her disgustedly and came over to the big bed where Miss Hallie's flabby pink face was only a blob against a mound of pillows whose cases were trimmed with wide crochet. He considered trying to win her over and decided that the odds were all against his succeeding even if he had the necessary time and patience.

The faded blue eyes could be vindictive, he thought: the chin beneath the deceptively soft flesh was narrow and stubborn, and the Cupid's-bow mouth had loosened until its ends drooped petulantly. He smiled: the sort of smile calculated to make small dogs put their tails between their legs.

"I don't intend you any bodily harm."

Miss Hallie did not appear to find this state-ment reassuring. She made whimpering noises against the back of her hand.

"But there is something I must know that only you can tell me and I haven't time to drag a duly accredited officer of the law up here to question you. What did Adela say to you when she came into this room Tuesday evening just before din-ner?"

Miss Hallie closed her eyes. One fat hand groped among the bottles on the bedside table and closed over a bottle of smelling salts. These revived her to the point of querulous defiance.

"If you think I'm going to say one word to any-body who's related to Ian Maclean—"

"What did Adela say to you?" Michael repeated.

The quality that Dr. Carter labeled "driving force" was never more apparent than now. After-ward he felt as weary as if he had really been beat-ing a feather bed, trying to make some lasting impression on its stubborn softness. But Miss Hallie answered his question.

"Adela came in and said she'd been walking—"

"Where?"

"She didn't exactly say. She said he'd dropped in on Mrs. Twelvetrees and hadn't Mrs. Twelve-trees failed dreadfully—and she has too. She's quite childish, poor old thing. It was mighty nice

of dear Adela to bother with Mrs. Twelvetrees her
first day here and—"

"Yes. Then what did Adela say?"

"She wanted to know if I was feeling better,"
Miss Hallie answered as obediently as a ventrilo-
quist's dummy. "I hadn't been well that afternoon.
Finding out Cook had been drinking rum in her
tea and two silver spoons missing . . . but I was
feeling better after a good nap. I told Adela she
didn't need to help me dress and she'd better get
dressed herself because—"

"Was that all? What did she do while she was
talking to you?"

Miss Hallie looked at him blankly. "Do?"

"Were you still in bed?" Miss Hallie nodded.
"Did Adela stand here, as I'm doing now? Did she
move about as she talked to you? Think, woman!"

This had the force of an electric shock and
stimulated even Miss Hallie's sluggish mental pro-
cesses.

"She did keep moving around, which wasn't like
dear Adela. She always had so much poise. She—
Oh, she picked up things off the dressing table
and put them back and straightened the doilies on
the bookcase."

Miss Hallie pointed to a small bookcase that
contained very nearly everything but books. There
were more photographs on top of it: one of Evelyn

Ferrell with her daughter and one of the Maybrys, the doctor appearing slightly harassed while Sitting Bull leered horridly into the camera.

"Adela picked up those pictures while she was talking to me and then put them back," Miss Hallie recalled. "I reckon she wasn't thinking what she was doing because she came back to the bureau and did the same thing. With the pictures, I mean."

"Oh." Michael looked from the bookcase to the dressing table and back to the bookcase again. "Oh, so that was it? That's all I wanted to know, Mrs. Durdan. Thank you."

He went toward the door, and Miss Hallie collapsed like a rickety piece of furniture whose prop is suddenly jerked away. She opened her mouth and began to make hysterical noises.

Maria appeared with a damp cloth in one hand and a hot-water bottle in the other, and the glance she gave Mr. Dundas before she closed the door in his face was compounded equally of repugnance and awe.

II

Michael went on down to the living room to find Loretta showing signs of disintegration under O. B. Sanders' persistent pounding.

"You have to make up your mind, Miss van Horn. First you tell me you didn't take out your car last night. Then when I tell you that I just found out from the man I had check with the garage that Mr. Prince turned that car over to you fresh-cleaned and polished—"

"Y-yeth, he did," Loretta stammered. "Of courth Wichard did—"

"Then when I ask you how the car got rained on if you didn't take it out last night you change your mind and say that you did take it out."

"I went widing for a little while about seven-thirty. Just to get a bweath of fwesh air."

"That's always a nice thing to do on a rainy evening," Sanders remarked. Michael grinned, not because Mr. Sanders intended to be sarcastic but because he did not.

"The only thing," Obie went on placidly, "is that Maria says you were here at seven-thirty. She can't say if you went out later and came back."

"Well," Loretta said desperately, "perhapth it was later than seven-thirty. I'm afwaid I'm stupid about time. I never pay attention to clocks."

"You must have had to pay attention to them if you've given music lessons all these years," Sanders said reasonably. "Well, that garage you keep the car in is on the opposite side of the Kelseys' house from their dining and living room. The man I had talk with the Kelseys tells me their hearing isn't too keen. But Mr. Kelsey does think he heard a car being driven out of their garage sometime during the early evening. He knows it was before eight o'clock because there was a radio program he wanted to listen to at eight."

Loretta swallowed. "Then it must have been me," she said stubbornly. "I don't leave my keys in the car and I lock Mr. Kelsey's garage very carefully."

Sanders shrugged ponderously. "Well, if that's your story, Miss van Horn. Where did you ride?"

"Just—just awound these hills—"

Obie sighed. "Well, if that's all—"

"No," Michael said, "I want a word with Miss van Horn, if you don't mind. I may as well tell you that Antonia overheard part of a conversation you had with Dr. Carter yesterday afternoon."

"Part of a— Oh!"

"Yes. You told the doctor what you and Adela said to each other in the upstairs hall before dinner on the night of her death. And I want to know what happened eight years ago to make you despise Adela so heartily."

"I—nothing," Loretta said tremulously. "I just didn't like Adela, that'th all."

"Is it? What did you mean when you told Dr. Carter that he should have guessed that Adela would be the first person his niece Rosalie would have confided in? What had Rosalie to confide?

What had you wanted to tell Dr. Carter for 'so many years'? Why could Adela—?"

"Toni was very wrong to listen! But I'm not going to explain, no matter what you do to me!" Loretta said and dissolved into tears.

Obie clucked commiseratingly. "You oughtn't to make them cry," he said and offered Loretta a large clean handkerchief.

She managed a watery smile, dabbed at eyes and nose, and then began to sneeze violently. Tears began to run down her cheeks again, and she cast the handkerchief in Obie's general direction.

"It's—it's perfumed," she said and sneezed again.

Sanders looked as guilty as if he had been caught using a curling iron on his hair. "Just a little lavender after-shave tonic."

"I know, but I'm very allergic to any kind of perfume. If I have to inhale it it gives me hay fever. It isn't your fault," Loretta said and moved casually toward the door.

"I haven't finished," Michael said. "I was just going to ask you what you meant when you told Dr. Carter that Adela could say she had done nothing wrong. Didn't you underline the 'she'? Does that mean that you couldn't say the same thing? Or—"

"Oh," Loretta said, "I wish you would go away and stop hounding me! I wish—"

"What's going on here?" demanded an unfamiliar voice that had many of the qualities of a trumpet blast. "What the—? Loretta!"

A tall man with a mane of silver hair scudded across the room, knocking two chairs out of his way. He lifted Loretta off her feet, kissed her soundly and without embarrassment, and turned on Michael.

"What the hell do you mean, bullying her until she cries? Loretta, I drove all night to get here after I got your letter about this Maclean woman. That's a nice way to repay hospitality: get yourself killed in your host's living room. I've a good mind to paste you one!"

"Me?" Michael said, prudently putting Obie Sanders between himself and Richard Prince. "I don't think Mr. Sanders would like that, and he is an officer of the law. My name is Dundas."

"Oh, so you're Dundas. Glad to know you." Mr. Prince was, Michael decided, as gusty and forthright, as forceful and as variable as a strong wind. "I know a lot of people who know you. But I can't have you annoying Loretta."

"If Miss van Horn could be persuaded to tell the truth occasionally she needn't be annoyed. Did you know Miss Hallie's daughter Rosalie, Mr. Prince?"

"What? Rosalie? Oh."

Prince's features were too piratically bold to be especially expressive. One could not imagine that he would ever appear apprehensive, but for just an instant he eyed Michael speculatively. Then:

"I saw Rosalie around after she came home from school," he said easily. "I met her at Evelyn Ferrell's. Evelyn Blake, she was then. I don't—"

Loretta had wiped her eyes on Prince's breast-pocket handkerchief while clinging tightly to his arm. Now she said sharply:

"Mr. Dundas is simply curious about everything, whether it has anything to do with Adela's death or not."

"Do you think so?" Michael said pleasantly. "But I won't bother you with my curiosity any longer—unless Mr. Prince would like to tell me how long he's known Mrs. Ferrell?"

"Evelyn used to work for me in my music store. She was the best stenographer I ever had. She came back to the store after she and Blake split up, but she was only there about a year before she married Bruce Ferrell."

"Thank you," Michael said as the sound of a car stopping before the house was followed by the slamming of the front door. He smiled at Loretta. "Isn't that 'Dr. Carter? Perhaps I can get farther with him than I have with you."

Loretta's little flicker of self-assurance wavered and went out. "You—you aren't going to talk to Cousin Doc!"

"Would you rather I talked to Cousin Hallie?"

"No! She wouldn't—she doesn't—"

"That's what I thought," Michael said and went off to find the doctor in his study, looking through the contents of his dilapidated black bag.

"Ought to get a new stethoscope, but I thought I could make the old one do. . . . Oh, it's you again? What do you charge to haunt a house?"

"How many rooms?" Michael said, grinning. He sat down on the edge of the big desk.

"Doctor, I'm going to ask you a question without bothering to be at all tactful and then I'm going to give you ample time to make up your mind whether or not you'll answer it—if you must have time. What was the true cause of your niece's death?"

"The true cause of Rosalie's— You impudent, prying young—"

"You know," Michael said thoughtfully, "that sounds more like a line from a play than Dr. Carter. If you had only said: 'Why, damn your impudence, sir!'"

The old man smiled sourly. "Very well; give me one good reason why I should answer your question."

"If you did you might explain why Loretta disliked Adela so much. As well as certain intriguing
statements made by you and Loretta in a conversation Antonia overheard yesterday afternoon."

"I thought Toni looked too much like a kitten
that's been at the cream *not* to have been listening," Dr. Carter said grimly. "Go on."

"You might also be able to account for the fact
that Adela, once she was back in Wisconsin, sel-
dom spoke of Rosalie and had no photograph of
her. Perhaps you could explain why Adela left here
so suddenly eight years ago and why she wasn't
too enthusiastic about visiting here again."

"Oh, wasn't she?" Dr. Carter muttered.

"Ian thinks she wasn't, and Loretta believed
that Adela never would come back. Perhaps. . . .
But that's all I'm going to say except to assure you
that I'm not talkative. That is, not very often,"
Michael added, remembering Nicholas Prevost's
bachelor dinner. "But I promise that I'd never repeat anything you might tell me if it had nothing
to do with Adela's death. You may want to talk
to—others before you see me again. Could I come
back this afternoon?"

"Better make it after dinner," Dr. Carter said
abstractedly. "I've a busy afternoon before me
and—make it around eight."

III

Michael found Sanders waiting for him at the front door. "Miss van Horn is crying again, and Richard Prince is tearing his hair," Obie reported with some satisfaction. Michael laughed.

"Do you know that some foolish women always refer to that head and hair as 'leonine'? Also, he used to be called 'Prince Richard' or 'the Lionheart' by certain fluttery females. They're an odd pair, but it must be love. He did not object when she used his beautifully folded breast-pocket handkerchief to dry her tears."

"I think it's true love and very nice," Obie said seriously. "But I'd like to know what's behind some of your questions. Nick Prevost told me that there comes a point when you are very exasperating. I am not easily exasperated, but I think that point has come."

"'Where two ride on one horse one must ride behind.' But I'm getting off for a while."

"What do you mean?"

"Dana Clyde promised to have a report ready for me by noon and, since I—or Ian—am paying him plenty for it, I want to see it. After that there's nothing I can do until evening. I must wait for a telegram to come from Wisconsin and I can't see Dr. Carter again until eight o'clock.

"But," Michael said, getting into his car, "I will have something to tell you after that. I don't know just what, but keep a man on Dr. Carter, will you?"

Obie nodded. "We'll do that and— Wait a minute. I sent a fellow up into the canyon to look around. Here he comes now. He's young and active; and anyway, my feet hurt." He lifted one surprisingly small foot and shook it gingerly.

"Perhaps you should have larger shoes?" Michael suggested.

"No. I wear nines, but tens feel so much better that I buy elevens. Well, Appleton?"

"If there were any footprints left on that path in the canyon of course last night's rain washed them out," Appleton said. "And I dug all around the bushes."

"Where?" Michael asked.

"Why, where they grow low to the ground all around that bench. I didn't find any signs that anything, any—any object had ever been concealed in there, so short of tearing up the bushes by the roots—"

"Oh, I'm sure that would be wasted effort. I see you also got down on your knees," Michael remarked, glancing at Appleton's trousers.

"Yes, I—"

"Who else got down on his knees up there?" Sanders interrupted.

"Bruce Ferrell, yesterday morning. Sorry, I thought I'd told you," Michael said, let in the clutch, and drove away.

Dana Clyde lived in another of Berkeley's sturdy, brown-shingled, vine-grown houses on a quiet block of Benvenue. Clyde was a stooped man, all gray: eyes, hair, and skin. Sparing of words, he simply handed Michael the report that his daughter, who had been his secretary for fifteen years, had just finished typing.

Michael sighed over the length of the report but, being given a comfortable chair and a good light, sat down to read. The light and chair were furnished by Miss Clyde, who was as neutral as her father and as unobtrusive as furniture.

She retired to a corner, and no one, least of all Mr. Dundas, could have guessed that she was fervently admiring his eyelashes. She watched him reading, guessing by his rate of progress that he knew how to skim, gathering the cream without paying too much or too little attention to the milk below.

Dana Clyde had dealt with Judith Maybry first, and the first interesting item in her career was the fact that she had been asked to discontinue attendance at a select girls' school in Berkeley at the age of seventeen.

Reason, as stated by Dana Clyde: "She was supposed to be carrying on an affair with the visiting musical instructor, a young Frenchman." Judith had then transferred to Berkeley High School, spent eighteen months there before graduating and the same length of time at Armstrong's Business College—without graduating.

She was twenty when Adela Maclean visited Rosalie Durdan in Berkeley. She had married James Maybry two years later, shortly after Dr. Carter took him into partnership. Judith's father, a retired civil-service employee, now lived with an older daughter in Sacramento. . . .

Mr. Dundas turned a page. Dr. Maybry came next, Miss Clyde remembered, and Father was not at all satisfied with that portion of the report. You could guess at a background of genteel poverty. Maybry's parents were farming folk in the San Joaquin valley. He had worked his way through Stanford, gone to medical school in the Middle West, returned to hang out his shingle in Oakland.

Not one of the nicer sections of Oakland, and few people there seemed to remember him now, though he had been in that one neighborhood for four years. Neither was there any information as to how he had happened to meet Dr. Carter.

But they had met, and apparently the old doctor had taken a fancy to him at once. At any rate,
they had been working together for a little over
six years. . . .

Seeing Mr. Dundas frown, Miss Clyde wanted
to assure him that the next dossier, that of Evelyn
Ferrell, was more satisfactory, even though Mrs.
Ferrell had been born and educated in San Diego.
Her parents still lived there.

Mrs. Ferrell was thirty-three, three years older
than Mr. Ferrell. She had come to Berkeley when
she was twenty and found a position in Richard
Prince's music store. She left it to marry Charles
Blake, who was a rather well-to-do realtor.

They had been divorced four years later. Very
amicably: there had been no question of alimony,
because Mr. Blake had taken custody of their two-
year-old son. That is, his mother had been foolishly fond of the baby and assumed responsibility
for its care.

Mrs. Ferrell went back to work for Richard
Prince again until she married Bruce Ferrell. But
she had not known him until some time after her
divorce. Father, Miss Clyde thought, had made
that quite clear.

As to Mr. Ferrell, he had gone through high
school and into the university but had not finished his junior year there. Miss Clyde thought

that it was a pity that no one seemed quite certain whether Mr. Ferrell had been advised to leave college or had done so of his own accord.

Mr. Ferrell's father was only a salaried clerk, but he had supported Bruce several years longer while he dabbled at various types of art. He had even lived one summer in Carmel, attired in sandals, shorts, and long hair.

Then Bruce had filled—very inefficiently— several clerical positions. However, he had had a large acquaintance among what Miss Clyde termed "the better people" in Berkeley. It was during this period that his name was linked with that of a very pretty woman whose husband was elderly and whose hobby was the collection of promising young artists.

Following that a young night-club entertainer had swallowed poison—but, Miss Clyde reflected scornfully, only enough to make her ill. Miss Clyde had no patience with inefficiency of any sort. However, the girl's farewell note had featured Bruce Ferrell. But he had lived that down and met and married his present wife. . . .

Then there was Loretta van Horn. Miss Clyde knew her by sight from industrious attendance at musicales. Loretta's people had been well to do and had meant her to be a concert pianist. But in 1932 Mr. van Horn had finally realised that he was never going to get back the money he had lost in '29 and '30.

Mr. van Horn had put a gun into his mouth and pulled the trigger. Mrs. van Horn promptly took refuge in melancholia and a sanitarium whose fees Loretta paid for two years before her mother died.

The rest of Loretta's life was as humdrum as Miss Clyde considered her own had been—except that suddenly Miss van Horn was going to marry Richard Prince. Miss Clyde sighed.

Mr. Dundas was reading even more rapidly now. However, there wasn't a great deal of information on Fredric Carter; no outstanding or especially interesting facts, that is. Dr. Carter's dossier covered at least two pages.

But probably his early life wasn't important or his sister's, either. Now they were just two elderly people whom everyone in their neighborhood knew. And Rosalie Durdan's life history in Dana Clyde's report was as short as her life had been.

"Well," Mr. Dundas said, looking up, "I don't see how you did this in such a short time."

"I've only skimmed the surface," Dana Clyde said disparagingly. "This case strikes me as the sort that's most difficult for the police to handle satisfactorily."

"Why do you say that?"

"Of course one must first accept your belief that your cousin did not kill his wife."

In her corner Miss Clyde nodded approvingly. Father knew that you can't erase a possibility simply by ignoring it. You have to consider it carefully first and then make up your mind whether or not to reject it.

"If your cousin didn't kill Mrs. Maclean and one of these people did, any one of them would be a clever amateur," Dana Clyde said. "It still seems to be the 'why' that's the big question. The answer to why Adela Maclean was killed must lie in the characters of these people and their relations with one another, and I'd say those are discouragingly complex.

"The police," he went on, "don't get far in that sort of case by questioning those concerned. For example, I picked up that gossip about Mrs. Maybry and Mr. Ferrell. But O. B. Sanders can't just ask Mrs. Maybry pointblank if Ferrell is her lover or suggest to Dr. Maybry that one of his sons isn't his. Well, will this do?"

He pointed to the typed report. Mr. Dundas glanced at the top page, flipped over several more pages, read the last sheet of the report again. Then he turned back once more, and Miss Clyde was vexed because she could not guess what page his finger rested on when he said:

"I'd like more information on this as quickly as you can get it for me."

Miss Clyde thought that Father looked rather surprised, and Mr. Dundas added: "Don't you think it needs explaining?"

"Well, perhaps it does," Dana Clyde said. "Will you accept rumor if I can't get facts as quickly as you want them?"

"All donations gratefully received. I also would like any interesting high lights you might be able to gather on Richard Prince. Not the sort of twaddle that's written about him in the Berkeley *Gazette*. He's back in town now. I don't know where in the south he was—probably Los Angeles—but I'd like to know when he left there. And it might save you a good deal of trouble if you'd just ask him if he—"

The telephone rang in an adjoining room, and Miss Clyde went to answer it, reflecting that even if Mr. Dundas didn't trust her Father did. She would get it all out of him when Mr. Dundas had left. When she came back to the living room and found that he had gone Miss Clyde sighed and said: "I wonder what sort of person his wife is. . . ."

Mr. Dundas' wife was, at about five o'clock, a very surprised sort of person to be invited to join her husband for cocktails at the St. Francis. Nor, when they were sitting in the patent-leather lounge, did he object to her ordering a rum collins instead of Coca-Cola.

"Though," he said morosely, "rum is a pernicious beverage. If Miss Hallie's cook hadn't added rum to her tea perhaps none of this would have happened."

"I suppose," Valerie said, "that you'll tell me next that Adela was killed because, besides ferreting out the cook's sins, she also discovered that two silver spoons were missing."

"Hmm? Yes, the silver spoons were important too." Michael looked at his watch. "I'll wait another ten minutes and then call Patton."

"To see if that telegram has come? Suppose your grandfather turns out to be even more stubborn than you are, darling?"

Michael smiled acidly. "Don't rub it in. Besides, I asked him to help Ian, not me. And to do Grandfather justice, he would have given me any aid I asked for at any time during the last fourteen years. I'd only to ask—"

"That's all," Valerie said a trifle sardonically. "My imagination balks at you in the role of prodigal grandson. I don't think you'd care much more for fatted calf than you would for humble pie. How long have you been back in the city?"

"Since early afternoon. I tried to work. You may ask Fanchon if I didn't," Michael said as Valerie smiled. "But all my sketches resembled shrouds, and Fanchon said I'd better knock off. Well, Grandfather may be having trouble with Adela's mother,"

"And what about George?"

"George?"

"The family representative Adela's mother was sending out here in her place."

"Oh, good lord! It would take only George's arrival to make my life complete. But he evidently isn't flying out and he can't get here by train for several days. . . . I could try to talk to Mrs. Twelve-trees again," Michael muttered.

"Yes indeed," his wife said amiably. "Why?"

"She must sit up late at night if she only sleeps six hours. And Adela went to see her instead of going straight from the canyon back to Dr. Car-ter's house."

"I wonder why I don't feed you arsenic when you act like this."

"A small dose of arsenic couldn't be much more painful than this. I'm worried about Antonia too."

"So am I. How long will it take Ian to realize how she feels about him?"

"That," Michael said, "is one thing I refuse to worry about. But I warned her this morning that the police are watching her and that she must not lead them to Ian. She only said: 'Of course I won't.' *That* does worry me. Well, I'll take you to dinner at Cathay House."

Valerie laid her hand against his forehead. "No temperature? You know you don't like Chinese food or not being able to get coffee at Cathay House."

"I don't need more coffee. I'm merely a walking collection of liquids now. Come along. I'll telephone to Patton on our way out. . . ."

Patton regretted that no wire had arrived. Michael sighed and called O. B. Sanders at Berkeley. Obie said plaintively that "none of our routine inquiries have gotten us very far.

"Only," he went on, "I didn't suppose Ferrell had access to a car, but it seems a friend of his about two blocks down is out of town. He was afraid of car strippers and asked Bruce to keep an eye on his car. So Bruce could have used that guy's car to pick Lulu Mae up in."

"Did you ask Mr. Ferrell why he strolled up to the canyon yesterday morning?" Michael said.

"Yes. He said it was thinking of Adela and old times that made him do it because they used to call that the sparking bench."

"Up to a certain point I imagine Ferrell spoke the truth. Anything more?"

"A boy about the age to notice cars lives next door to Lulu Mae's house. He claims he noticed

the same car come by there at least twice sometime after seven last night. He knows Jerry Flanigan and his car, and saw him too. This other car,
as the kid describes it, would be that roadster of
Richard Prince's, and he thinks a woman was driving it, but he's not sure.

"And Mrs. Ferrell comes close to having an
alibi for last night. We turned up a boy that puts
books back on the library shelves. He remembers
seeing her two or three times while he was working around. But I've been having a talk with Mr.
Carter and I'm not done with him yet. It seems—"

Sanders stopped and spoke to someone else.
Then: "Could you wait a minute?" he asked.
"Here's a fellow I have to talk to."

"Is it anything that can't wait until this evening? No? Then I won't wait. Don't forget to keep
an eye on Dr. Carter. I'll take my wife to dinner
now. . . ."

While Valerie consumed an enormous platter
of chicken chow mein and innumerable tiny cups
of China tea Michael dabbled in fried rice. He
did not suggest that she hurry, but Valerie began
to feel, sooner than she liked, that he wished she
would.

"Let me go with you," she said when they came
out onto California Street again and had walked
down to Grant Avenue where, in the gray evening,

old St. Mary's sat red and solid in the midst of its pagan flock of oriental bazaars.

Michael shook his head. "I'd like to take you with me, dear. But if that telegram arrives you will have to bring it over to Berkeley in a taxi. I'll take you home now instead of calling Patton. I have a notion I'll have to leave you there."

And when Patton again reported that no wire had arrived he drove on toward the Bay Bridge alone. When he reached the end of Vincentino Road a fine drizzle was falling, and it was quite dark at five minutes of eight.

There were no lights showing in the Carter house, but the doctor's old car was parked in front of it. Michael looked about for some loiterer that would be the man O. B. Sanders had detailed to watch Dr. Carter. He saw no one, and when he reached the front door it swung open under his hand.

IV

Antonia leaned back against the front door after closing it on Freddie Carter and shook her head in silent exasperation. This, she thought, was a nice time for Freddie to choose to propose to her again.

But of course Freddie didn't know that she had any plans for the evening, and it was still too early for her to leave the house: only six o'clock and not dark enough. She could get things together now, though, since she had seen the cook and maid start off together to an early movie.

She went into the kitchen, started coffee brewing, opened a can of soup, and put it to heat while she filled two thermos bottles with hot water. She buttered bread, inserted thick slices of ham, cut cake, wrapped it in waxed paper.

When the thermos bottles were filled with soup and coffee she went upstairs for her father's thickest sweater, a bottle of his best scotch, cigarettes, and two blankets. She found the big lunch basket they used on picnics, took it down to the kitchen, and packed it.

Freddie, she thought, had really meant to be sweet. It was nice of him to propose again just now. Bruce, Freddie said disgustedly, had told the police about that unfortunate scene on the balcony.

Only those, Antonia remembered, smiling, were not Freddie's words. He had called it "your little spot of canoodling." But he had not been facetious when he remarked that "sooner or later the police are bound to catch up with Ian. Then you're going to be in for it too, Toni."

"I had a detective here this morning wanting to know if it was love at first sight between Ian and me," Antonia said. "I asked him what he would do if he were alone on a very small balcony with a pretty girl. But he was a serious-minded man."

"So was Adela serious-minded about such things, and everyone knows it," Freddie said with unusual sharpness. "She probably gave Ian hell for that and if she kept at it long enough—well, the police believe that they did quarrel violently. And since they know about you and Ian, Toni, they know two reasons why Adela and Ian might have quarreled. And her refusing to give him a divorce is just one of them."

"I know. But"—Antonia shrugged—"that's water under the bridge, Freddie."

"Well, it would help if we were engaged and when all this comes out I just laugh and say that I thought nothing of it."

Freddie turned pink and passed a hand over his hair. "That sounds corny, doesn't it—offering you the protection of my name? But you know—"

"I know what you mean, and it's nice of you— and the answer is 'no.' And was I mistaken in thinking you looked a bit ruffled when you turned up here, Freddie?"

"Did I? Well, I was. I'd just had a session with O. B. Sanders. You know I don't have a full-time stenographer but get a girl in from an agency when I need one. She was with me yesterday just before five. The telephone rang, and I asked her to answer it.

"Maybe it was a girl's voice, as the stenographer claims. She told Sanders that a 'soft, girlish voice' asked for Mr. Carter. I took the phone and said hello about four times. Then"—Freddie snapped his fingers—"she just hung up. I don't mind admitting it's got me worried. Sanders already had the bright idea that Lulu Mae might have wanted to consult a lawyer."

"You, Freddie?"

"Lulu Mae distrusted lawyers, but Sanders suggested that she knew me and might have been willing to consult me. He did say, too, that someone might have recommended me to Lulu Mae. If someone did and that was Lulu Mae calling yesterday afternoon why did she hang up?"

"She might have gotten frightened and backed out when she realized there was someone with you. Who would recommend you to Lulu Mae? And did anyone know you wouldn't be alone in your office yesterday afternoon?"

"Why"—Freddie frowned—"while we were playing bridge the night Adela was killed I said that I had enough work that I'd have to call in a stenographer two afternoons running. We were discussing business in general and income taxes and— But hell! That's too farfetched if you mean what I think you might."

"Everything about this business is farfetched. Lulu Mae could have been acting on the orders of someone who wanted to incriminate you. Or she might just have thought she'd talk to you and then decided not to risk it."

"And it may not have been Lulu Mae at all," Freddie said. "If she hadn't asked for Mr. Carter I'd suppose it was a wrong number. I'm glad my visiting stenographer testified that the mysterious female did hang up. But I don't like it. Sanders gives me the jitters."

"Not Michael?"

"Not so much. Dundas is sort of cyclonic: here one minute and gone the next. But Sanders is like a mountain moving, kind of slow and irresistible. Dundas springs around from one idea to another like a grasshopper, but when Sanders gets an idea he keeps chewing on it. I don't want him chewing on me," Freddie said decidedly. "I hate to leave you here alone, Toni. If your folks knew about this they'd have hopped a plane home before now. Why don't you come out to dinner and a show with me?"

"I had practically no sleep last night and I'm going to bed early," Antonia said and finally managed to herd him into the hall and out of the house. . . .

It was still only six-fifteen, but suddenly she closed the lunch basket, bundled the blankets and sweater over one arm, and started down the stairs that led from the hall to the basement garage.

If I'm to be followed I'll be followed any time, day or night, she thought. And he's been alone in that big, cold, empty house all day. I don't care what Michael told me. . . .

She started the car and left it running while she opened the garage doors. Fortunately they opened easily, and she had backed into the garage the last time she used her car. That made it possible for her to get away to a running start. She was in high gear by the time she turned into the street and promptly stepped on the gas.

She was certain that a black car which had been parked on the street all day was following her— and laughed a little. She was an expert and fearless driver, and she knew her Piedmont hills. Her course was very nearly as devious as Michael's had been in San Francisco last night, and her handling of the car would have won a word of praise even from him.

When finally she slowed down a little she was well into East Oakland. But remembering Michael's tactics, she took the most roundabout way back to Berkeley and the house on Spruce Street.

Instead of entering it at once she rang the bell of the house next door. "I thought I'd tell you," she said to the middle-aged woman who answered the ring, "that I have to look over the kitchen to see if it has to be painted before we can rent the house. I was afraid you might notice the light and wonder if there were prowlers there."

"Well, I do keep a sort of eye on the place," Mrs. Welch admitted. "My, property is a responsibility, isn't it? Vandals, that's what renters are—just vandals. And with workmen so independent and the war and priorities and all, keeping a place in repair just eats up your profits before you get them."

"That's what my father says," Antonia agreed politely. "But I thought I'd better look at the kitchen. Good night, Mrs. Welch. . . ."

She drove the car around to the garage in back of the house so that she could unload her supplies without being seen. Then she rapped five times on the back door and, when it swung open, stepped in and turned on the large flashlight she had brought with her.

"Good lord!" Ian said. "You shouldn't have—"

"Are you sorry I did?"

"No. I— You'd better not do that," Ian protested as Antonia produced another light: a large electric lamp that she put on the drainboard.

"It's all right," the girl said calmly. "Here, take the lunch basket. You were saying?"

"If you have ever seen a six-foot-two, one-hundred-and-ninety-five-pound hunk of flesh in a blue funk, on the point of shrieking like a hysterical woman—well, take a good look at me. I ran out of cigarettes around noon. My fault; I should have rationed them. I've sat on this couch and shivered like a whipped pup. Well, never mind."

But he put out a hand, touched hers almost fearfully, and then tightened his hold on it.

"You're alive, aren't you? Alive and warm. Any cop could have had me for the asking this afternoon if I hadn't promised Michael—"

He broke off and grinned. "Did I promise Michael I'd stay here until he came or did he only tell me that I had? The question occurred to me about an hour ago. Lord, that looks good. Coffee."

"And soup and scotch," Antonia said proudly. "But you'd better have soup and a sandwich before you sample the scotch. And put on Dad's sweater. . . . Ian," she said presently, sitting on one end of the comfortless old box couch, watching him eat, "what are you going to do when Michael clears you of this?"

"'When?' If, my dear."

"I'm sure he's making progress."

"Oh, I do have a reasonless sort of faith in his ability to get me out of this—sometime. And as to your question, that's something I've been thinking over, having had unlimited time for thought. And I've come to the conclusion that the family business can struggle along without me.

"I fancy it always could have, even before Pearl Harbor, if I'd had the guts to say so to my wife and grandfather. I think I will join any branch of our armed forces that will take me."

"They'll take you," Antonia said. "You look very healthy—or did, three days ago."

"But I have a feeling that first I'd like to crawl away somewhere for a while. Somewhere in the mountains or by the sea. Just," Ian said apologetically, "for a day or two until I get my bearings again."

"Carmel is nice. We have a cottage there you could have. If—" Antonia turned scarlet, but she went on steadily: "Will you take me with you?"

"Will I—?"

"Will you take me with you for as long as it takes you to get your bearings? I know you don't want to marry me," Antonia said rapidly. "I wouldn't blame you if you never wanted to marry anyone again. I swear I'll be a—a gentleman and never, never consider I have any claim on you at all. I—

But can a man ever believe a woman when she promises that?"

"Yes, I think a man might believe one woman," Ian said slowly. "But, Toni, why?"

"I couldn't bear the idea of your going off alone. Oh, darling, I couldn't!—any more than I could leave you alone any longer in this awful cold place. I know Adela would rather have been burned at the stake than ever to have offered herself—"

"Adela certainly would. But let's forget Adela." Ian got to his feet and took her hands. "Come here, sweet. . . .

"I do," he added presently, "realize that I'm kissing you this time: Antonia Jordan, not only a pretty girl I've just met. That's what you were wondering, isn't it?"

A heavy fist thumped on the door before a large foot kicked it open. A middle-aged, red-nosed man stood regarding them benevolently.

"Well, that was quite a chase you led us, little lady," he observed. "Ain't this cozy? A reg'lar love nest. Now, miss! You take it easy or I'll have to put the bracelets on you too. Come along, Maclean, and tell it to the boys at headquarters."

V

The old doctor was dead. He sat in his worn creaking chair at the big desk with his old black bag at his elbow and he had been shot through the chest at close range.

In the hall an old grandfather clock struck eight deep, slow chimes. It set a refrain going in Michael's mind that persisted for hours: "Tick, tock, tick, tock, His life seconds numbering, Tick, tock, tick, tock, It stopped short never to go again When the old man died."

He left the study and went upstairs. In one big front bedroom Miss Hallie lay on her back with her teeth in a glass of water on the bedside table, mouth open, snoring genteelly. She mumbled and turned over on her side without waking when Michael shook her fat shoulder gently.

No other bedroom on the second floor was occupied. There was a bathroom and two small bedrooms on the half story above. One bedroom was empty. In the other a rawboned woman with carroty hair also lay snoring, but not genteelly. An empty rum bottle and the aroma that pervaded the room proclaimed the cause of her slumber.

Michael returned to the study. He stood behind Dr. Carter, looking at the desk. The old man's right hand lay on the desk blotter, its forefinger ink-stained. There was no fountain pen in his vest, but in an instant Michael saw that one was protruding a little from a pocket of the doctor's baggy trousers.

He did not touch the pen but, dropping to one knee, made certain that the doctor had thrust it point down into his pocket without screwing the cap on first. He stood up and looked at the desk blotter. But it was old and cracked, crisscrossed with innumerable words and bits of words and sentences.

Michael turned away, then muttered: "But if your pen went into your trouser pocket so quickly what were you doing with your other hand?"

He lifted the blotter. A crumpled sheet of paper lay under it. Beneath his printed name and address Dr. Carter had written in the hand that had been the despair of pharmacists:

> DEAR DUNDAS:
> *One of my patients is very ill and I may be called out again before you get here, in which case I will leave this for you. Remembering your promise, I have decided to answer your question. My niece Rosalie died as the result of an abortion performed on her. I will tell you the story in detail if you want to—*

The last seven words were badly smeared, as if the ink had not been dry when the paper was thrust beneath the blotter. Michael put the letter in his pocket and started toward the telephone.

The doorbell rang before he reached it. Michael said: "Come in. The door is open," and James Maybry stepped into the hall. He raised his eyebrows.

"We haven't met, but you're Dundas, aren't you? Where is the doctor? It's very quiet here."

"Very. The doctor is in his study. You will have to go to him," Michael said.

Maybry stared at him. "What do you mean?"

Evidently Michael's expression alarmed him. He went into the study to emerge in an instant, white and sweating.

"Good God! I talked to him around seven. He was alive then. I can't—"

"You can't believe it," Michael said unpleasantly. "But you are a doctor. Death is an old story to you."

The corner of Maybry's mouth and an eyelid twitched nervously. "I happen to owe Dr. Carter a good deal. Besides, everyone who knows him will feel that others die but he's always there, fighting death—"

"Oh, spare me a premature funeral oration!" Michael said savagely.

Maybry's eyelid stopped twitching, and he eyed Michael professionally. "Your own nerves are strung so tight they're ready to snap," he said. "Have they ever?"

"No. I take it out in snapping myself—at other people. And while I always appreciate free medical advice—"

"This is not the time for that? I suppose you're right. But where is everyone? We heard no shot, but surely Miss Hallie—"

"The cook is thoroughly swacked, and I think Miss Hallie is doped."

"That's possible. She insists she hasn't slept a wink if she stays awake for two hours," Maybry said. "Dr. Carter was always careless about guarding the drugs he kept here. I'm certain Miss Hallie always managed to have a private supply. You brought about a relapse by talking to her this morning."

"Did I?" Michael said indifferently.

"That is her diagnosis. When I talked to Dr. Carter about seven he said he was going to give Miss Hallie some allonal 'to shut her up.' Yes, and because this is Maria's evening off and she insisted on taking it. I'd forgotten that, but I think Maria had already left."

"And the others?"

Maybry frowned. "Freddie and Loretta weren't here. Dr. Carter said the cook was in no condition to provide dinner for them. She wanted to leave, but the police wouldn't let her, and I suppose she must have been pretty drunk by seven. And— Oh lord!"

Maybry bit at his mustache. "I forgot to tell you why I came back here. Well, the cook must have retired to her bed early, and if Miss Hallie has slept through the telephone's ringing my bet is that she augmented the allonal Dr. Carter gave her with some of her private stock."

"Has this telephone been ringing?"

"A little girl Dr. Carter was very fond of is dying. The Harlans have been trying to get him here and finally called me. That's why I came over now. I—yes," Maybry said, squaring his shoulders, "I must go since he can't. I'm afraid I can't wait for the police. And why haven't they arrived?"

"Probably because I haven't notified them," Michael said, turning back toward the telephone.

"You haven't—? Well, I can't stop to discuss that. But you'd better. . . . I wonder if that is the Harlans again."

Michael picked up the telephone. "No," he said as he heard Antonia's voice, "it's not the Harlans. You'd better go. . . . Well, Antonia?"

"Michael, I led them straight to Ian! They— they handcuffed him! And he insisted on answering their questions, and they wouldn't let me telephone right away. I tried to get our lawyer, but he isn't home, and then Valerie said you should be at Dr. Carter's. And you must get a lawyer   "

"¡*Basta!* What time did they pick Ian up?"

"What does it matter what time? Oh, it wasn't quite seven. . . . Michael, what is there to laugh at? And I don't like the way you—"

"Don't worry," Michael said. "I think Ian is probably cleared if you were with him at a little before seven. Of course it took another man's death to do it, but that needn't worry you."

"I— Michael, what man?"

"Dr. Carter. I'm afraid Ian isn't going to like that. Get Sanders to the telephone for me, Antonia. I want Sanders: no one else."

VI

The machinery was in motion. Fingerprint men and photographers and a police surgeon in the study, O. B. Sanders and a small corps of helpers roaming about the rest of the house.

Loretta was lying across her bed upstairs while Richard Prince paced back and forth before the door. Miss Hallie had been roused, had testified that Dr. Carter was alive at seven o'clock. She admitted that "maybe I did take just one more pill than he gave me. Just one more. Well, maybe a half one I happened to have too."

Evelyn sat on one side of her bed now, Freddie on the other. They listened to her ceaseless and hysterical laments, Evelyn patiently; Freddie pale, patting the fat grasping hand, unhappily trying not to appear embarrassed.

Bruce wandered in, uttered a few smooth sympathetic phrases, and kissed Miss Hallie's sodden cheek. His wife's lips curled a little, but Miss Hallie hiccupped gratefully.

Bruce went back downstairs and out to the kitchen, where Judith was tending a large kettle of hot water with nearly two pounds of coffee bobbing about in it, tied into half a tea towel.

As it developed that there was nothing of interest on the second and third floors except the cook and as they finished inspecting each downstairs room, Sanders kept sending men away to carry on the investigation outside of the house. At last Antonia, Ian, and Michael were alone in the big living room.

Antonia began: "Michael, why, of all the people it might have been, was it Dr. Carter?" But Ian jogged her elbow warningly.

He had seen Michael more than once in this mood of black anger. He was better qualified than Valerie to recognize it. She had not known Michael before he was thirty, by which time he had acquired a very tough, highly polished outer shell. But Ian had known the boy of twenty and, besides, that vein in Michael was pure Maclean. Ian tried to be facetious, whispering to Antonia:

"If you do you'll get your fingers hurt in the buzz saw, darling."

The girl bit her lips and said nothing more. Ian sat beside her, recalling vague pictures of a man who had been himself telling a story to other men at police headquarters.

It had been a long story, and they had kept interrupting him, asking questions, smiling at some of his answers. They had been polite and taken down his statement—and hadn't believed him.

There had been a great glare of lights. The sweat ran down his face, under his collar, trickled over his chest. That had annoyed him more than anything else. Then O. B. Sanders had come in and the interrogation had taken on a quieter, slower tempo.

Until there had been an interruption. Sanders had been called from the room; that was it. And presently they heard his voice, not shouting, but twanging like an indignant bass viol.

"Suffering Saint Simeon Stylites! You're not going to say Dr. Carter's death isn't directly connected with Mrs. Maclean's, whatever you may have thought about Lulu Mae Brown's! And if Dr.

Carter was alive at seven, as Dundas says, Maclean couldn't have killed him. Neither could Miss Jordan, and she is the only possible confederate Maclean could have had. You have to accept the testimony of our own men as to what time they nabbed Maclean.

"Yes, and I want a man put on Dr. Maybry right away. Dundas says he is supposed to have gone to the home of some people named Harlan. Where is Simpson? He knows where the Harlans live. The old doctor was there last night, and Simpson checked on it. Send him right away. . . ."

Then after a few minutes Sanders had come back and invited Ian gruffly to "come along up to the doctor's house." And here was Sanders now, looking at Michael sadly.

"I found out what became of the man who was supposed to watch this place and the old doctor. One man did watch until he was relieved at seven. But meantime we had word the fellows that were tailing Miss Jordan had picked Maclean up. So, being shorthanded and without consulting me, the man who was to relieve Chase at seven relieved him all right—but didn't stay himself. And the doctor was killed between seven and eight. Someone may have been seen coming into the house, but I don't know. If someone wanted to sneak in at the back by way of the canyon—"

He eyed Michael hopefully. "You want to talk to me? No? Well, what—?"

"'*Paciencia y barajar.*'"

"'Patience and shuffle the cards.' *Don Quixote*. Yes, I know some Spanish," Obie said. "I wrote my doctor's thesis on Don John of Austria. I wish I'd stuck to history. A competent historian has to be a pretty good detective, but it's all on paper. That nice old guy . . ."

He went out, shaking his head. Antonia smoked two cigarettes before she realized that finally Michael was looking at her as if he really saw her.

"I'm—I'm a mess," she said nervously, putting her hands to her hair.

"Yes, you do look as if you'd made a night of it," Michael agreed.

He fights it off more quickly than he used to, Ian thought. And a good thing. Though when I think of Dr. Carter myself . . .

"I'm going down to talk to Mrs. Twelvetrees," Michael went on. "No, I don't want you to come with me, Toni. If Valerie receives a wire I've been expecting she'll bring it over. You might watch out for her. . . ."

They heard him leave the house. Ian moved to the chesterfield where Michael had been sitting and beckoned to Antonia. She hesitated for an instant before she sat down beside him.

"I feel guilty," she said unhappily, "because I can't help being glad that this seems to clear you. And Dr. Carter would be glad it does, too, if he had to die. Oh, I'm all mixed up. But—but don't kiss me. I suppose it won't matter if you put your arm around me and we just sit here quietly."

She closed her eyes and presently, since she was so very tired, dozed a little. When she jerked awake it was because Ian had stood up. Then, hearing a familiar voice that she had never heard outside its owner's own home, she wondered bewilderedly how she had gotten into Mrs. Twelvetrees' living room.

But Mrs. Twelvetrees had left her home port for strange seas. She limped into the room, honking at Michael:

"Don't jiggle my elbow! I can walk when I've a mind to. Rather make people come to me, that's all."

She settled herself in a large chair and demanded a footstool. She blew her nose vigorously, and Antonia realized that Mrs. Twelvetrees had been crying. That was almost as startling as if tears had suddenly rolled down the cheeks of the bust of Robert Edward Lee on the mantelpiece.

"I'm an old fool," Mrs. Twelvetrees said. "Haven't cried since my husband died, and God knows he wasn't worth my tears. But Breck Carter was the last person I knew who had known Twelvetrees. Well, get along with your business, young man. I don't want to stay here all night. Antonia will look after me."

"I don't believe the police would object if I changed clothes," Ian said. "Perhaps I'd have time to shave too."

"Go ahead and don't ask them if you may," Michael advised. "I'm going upstairs too."

As they reached the second floor Freddie Carter came out of Miss Hallie's room. "She's finally talked herself to sleep." He wiped his forehead on his handkerchief. "Evelyn will stay with her for a while longer."

"I wouldn't worry about her so long as she can talk," Michael said.

"You mean it's better for her to be hysterical than like Loretta? I suppose so." Freddie glanced down the hall at Loretta's closed door.

"I wonder where Richard Prince has gone to. I'm rambling. I guess I never really expected Uncle Doc to die. He seemed eternal. I can't imagine how Aunt Hallie will get along without him. She'll miss him more than she ever did her husband; she's lived with Uncle Doc so much longer. I suppose she'll go on living here. She's thought of this house as hers for a good many years, and it will be hers now."

"Is that all the doctor left Miss Hallie?"

"Yes. Her husband left her a lot of money, and she's spent very little of it for years."

"Has she made a will? Yes, I know this is no time to talk of such things," Michael said as Mr. Carter frowned reprovingly. "But she has? Well, by her will does Mr. Ferrell cut himself a slice of the cake?"

"A very nice little slice," Freddie said cautiously. "But Uncle Doc ate his cake or gave it away. He never pressed his patients for payment. This house is mortgaged. What's left when his just debts are paid will go to Loretta. Well, I hear that Sanders wants to talk to me again. I'd better try to find him."

He went downstairs. Ian opened the guest-room door and stood looking at Adela's bags, Adela's silver toilet articles. He realized that Michael was watching him, said: "I can't put it off forever, can I?" and entered the room.

When he went into the adjoining bathroom its door into the hall was open. He heard Michael speaking outside Loretta's bedroom door.

"Miss van Horn, I want to talk to you. I want to show you the letter Dr. Carter was writing to me when he was killed. I think it may interest you. If you don't want to talk to me alone—"

"She isn't alone," Richard Prince's clarion voice announced. "And she—"

"I want to talk to you too, Mr. Prince. I've just had an interesting telephone conversation with a private detective named Dana Clyde. You know him? He talked to you this afternoon. Incidentally, Miss van Horn, I called him from Mrs. Twelve-trees' home. I've been talking to her, and her advice is that you talk to me."

Ian heard the soft murmur of a woman's voice for a minute or two before Prince spoke again.

"All right, come in," he said. A door opened and closed; Ian locked himself into the bathroom and began to shave.

He did not hurry, and nearly half an hour had passed before he went downstairs to find O. B. Sanders talking to Michael in the hall. Ian stopped and listened.

"The trouble is," Obie said, "that anyone could come here from the Ferrell or Maybry houses, kill the doctor, and get home again in fifteen minutes at the most. Of course that wouldn't give the murderer time to have a talk with the doctor first. But say the murderer had already talked to him earlier."

"How many people did do that?" Michael asked.

"All of them," Sanders said mournfully. "Miss van Horn and Carter had lots of chances to talk to him; you can see that. Dr. Carter got home about six after getting his dinner downtown."

"And when did Freddie and Loretta leave here?"

"Both of them a little after five. I'll come back to that. The Ferrells came over to ask after Miss Hallie. They weren't together all the time. Miss Hallie says they were in her room at different times and not with the doctor. He stayed downstairs. Then they went home to their dinner, which they had at six-thirty.

"Well," Obie continued, "Dr. Maybry wasn't home then. By the way, he came back just now. Well, Mrs. Maybry called over to Dr. Carter as the Ferrells were leaving and asked him to come over and see if one of her boys was running a temperature. He went but he didn't stay more than ten minutes. Mrs. Maybry says he'd just left when Dr. Maybry got home and came over to talk to him just before seven o'clock."

Sanders produced a match and looked at it thoughtfully.

"Cigarette?" Michael said.

"No, I smoke cigars, but I'd rather chew, so I'll light my pipe. Well, that brings us up to the time between seven and eight when Dr. Carter was killed, and our doctor favors seven-thirty rather than seven or eight.

"Freddie Carter went to see Miss Jordan and left her about six. He ate downtown and then he says he went to his office again to work on those income-tax reports. A dentist in the Acheson Building who was working late this evening saw Carter go into his office about seven, but of course that doesn't mean that Carter stayed there."

"No. But he would have to return here in his car," Michael said. "It's too far for him to have walked all the way. Of course he would have parked his car a safe distance from here."

"We're trying to find out if he did, but people aren't apt to notice just a parked car. Well, Miss van Horn had dinner with Mr. Prince at his home."

Sanders pursed his lips rather disapprovingly. "Naturally they alibi each other. Prince has an old Chinese servant who'd never give him or Miss van Horn away if he knew anything. It looks like they're in the clear, *but* if either of them had slipped back here between seven and eight they'd have had to use a car. Prince lives on LeConte, on the other side of the campus."

"And the Ferrells and the Maybrys?" Michael said.

"Wouldn't you expect they could alibi each other? But, no: the Maybrys had dinner late. What time did Maybry join you here?"

"At about ten minutes after eight."

"Mrs. Maybry says she put dinner on about ten of. Maybry didn't get to finish it because these Harlans, whose little girl just died, telephoned, wanting to know why they couldn't raise Dr. Carter. Incidentally, they began calling him about seven-thirty, so he must have been dead by then. Well, Maybry says his wife was in the kitchen from seven on, and she says he was in his study.

"But they both had about three quarters of an hour unobserved by the other. And Maybry knew the cook was tight, that Maria was out, and that Miss Hallie was going to be given sleeping tablets. Those things mostly take hold in about half an hour, don't they? Maybry could figure Miss Hallie would be dead to the world by seven-thirty. Mrs. Maybry couldn't, but she could have slipped out her own back door."

Sanders stopped to relight his pipe for a fourth or fifth time.

"And the Ferrells were through dinner before seven-thirty," he went on. "The little girl was in bed, and the maid was in the kitchen. She doesn't live in, but she does stay with the little girl if the Ferrells go out, so she's still there now.

"She says Mrs. Ferrell was in her upstairs sitting room and Ferrell in the back room downstairs where he works. The Ferrells tell the same story, but of course they knew we'd check with the maid. The thing is that so little time was needed to slip over to this house and home again.

"We got hold of the maid here, Maria, at her sister's. She can't tell us anything. She isn't very bright, and Miss Hallie kept her trotting all day long. Besides, she did what cooking was done—"

"Just a minute," Michael said, walking toward the door. "I think a car has stopped outside. Yes, a taxi—"

He went out to meet Valerie, brought her in, and held out his hand. "It came?"

"Yes." Valerie smiled briefly as she opened her purse and took out a telegram. "*And* collect. Ian, I am glad to see you."

Michael read the telegram and handed it to Ian. "It wasn't absolutely essential, but it will help. Let's go. Well, the study is empty now, isn't it? Let's go in there, Sanders. I want to talk to you. Ian, will you look after Valerie? And I'll take that."

"Just an instant," Ian said and reread the telegram before he handed it back to Michael.

Their grandfather had wired:

DEAR GRANDSON I MADE ADELA'S MOTHER LET ME READ THOSE LET-TERS THEY WERE WRITTEN BY A LAD WHO SIGNED HIMSELF BRUCE

WHEN NOT AS YOU PUT IT WITH
SOME NAUSEATING PET NAME
THEY WERE THE SORT OF SICK-
ENING DRIVEL SOME YOUNG MEN
BUT THANK GOD NOT MACLEANS
DO WRITE TO YOUNG WOMEN
AFTER READING THEM I COULD
NOT UNDERSTAND WHY ADELA
CAME HOME AND MARRIED IAN
INSTEAD OF STAYING IN BERKELEY
AND MARRYING THIS BRUCE YOUR
LAST INQUIRY MAKES ME WONDER
HAVE YOU GONE QUITE DAFT BUT
AFTER READING THE NOTES SEV-
ERAL TIMES I BELIEVE THAT THEY
WERE NEVER MAILED THAT IS THEY
NEVER PASSED THROUGH THE
MAILS BUT WERE LEFT IN SOME
SORT OF SECRET HIDING PLACE
ADELA AND BRUCE HAD AGREED
ON THE FACT THAT ADELA KEPT
ENVELOPES TOO BUT THERE ARE
NO ENVELOPES TO THESE LETTERS
SEEMS TO BEAR OUT THIS IDEA I
AM FORWARDING THE LETTERS TO
YOU AT ONCE AIR-MAIL GET IAN A
GOOD LAWYER GRANDFATHER

PART EIGHT

I

"Now," Obie Sanders inquired benevolently, "is everyone comfortable?"

He was answered by an uneasy sort of mass movement that was not exactly dissent but which certainly verged on it. There were twelve people in the living room, occupying chesterfield, wing, lounge, and occasional chairs, besides four dining-room chairs commandeered for the emergency. Some of the company cleared their throats; others settled themselves more comfortably; one or two abandoned comfort to sit forward in their chairs.

Miss Hallie was still upstairs, attended by the cook, greatly chastened now that she understood that Dr. Carter was dead. O. B. Sanders stood on the hearth, eclipsing the fireplace. Michael managed the difficult feat of appearing at ease on a piano stool, and two of Obie's official family lounged a little too casually in the doorway.

"Well, that's just fine," Sanders went on. "I know it's late and you're tired, but pretty soon most of you can go home. We'll begin with Dr. Carter's death, though that's not good historical method. But, you see, the doctor was writing a letter to Mr. Dundas when he was killed.

"He hadn't written much, and it's plain enough that when his murderer entered the study the doctor didn't want the murderer to know he had been writing. He stuck his fountain pen into his trouser pocket without waiting to screw the cap over the point, he acted so quickly.

"At the same minute he must have thrust the letter under his desk blotter. The ink on the last few words was so wet that it smeared. Well, I'll read you what he wrote. . . ."

Sanders dug a sheet of paper out of one sagging pocket and read the three completed and the one unfinished sentence of the old doctor's letter.

"Well," he continued in a slow, meditative voice, "as Mr. Dundas says, we'd have made headway a lot quicker if one of you could have been persuaded to tell the truth about Miss Hallie's daughter Rosalie. Mr. Dundas noticed that quite a few people shied away from talking about Rosalie.

"Dr. Carter did, too, but he thought better of it—a little too late. So it's a lucky thing Miss van Horn knows as much or more than Dr. Carter did,

though no one knew she did except Dr. Carter
and, finally, Mrs. Maclean. Miss van Horn seems
to be able to keep a secret, but she's going to talk
now."

"Y-yes," Loretta said faintly, "but I—I don't
know how to begin. Or how to tell—"

"Don't be a ninny, girl," Mrs. Twelvetrees
honked. "This is no time to be missish."

"Don't bully her!" Richard Prince trumpeted.
"Tell it your own way, kitten."

Someone snickered, but Valerie was unable to
find it amusing that Mr. Prince should address
Miss van Horn as "kitten," even though as a de-
scriptive term it was singularly inappropriate.
Prince appeared not to know that he had been
amusing, but Loretta flushed.

She sat erect and pushed her hair behind her
ears, looking not at all girlish or apologetic but
very nearly handsome.

"The summer Adela was here Rosalie had an
affair with a man named Edward Hall," she said.
"He is dead now too. If any of you remember him
you probably also remember that he was married.
I think I'm the only person who knew that he
was—was what is usually referred to as 'the man.'

"All of you who knew Rosalie should realize
that though she was very sweet she hadn't much
character. She was easily persuaded. You know

how strictly she was brought up. And," Loretta said bitterly, "how Cousin Hallie wanted to know her every waking thought besides ordering every minute of her day. Rosalie loved her mother. She loved everyone. She was as affectionate as—as a puppy and as easily frightened. She was afraid of Cousin Hallie."

"Oh, now, Loretta," Bruce began.

"That's true," Mrs. Twelvetrees snapped. "Hallie never failed to punish Rosalie for every childish trick she ever indulged in. Oh, sorrowfully, of course—and severely. Go on, Loretta."

"So when Rosalie knew she was pregnant her greatest fear was that Cousin Hallie should ever know the truth. But she had to talk to someone. Naturally she confided in her dearest friend, Adela. I suppose she knew Adela would be shocked. But I'm sure she didn't expect that Adela would turn away from her like—like—"

"Sir Launfal spurning the leper at the gate," Michael drawled.

"Yes. I'll try not to be unfair. It was a shock to Adela. As Cousin Doc said, Adela was really very inexperienced. Her mother had brought her up strictly, too, and shielded her, and as she was strong-willed and not of an affectionate nature, she never had any difficulty in obeying her mother's and Cousin Hallie's precepts.

"Cousin Doc said, too, when I told him all this yesterday evening, that what happened to Rosalie probably had a lasting effect on Adela. He said that the whole incident may have set her more firmly on the way to becoming the sort of person she did become. Because Adela thought that Bruce was Rosalie's lover."

"What!" Bruce gulped and lowered his voice. "My God! So that was it? All these years I've wondered why Adela acted as she did the last time I saw her before she went back to Wisconsin. I didn't know—"

"And Adela was too ladylike to tell you," Loretta said dryly. "Besides, I will admit that she never betrayed Rosalie's secret. But she didn't believe Rosalie when she said you weren't the man."

"But, Loretta! You know—"

"I know that you looked on Rosalie as a sister," Loretta said even more dryly. "Besides, it would have been most impractical of you to seduce Cousin Hallie's daughter. You were remembered in Cousin Hallie's will even then. But Rosalie couldn't convince Adela. If she was in love with you, Bruce—what passed as love with Adela—she saw no reason why Rosalie should not have been too.

"At any rate, Adela went home as soon as she could. And Rosalie died. You see, she'd gotten the address—I don't know from whom—of an abortionist in East Oakland."

"East Oakland!" Freddie repeated, whistled involuntarily, and then looked nowhere but at his own feet.

"Yes," Loretta said, "but Rosalie wouldn't tell Cousin Doc anything because she did realize that if he knew the names of the people responsible for her death he would feel he must expose them. That would have meant that Cousin Hallie must know the truth. Rosalie died, certain that her mother would never know why she had.

"She knew Cousin Doc had influence enough to call her death acute appendicitis and be sure that the few people—in the hospital—who knew differently wouldn't talk. And Cousin Doc admitted that he was glad Rosalie wouldn't confide in him. He wanted to spare Cousin Hallie too. So—"

James Maybry got to his feet. "It's true I practiced in East Oakland," he said. "And in an unsavory neighborhood."

"And Adela," Bruce remarked thoughtfully, "was so anxious to meet you. I mean to say, she'd caught a glimpse of you when she was out walking."

Maybry went on as if he had not heard Bruce. "But though I very nearly starved to death for the first year and ate sparingly for three more, I never indulged in malpractice, for all the opportunities that came my way. I—"

Loretta stood up. "You don't understand," she said. "Adela didn't help Rosalie. She went home, and Rosalie came to me then. I went with her to that—that place in East Oakland. We didn't ever see the face of the doctor there. If she was a doctor. Because it wasn't a man; it was a woman. It wasn't Jimmy; the place was nowhere near his old office. Besides, Adela wasn't there. I was."

II

"Then why," Evelyn said finally, "have we had to hear this story?"

"Because it is necessary to an explanation of Dr. Carter's letter to me," Michael said. "That letter can't be withheld. Yes, Miss van Horn?"

"I don't think I've quite finished," Loretta said. "Cousin Doc and I talked things over yesterday around dinnertime. He never knew until then how much I knew. I kept silent because Rosalie had asked me to. When Adela ran into me upstairs the evening she was killed we talked for a few minutes.

"She wanted to know why I seemed to resent her being here. I told her that I'd despised her ever since she acted as she did toward Rosalie eight years ago. I didn't expect her to understand that and I didn't want to discuss it. She said she thought we must discuss it again, but I left her and went to my room.

"I know Toni heard me tell Cousin Doc early yesterday afternoon that at least Adela could say she'd done nothing wrong. Intolerance and shocked virtue aren't wrong. But I let Rosalie go to that place and I helped to kill her."

"What would Rosalie have done if you hadn't gone with her?" Michael said gently.

"She would have gone alone—or I think she would have killed herself before letting her mother know the truth. She threatened to if I told Cousin Hallie or even Cousin Doc. And—my father had killed himself two years before. I—well, I did what I thought was best. That's all."

"Yes," Michael said. "Mr. Sanders wasn't being purposely misleading when he said that we could have made headway more quickly if someone had told us what Miss van Horn just has. We could not ignore the fact that too many of you objected to discussing Rosalie's death if we wished to be able historians."

Obie chuckled and, when Michael glanced at him questioningly, shook his head. "You go on. You have the gift of gab and, anyway, you pieced this together. I didn't."

"There were other questions that cropped up and had to be answered before we could be certain that one of them wasn't important. We wanted to know why Adela had left here so suddenly eight years ago; why she had never talked of Rosalie again; why she did not even have a photograph of her. I think Miss van Horn has answered all those questions. Dr. Carter also finally realized that they must be answered, though yesterday he had warned Mrs. Twelvetrees not to talk about Rosalie. That's right, isn't it?"

"Yes, though he could have saved his breath," Mrs. Twelvetrees said. "I've got the gift of gab, too, but it's well under control. However, Breck Carter guessed I had guessed the truth about Rosalie and he did warn me. Yesterday afternoon he saw no reason why your curiosity should be satisfied."

"But today he saw that not knowing the answers to those questions I just sketched was holding us up," Michael said. "His letter should have told you that he knew that the circumstances of Rosalie's death did not furnish the motive for Adela's murder. He said: 'Remembering your promise, I have decided to answer your question.'"

"But," James Maybry pointed out, "we don't know what your promise was."

"That's true. I promised not to repeat anything he might tell me unless it was necessary. But he added: 'I will tell you the story in detail if you want to—' He wasn't able to finish that sentence, but it is fairly obvious that it would have gone on: 'hear it after you hear what else I have to tell you,' or words to that effect."

"I don't see anything so obvious about it," Bruce began, but his wife frowned at him and he scowled sulkily and did not go on.

"So," Michael said, "to understand why Adela was killed we must go back to her activities on the day of her death. She spent the day bringing the iniquities of the servants to light. Miss Hallie was so overcome by this pleasurable excitement that she took to her bed. Dr. Carter told her to stay there and rest if she wanted to receive the guests she had invited to dinner that night.

"So Adela went out for a walk. Very naturally she went up into the canyon first. Even Adela would think it proper to pay old scenes the tribute of a passing sigh. She sat down on the sparking bench."

"How can you know that?" Maybry said.

"Your oldest son told us so. Lulu Mae could have told us more since most of the time she blocked your sons' view of Adela but must have been able to see Adela clearly herself. But your son did tell us that finally Adela got up and felt about in the brush that grows around the sparking bench.

"Lulu Mae could have told us that Adela found something in that brush. I'm not certain just what, but I'd guess it was some sort of box. Some weather-resistant container at any rate. Because, again naturally, while Adela sat on the sparking bench she remembered how she and Mr. Ferrell used to exchange letters and, being young and rather elaborately romantic, had arranged their own post office."

"You're crazy," Bruce said flatly. "And—and you can't prove that!"

"I will, Mr. Ferrell. You see, Adela kept your notes. Don't you find that touching? Ian saw but never read them. He did remember that they were not in envelopes. Now our grandfather has read those notes and wired me."

Michael took the elder Maclean's telegram from his pocket and read it aloud. Certain phrases in it called forth a general smile and a momentary lessening of tension.

"I suppose that in at least one note you spoke of—oh, perhaps of 'leaving this letter in the usual place.' Or of having collected one of Adela's from your private post office. I don't expect you to re-member, but when those notes arrive here we'll see, Mr. Ferrell. Did you ever speak to your wife of this phase of your romantic youth?"

"He did not," Evelyn said. She smiled rather sardonically. "I understand now why he never discussed Adela with me. Male vanity—he never knew until now why she loved him and left him."

"Well, if you can't help us and Mr. Ferrell won't, I see that Mr. Carter is acting as if the seat of his chair was filled with tacks."

"It was a box," Freddie said. "A small black enameled box with a sort of little hook to hold the cover down tight. You know the kind. They kept it under the bushes and put their letters in it. Loretta remembers how I used to tease Adela about playing post office."

"Yes, but we all thought you meant the kissing game, Freddie."

"Adela and Bruce knew what I meant. But I haven't thought about that for years."

"And neither have I!" Bruce said angrily. "I did remember it the morning after Adela was killed. Say I was feeling sentimental when I strolled up the canyon then. I wondered if the old black box was still there because I'd never taken it away. I even got down on my knees to look, but I couldn't find it. I'd really thought it would be there."

"It was removed, along with Adela's footprints and, probably, Lulu Mae's and the children's," Michael said. "But Lulu Mae saw Adela take a black box from the bushes, open it, and take something from it. Yes, I'm guessing now! But Lulu Mae was killed. If you won't accept my guess tell me why she was killed.

"'What, silent still and silent all?' You are also going to have to accept my guess that Adela discovered that the old post office was still in use."

"That's the only reasonable working hypothesis," O. B. Sanders remarked.

"Thank you. It is also reasonable to suppose that anyone writing letters that must be exchanged in that fashion would not be apt to sign his or her name to one. Anyone whom Adela knew, that is— and whom did she know well here except those present? But even unsigned letters betray their writers by allusions or phraseology. Let us say that Adela thought she knew who had written the letter she took from the old post-office box but that she was not entirely certain.

"So she went down to call on Mrs. Twelvetrees. Later on I will ask Mrs. Twelvetrees what she thought Adela wanted to know. Then Adela came back here, talked to Miss van Horn, and then went into Miss Hallie's bedroom, ostensibly to ask if she was feeling better.

"But even Miss Hallie noticed that Adela had lost a little of her usual repose of manner. She moved about the room, picking up photographs and putting them down again. Think of your own photographs that you have bestowed on Miss Hallie at various times, and if you remember them at all well you should know what the real purpose behind Adela's movements was. She left Miss Hallie and stood for an instant in the hall. Ian can describe that."

"I had seen Adela just before she went into Miss Hallie's bedroom. I thought then that she was thinking something out, came to some decision, and was pleased with her own cleverness. After she left Miss Hallie she stood under one of the hall lights for an instant," Ian said. "She seemed to be studying the palm of her hand—or something she held in it.

"The latter, I fancied, because when she saw me she put her hand quickly into a pocket of her coat. Later on, before we went downstairs, I was certain she had her knife out for someone. I couldn't tell that to a jury, but I did know Adela. Then we went down to dinner—"

"But Adela never acted hastily," Michael said. "We have her own word for that. During the evening she watched one person in particular. Then most opportunely Mr. Carter fused the lights."

Freddie moved uneasily. "What do you mean—'most opportunely'? Do you think I—"

Michael shook his head. "I think you were only bored and, as there had been several unfortunate incidents during the evening, you thought it would be best to break up the gathering. But the black-out did give Adela an opportunity to speak to the person she had been watching all evening. And because the lights were out Ian happened to overhear part of that conversation. Ian?"

"Yes. Adela was saying, when I first realized she was speaking, 'But you haven't changed, you see. And I've watched you very closely all evening. I never act hastily.' Then Dr. Carter shouted something and drowned her out.

"After that I heard Adela say: 'I hope I know my duty. You can't say I didn't take this opportunity to warn you. I have all the proof that's needed. Don't expect me to pity you.' I think the person Adela was talking to spoke then but in a whisper I couldn't hear," Ian said. "And in a minute or two the lights came on."

"You see the importance of the fact that Mrs. Maclean said she had proof," Sanders pointed out. "So it isn't so farfetched, after all, to assume she'd found a letter in the old post-office box in the canyon. She must have kept it on her and the murderer got it.

"It would help if anyone else had heard that conversation. I mean, it would help Mr. Maclean, and it seems to me that since Dr. Carter's been killed some of you who mightn't have been willing to talk before would feel differently now."

III

"Yes," Evelyn said. "Yes, I do feel differently about Dr. Carter and Lulu Mae than I did about Adela. I heard part of what Adela said there in the hall. I'd gone into the kitchen and meant to go from there into the hall and on upstairs to find my purse and flashlight. But Freddie came through the kitchen, going downstairs to the basement to the fuse box. He went clattering through and he wouldn't have heard Adela—or did you, Freddie?"

"I didn't hear anything but my own feet. I didn't even know you were in the kitchen then."

"I was out of your way, near the door into the hall. I knew the lights would come on in an instant and I—I didn't want to—to embarrass anyone."

"Whom didn't you want to embarrass, Mrs. Ferrell?" Michael said. "That is, why didn't you tell this before?"

"Because I thought Adela was talking to Bruce. I— Please don't!" Evelyn jerked away from her husband's placating hand. "After all, Adela said: 'You haven't changed.' I took it she was speaking of character, not appearance. She certainly had known Bruce better than she knew anyone else who was here that night. And when she said, 'I've been watching you all evening,' it seemed to me that every time I looked at Adela she had been watching Bruce with a—a peculiar sort of expression."

"Pitying, perhaps?" Michael suggested.

"Perhaps. Of course I couldn't think what she meant when she said that she never acted hastily. I'm sorry, Bruce; I don't really enjoy washing our dirty linen in public. But I'm a little tired of keeping up appearances. I've always known when you, to put it vulgarly, have gone on the loose again. But I didn't see how Adela could have ferreted out anything along those lines in the time at her disposal. Still—"

"Yes, Mrs. Ferrell?"

"I did hear Adela say she had all the proof that was needed. That puzzled me. What sort of proof but her own observations and some gossip could Adela have—of anything?

"And in spite of what you're all probably thinking, Judith's name didn't immediately pop into my head," Evelyn went on. "I thought of Lulu Mae. Apparently it's never occurred to any of you that Lulu Mae might have been rather flattered by Bruce's gallantries."

"I thought she was," Judith said. "She was a nice kid, but she was sort of coquettish. She liked to make Jerry Flanigan jealous."

"Yes, she did. So I did think it remotely possible that Adela could have—have seen Lulu Mae and Bruce together when she was out walking that afternoon. In—in the canyon, perhaps," Evelyn said with a little grimace of distaste.

Mr. Ferrell said nothing. The muscles that made his jaw a jaw seemed to have lost their elasticity, and his self-confident chest sagged slightly.

"Of course it all seemed very fantastic," Evelyn said. "Bruce and I have carried on our marriage for quite a while according to rules we've never discussed but understand perfectly. I can't see Bruce killing Adela to keep her from talking to me. I can't see him killing anyone."

"Yet three hours after the conversation that you and Ian overheard Adela was killed," Michael said. "Killed in this room. The police believe that she came down here because she found that Ian was gone, couldn't sleep, and preferred to wait for his return down here. Or that she heard him come in and came down. Those are reasonable explanations, but if you recall what the situation between Adela and Ian was that night there is another way of accounting for her coming down to this room."

He stood up, thrusting his hands into his pockets. Here it comes, his wife thought. He's preparing to underact this scene, which means it's the big one. . . .

"So that you won't accuse me of guessing again, I'll ask you this. If you knew that two of you here were using that old hiding place in the canyon for the exchange of letters, what would you suppose those two people were engaged in—besides letter writing?"

For an instant no one answered. Then: "In an illicit love affair," Richard Prince said baldly. "And that at least one party concerned was married so that they couldn't risk letters that came through the mail being opened by a husband or wife."

"Exactly. Well, we have three women available," Michael said as casually as if he were discussing the weather. In fact, his wife thought, he could be very eloquent when dealing with the weather.

"Anyone just looking at the three of you would immediately cast Mrs. Maybry in the role we are considering. Mrs. Maybry looks the part, but I suspect she is as virtuous as she is beautiful. I imagine that when she looks most seductive she is merely thinking about seven-minute frosting or the deplorable fact that children go through their shoes so quickly."

"Now, Jimmy," Judith said, "sit down. I don't think Mr. Dundas is insulting me. He didn't say I'm dumb, but *you* say so when you listen to me instead of look at me. He's right. I'd have at least six babies if you'd let me and I don't like Bruce's pictures of me or posing for him and I wouldn't do it if it wasn't that I like to buy things for you with the money he pays me. You know that."

Maybry sat back in his chair. "I know," he said, smiling briefly. "I really do know—but, as you say, I look at you too often and forget."

"I do dumb things too," Judith said placidly. "Like last night."

"What did you do last night, Mrs. Maybry?" O. B. Sanders asked quickly.

"Well, after I had to take care of the kids all afternoon after Lulu Mae left I was a wreck," Judith said. "I couldn't phone Lulu Mae and I thought I just had to get her back this morning. Jimmy was out in our car, so I asked Loretta if I could borrow the roadster Mr. Prince had loaned her.

"It was a silly thing to do, and I shouldn't have left the boys alone, though I wasn't gone half an hour. I intended to offer Lulu Mae more money if she'd promise not to run out on me again. I didn't tell Jimmy because he can't understand why I depended on her so. He's never had to take care of our children for a whole day," Judith said without rancor.

"Anyway, there were no lights in her place, though I drove by the house a couple of times. I decided she wasn't home and I came home. But I was thinking today that maybe you might have found out that Loretta's car was out last night. I knew she'd never tell that she let me have it, so I thought I'd better mention it now."

"I'm glad you did, Mrs. Maybry. That's one more small item cleared up, and we can go on to more important matters," Michael said. "Taking up where I left off, we have Mrs. Ferrell, who is an admirable if somewhat long-suffering wife. And Miss van Horn, who is going to marry Mr. Prince. It's rather difficult to choose between them, don't you think?

"Please, Mr. Prince! Get off your charger and drop your lance and good broadsword. I was going to say that since I cannot see Miss van Horn in the role I cast my vote for Mrs. Ferrell. Or," Michael said pleasantly, "may I also call you Rapunzel?"

Mr. Ferrell came out of his corner, swinging. Mr. Dundas ducked. He had taken off on his left foot. He promptly brought his right down on Mr. Ferrell's toes. Bruce yelped. While he was still off balance Michael brought his left elbow up under the Ferrell chin. For an instant he viewed the result dispassionately. Then:

"I think I'll get a drink. So much talking makes my throat dry," he said and stalked out of the room.

O. B. Sanders had begun moving when Bruce did, but he was still only in second gear when Mr. Ferrell hit the floor. He picked him up and dusted him off.

"You aren't really hurt. You'll— Now, we don't want to hear any of that kind of language," Obie said disapprovingly, guiding Bruce to his chair. "Dundas spotted you about forty pounds, and he could have laid you colder than a dead mackerel if he'd really tried. I know what the top of your head feels like, but you just sit still and keep quiet."

Evelyn had not moved. She did not speak until Michael came back into the room. Then:

"Why must you draw this out?" she said. "Why can't you just name the murderer?"

"You've just seen what happens when I venture an opinion without backing it up with facts," Michael said, looking at Bruce. "But this is a fact. I was interested to learn that though you and your first husband presumably underwent one of these friendly divorces he took custody of your two-year-old child and did not pay you alimony."

The woman's lips whitened. "Yes," she said. "Yes, I—I gave up my baby."

"Well, why did you, Mrs. Ferrell? I didn't know why until a few hours ago. But though you do not parade your affection for your little girl I don't consider you the sort of woman who would give up a child simply because she doesn't want to be bothered with it. Mr. Prince says you are not that sort of woman."

"I wish you could leave me out of this," Richard Prince said.

"But you've known Mrs. Ferrell longer than anyone else here has, Mr. Prince. However, I got the same information that you could give us from a private detective, Dana Clyde. He discovered, Mrs. Ferrell, that you had to give up your child by your first husband because he could have and did threaten to bring suit against you if you didn't.

"You had given him grounds for divorce in any state in the Union, and he would also have been given custody of your child because he could prove that you were 'unfit' to have charge of it. That's true, isn't it?"

"Yes," Evelyn said desolately. "Yes, but that was so long ago!"

"You were divorced shortly after Adela was here eight years ago. No doubt she heard gossip about you then. You told Ian that Adela broke up your friendship with Rosalie. I will guess that Adela did not approve of you. So it could have been you to whom Adela was speaking when she said: 'But you haven't changed, you see.' Especially if you pleaded, as you just have, that all that was so long ago.

"Besides," Michael said, "here is another fact. Adela went from the canyon to call on Mrs. Twelvetrees. Mrs. Twelvetrees is apt to go to bed rather late. And your bedroom windows face her house, and from her favorite lookout she can see that corner of your house."

"I'm sorry, Evelyn," Mrs. Twelvetrees said gruffly. "I wouldn't have given you away under ordinary circumstances. But it's true that while Adela didn't come right out and ask, I was certain she called on me to find out how much I knew about your goings on.

"I didn't tell her anything. But I know, Evelyn, that you haven't always been alone when Bruce is away. And Adela said a peculiar thing that afternoon. She said: 'I understand Bruce is going to be away next week end.' But Mr. Dundas says that at that time Adela hadn't seen any of you yet."

"And Mr. Ferrell had only accepted that invitation for this week end that morning," Michael said. "So where could Adela have gotten her information—except from the letter she found in the old post-office box? The fact that Bruce was to be away would be reason for Mrs. Ferrell's writing to her lover, though I'm certain that it was his answer to Mrs. Ferrell that Adela found."

"How can you be certain of that?" Ian said.

"I'll tell you in a minute. There were other signposts that made me believe you were the person Adela had talked to during the black-out here the night she was killed, Mrs. Ferrell. Mrs. Maybry's perfume, your daughter's book of fairy stories—"

"Lynn's book? Oh. Rapunzel?" Evelyn said wearily.

"Yes. But first I think it should be pointed out that it's very obvious that both people who used that box hidden in the canyon for the exchange of letters must have had easy access to the canyon."

"That's right," Sanders said. "A person who didn't live in this neighborhood or visit it often so that he or she was well known around here couldn't keep depositing and collecting letters without someone getting suspicious. Mrs. Ferrell, it would save us much trouble if you'd just tell the truth."

"Tell him, Evelyn," Bruce said in a husky whisper that would have been ludicrous at any other time. "Tell him he and Dundas are just two damn fools."

Evelyn turned on him. "So you can't imagine how, having the good fortune to be married to you, I could love another man! But I have! You bore me. You have for a good many years. I haven't minded your silly, shabby little affairs. I didn't care what you did so long as we kept up appearances. It was fun, fooling you and Judith and Loretta and—and everyone."

For an instant she had seemed on the point of laughing, but now her face crumpled suddenly. "And yet I didn't ever intend to do it again. I meant to be good. I told you so, didn't I, Richard? I told you when you advised me not to marry

Bruce that I was going to make a success of this marriage. And yet what Mrs. Twelvetrees docs know is true. But she doesn't know enough, and I'm not going to tell you."

"Oh, but I think you will, finally, Mrs. Ferrell," Michael said softly. "I'm going to answer Ian's question now. I asked you to remember your photographs that Adela looked at in Miss Hallie's bedroom when she came back from talking to Mrs. Twelvetrees."

"I've tried to remember if there was anything unusual about mine," Loretta said. "But I can't. It was just a picture."

"But you signed it, Miss van Horn. The inscription was a fair sample of your handwriting, wasn't it?"

"Oh! You mean," Ian said, "that Adela wanted to check on the handwriting in the letter she'd found and she thought of that way to do it? That was why she stood in the hall and looked at the letter again under the light."

"Of course. But Mrs. Ferrell's photograph is not signed. That's why I said the letter Adela had was not written by Mrs. Ferrell. Adela would have remembered Mr. Ferrell's writing, which is an additional reason for counting him out. There is no picture of Mr. Prince in Miss Hallie's bedroom, and that eliminates him. The Maybrys are

represented by a family group which is not inscribed. Count Miss van Horn out and," Michael
said, "that leaves Mr. Carter."

IV

"Me?" Freddie bleated. "You mean you think
Evelyn and I—? But I'm in love with Toni!"

"Are you? I began speculating about you, Mr.
Carter, the first time we met. Everyone told me
that you wanted to marry Antonia. But the male
animal in love is fairly primitive. Your reactions
were all wrong."

"Oh!" Antonia said. "That's what you meant
Wednesday morning when you said that there
should have been a reaction and there wasn't.
You told Freddie and me that Bruce hinted that
I couldn't resist his charms. Freddie took it very
calmly. So did he take my kissing Ian right in
stride. I though he was just being nice, but—"

"Of course it was possible that Mr. Carter is
only civilized to the point of desiccation," Michael
said. "But I wondered. The instinct of self-preser-
vation is also strong in the average man. He doesn't
ordinarily ask a woman to marry him merely to be
obliging or unless he is enough in love with her to
resent one man's kissing her and another's sneer-
ing remarks about her.

"However, Antonia didn't intend to marry Mr. Carter, and he must have known that. And I have known a man to pretend devotion to one woman as a smoke screen to hide his feelings for another. So long as everyone accepted the fact that 'Freddie wants to marry Toni,' they weren't apt to speculate about you and Mrs. Ferrell, were they, Mr. Carter?

"I only speculated and only about you, Mr. Carter, that first morning. Lulu Mae's disappearance gave me other things to think of. But I was always certain of one thing. If you were using Antonia as a smoke screen your true love was someone of whom Miss Hallie wouldn't approve."

"And what," said Freddie calmly, "made you come to that conclusion?"

"You told me this evening that Miss Hallie is a wealthy woman. I'd already gathered that she was. It was also obvious that you must be her heir. Someone saw you through college after your parents died. Miss Hallie is the type who must have possessions. Her daughter died, and you were the logical substitute for the son she hadn't had.

"Miss van Horn has told us what Miss Hallie's attitude toward her daughter was. So Miss Hallie certainly would expect you not to do anything that didn't meet with her approval. I take it, from everything anyone has told me of your aunt, that she is a narrow-minded, stupid, intolerant, vindictive old woman. Her standards were precisely those of Adela Maclean.

"So you'd lose a great deal, Mr. Carter, if your conduct didn't meet with Miss Hallie's approval—or Adela's, which was one and the same thing, considering how much influence she had over Miss Hallie. It's also obvious that whatever Adela had learned late Tuesday afternoon was not merely a piece of gossip to be exclaimed over and enjoyed. What Adela knew was something that would excite Miss Hallie to the point where she wouldn't be able to appear at the dinner table that night.

"It's true Adela wasn't given to acting hastily. But I do think that if she hadn't been warned by Dr. Carter not to excite Miss Hallie again she might not have waited to tell her what she had learned. Once she'd checked the writing in the letter she had found against Mr. Carter's writing on his photograph Adela didn't really need to wait.

"But she'd been too industrious that morning. As I told my wife, the fact that Adela discovered two spoons were missing and that the cook drank rum was important. Those discoveries sent Miss Hallie to her bed under orders to rest and be quiet if she wanted to get up for dinner."

"And Adela was always so thoughtful," Ian said ironically. "Of course she would have enlightened

Miss Hallie at once if Miss Hallie could have tak-
en it in stride and been persuaded to go in for a
spot of watching and waiting too. And of course
Adela didn't want that dinner to be postponed.
She meant to enjoy herself that night, knowing
she had dynamite in her possession that would
blow this group sky-high."

"I'm sure you know, Ian. And I do know that
a woman of Miss Hallie's type always blames the
woman in the case more than the man. I wondered
if she would be sufficiently angry to disinherit
you, Mr. Carter, if she discovered you were, just
for example, carrying on an affair with a married
woman.

"I can't," Michael said almost apologetically,
"keep my mind from working the way it does. So
I thought: But suppose that Mr. Carter was Mrs.
Ferrell's lover? Miss Hallie had always been very
fond of Mr. Ferrell. Would she, under the circumstances just outlined, transfer her affections to
Mr. Ferrell?

"Well, Mr. Carter, you told me yourself just a
few hours ago that even under Miss Hallie's present will Mr. Ferrell cuts himself a very nice little
slice of cake. If Miss Hallie had known that you
were Mrs. Ferrell's lover it is not at all unreasonable to suppose that she might have changed her

will in Mr. Ferrell's favor—or at least that you were afraid that she might—"

"'Might have,'" Freddie repeated. "'Suppose'—'if'—that's not evidence."

"No. It is on the record, though, that you are very allergic to perfumes. Mrs. Ferrell has recently stopped using any sort of scent. Mr. Ferrell brought her a very expensive bottle of perfume from New York last autumn, supposing that she would like it. He was surprised when she said she no longer wore perfume and passed his gift on to Mrs. Maybry. That's so, isn't it, Mr. Ferrell?"

"Yes," Bruce said dully. "I don't know how you knew that. Oh, I did say that you can never pick out a present that will please a woman, didn't I? You put two and two together."

"Mrs. Maybry had already remarked when one of her sons soaked himself in that perfume that she couldn't afford to buy it herself. Today I found that the perfume came from New York. I connected it with your trip to New York and your remarks about bringing a gift to a woman and that gift's being unappreciated.

"That's not evidence, nor can I imagine telling a jury about Lynn Ferrell's book of fairy tales and poems. But it interested me," Michael said. "Lynn's favorite story and picture was that of

Rapunzel. She said that Rapunzel was Mamma because Mamma had such long hair. You remember that Rapunzel's lover said: 'Let down your hair and I will climb up without any stair'?

"Slightly nauseating, but love is apt to blight one's sense of humor. Lynn told me that the book was made up of her favorite stories that 'people' had told her. I asked her who told her the story of Rapunzel, and she said 'Fweddie.'"

"That's—that's true," Bruce said heavily. "And I—I remember Freddie and Evelyn looking at each other and smiling. That hair of Evelyn's, when she lets it down—"

"I have a fairly vivid imagination," Michael said. "But unfortunately I underestimated Dr. Carter. I only asked him to tell me about Rosalie. I wanted to clear away that obstruction and get on with it. I should have realized that he was a shrewd and wise old man who had kept a thousand secrets in his time. He wasn't apt to be deceived, either, by his nephew or Mrs. Ferrell. We'll have to guess that today he suddenly tied heaven knows how many loose ends together and knew why Adela had been killed."

Michael paused to watch Ian, who had just untied his shoelaces and seemed to be trying to locate a protruding nail under the shoe's inner sole.

"But," Antonia ventured, "Freddie is so much younger than Evelyn."

"I'm glad you mentioned that. Mrs. Ferrell is married to a man three years younger than she is. Her first husband was a little younger than she was. You don't know, of course, that the affair that led to her divorce was with a man some years younger than she was then. Mr. Prince knows that."

Richard Prince nodded reluctantly. "I suppose that's why Mr. Prince advised her not to marry Mr. Ferrell. Those things are apt to follow a pattern," Michael said impersonally. "Mrs. Ferrell attracts men younger than she is and, naturally, in time they bore her. She didn't marry her first lover after her divorce. And I don't think it would have been too long before she tired of Mr. Carter too. You might give that a little thought now, Mrs. Ferrell.

"And don't forget that Mr. Carter has always known of the existence of the post-office box in the canyon but didn't mention it until he suddenly realized that if he didn't remember it Miss van Horn might recall that he used to tease Adela about 'playing post office.' Mr. Ferrell, Adela, and Mr. Carter were the only ones who knew about that box hidden in the brush, if we accept Mrs. Ferrell's statement that her husband never discussed Adela with her."

"That's true. She told the truth," Bruce said. "I mean to say, I never told her about the box."

"Thank you. However, Dr. Carter did know that I was interested in Adela's afternoon walk. He said immediately that she might very well have gone up the canyon. I'm only guessing, Mr. Carter, when I say that it's not unlikely that you explained your little joke to your uncle eight years ago. But he, being an old man, honestly forgot—until this afternoon.

"However, leaving that, there is the fact that Adela was killed in this room. Has it never occurred to any of you that there was only one person in this house on the night of her death that Adela would have refused to talk to in her bedroom?

"She would have admitted Loretta, Miss Hallie, or Dr. Carter to her room. But not Mr. Carter. He was a young man, and since Adela had just refused to give Ian a divorce she certainly would not risk being caught by him talking to a man in her boudoir after midnight. What do you think, Ian?"

"Hmm? Oh, you're right," Ian said, retying his shoelaces. "Adela was a prude, and she would have judged me by herself, anyway. Of course. Freddie could have seen me leave the house and known I'd leave the door unlocked. It always would have been easier for someone in the house to kill Adela than someone from outside. Though I did think

I heard someone outside the house when I left it
that night."

"I was there!"

Evelyn Ferrell stood up. Her hands fumbled at
her hair, but her fingers only dislodged the hair-
pins she tried to push back into place. The heavy
braid swung loose over her shoulder.

"I was the one Adela talked to that night when
the lights were out."

"Don't be a fool, Evelyn," Freddie said coolly.
"Once they've taken it down in black and white
they have a case against you."

He nodded toward one of the men in the doorway who had just produced a stenographer's notebook and pencil. Evelyn looked at him vaguely.
Then light and anger come into her eyes, and she
turned back to Freddie.

"A case against me! Against *me!* That's it—
they'll arrest me, and I didn't kill anyone! You did
all of it, and I didn't want you to kill Lulu Mae. I
told you you wouldn't have to. I didn't even know
you were going to. You believe me, don't you?"

She appealed to O. B. Sanders. "I believe you,"
he said stolidly. "We're pretty sure you were in
the library too long to have had time to kill Lulu
Mae. She just called you on the telephone, didn't
she, after she left the Maybrys', because she wanted advice."

"That was it," Evelyn said eagerly. "She just telephoned me. All she knew was that she'd seen Adela dig a black box out of the bushes back of the bench in the canyon and take a piece of paper out of the box. She wondered if she should tell the police about it. She thought it was 'queer' and it worried her a little. I didn't want her to tell anyone, of course.

"But it was different with Adela. She had Freddie's letter to me. I'd written him that morning when Bruce decided to go away this week end. He picked it up in the early afternoon and left an answer, but Adela got it before I could.

"When she told me that, while the lights were out, I managed to tell Freddie what she'd said before we went home. But I couldn't sleep. I dressed and came back here. I just stood before the house, trying to think what we could do. Then I heard Ian coming out and hid. When I saw it was Ian and knew Adela would be alone I—I—"

"You realized that you could depend on Mr. Carter to deal with the situation," Michael said. "And to manage the business so that Ian would be blamed."

"I never set foot in this house again that night! I didn't know what Freddie had done until Wednesday morning. After all, he was the one who was bound he was going to have Miss Hallie's money.

I've never cared about money. Of course I didn't want Bruce to have grounds to divorce me and take Lynn away from me, and he's so vain he would if he found out I was cheating on him.

"Adela couldn't have been bribed or persuaded not to talk to Miss Hallie in the morning," Evelyn said sullenly. "It was different with Lulu Mae. I did suggest that she consult a lawyer. It was a shock, finding out she'd seen Adela find Freddie's letter. How could I know what I should do? I thought Freddie could persuade her that she'd only make a lot of trouble for herself if she talked.

"I told her to stay away from home so the police wouldn't find her there. I said they'd be watching Freddie's office so she'd better not go there and that he'd pick her up at the corner of Shattuck and Dwight Way as soon after seven o'clock as he could."

"And you turned her over to his tender mercies," Michael said.

"But he didn't need to kill her!"

"Hadn't you told him that I was trying to locate Lulu Mae?"

"I had to tell him that! I suppose when she got impatient and called him at his office in the afternoon—though she just hung up, he said, probably because she realized when the stenographer answered the phone that he wasn't alone—well,

I suppose that worried him, thinking she was
getting impatient. But he could have persuaded
her that what she knew wasn't worth telling. She
wasn't anxious to go to the police.

"And I hadn't anything to do with Dr. Carter's
death, either! I didn't know until Freddie told me
so a few hours ago, upstairs, that he'd guessed
about us. And told Freddie that he had before
Freddie went off to dinner tonight. Dr. Carter had
suspected the truth about us for a long time. He
wouldn't have told. He thought Freddie might as
well have Miss Hallie's money and that I'd better
stay married to Bruce and keep my baby. If Adela
had stayed where she belonged, in Wisconsin—"

"Mr. Carter told you this evening what Dr.
Carter had said to him?" Michael broke in.

"We whispered across Miss Hallie after she
was asleep. The doctor did remember, just as you
thought, about Freddie's teasing Adela about playing post office. Freddie had told him how Bruce
and Adela exchanged their letters eight years ago.
They thought it was funny—then.

"The doctor had wondered how Freddie and I
kept in touch when we never went out of the way
to talk to each other. He knew we couldn't write
through the mails. Bruce and Miss Hallie are curious about letters. So he put everything together
and told Freddie he was going to tell you.

"Of course Freddie insisted Dr. Carter was wrong and acted—acted hurt. Dr. Carter must not have been quite sure enough that he'd discovered the motive for Adela's murder to call in the police right away. Freddie thought he wouldn't. But he knew Dr. Carter would tell you what he'd guessed, Mr. Dundas, and he couldn't chance that. He went to see Toni, had dinner, went to his office, but slipped out again. He drove back and parked several blocks down, slipped in and killed the doctor.

"The doctor said, too, when he told Freddie that he would never have told anyone his suspicions about us if things had just gone along as they were before Adela came back, that he knew it wouldn't last. You and he were both right, Mr. Dundas; I just realized that," Evelyn said, suddenly calm again.

"A few more months and it wouldn't have been fun. I'd have gotten older and so would Bruce, and we'd have settled down and watched Lynn growing up and been comfortable and friendly. I didn't intend to give you away, Freddie, even though I'm afraid of you now. You might want to kill me too. And no man's worth it!"

"So it seems," Freddie said. He sleeked down his hair, smiled, and stood up. "Would you mind taking me to some other room while she spills her guts, Sanders? I reserve my defense."

V

Sanders came back into the living room, shaking his head sadly. "That Carter's a cool customer. You were right, Dundas. We didn't have enough proof even to arrest him. Our only chance was to make Mrs. Ferrell talk. But of course the odds were that she would. They always do.

"I guess she's told us everything we have to know right now. There are a few more details we can get straightened out when she's fit to talk again."

Freddie Carter had just left his uncle's home, handcuffed to a detective. Evelyn's sudden calm had been followed by hysteria. Dr. Maybry and a hastily summoned policewoman were dealing with her upstairs.

Loretta had managed to engage a nurse who would arrive soon and be with her before Miss Hallie wakened again. Richard Prince had announced his intention of sleeping in the guest room that night. He and Loretta were talking upstairs. The others had gone home: Bruce Ferrell to the telephone to engage a lawyer for his wife.

"She won't get more than life," Obie predicted sadly. "Maybe not that. I hate to think what effect all this will have on the little Ferrell girl when she's old enough to understand it. Yes, and this is going to be kind of hard on the old lady, Miss Hallie."

"She can adopt Bruce," Michael said callously. "She'll manage to make herself comfortable again before too long. Her sort always does."

"I suppose none of it would have happened if Miss Hallie had been a different sort of person," Antonia said.

"Or if Adela had. And I think," Valerie remarked, "that it's a good thing Mr. Prince is around to keep Loretta from allowing Miss Hallie to work on her sympathies."

"It may help, Mrs. Ferrell telling us where Carter picked Lulu Mae up," Obie mused. "There's a drugstore at Dwight Way and Shattuck. Probably Lulu Mae phoned her mother from there since she did that about seven, and that's when Carter was to pick her up. If someone happened to see Lulu Mae get into his car that will help."

"Will this?" Ian asked.

He threw a sheet of ruled paper down on a table: a page torn from a rather large notebook, covered closely with small writing. It was badly creased, as if it had been folded at one time into a three-inch square.

"Under the inner sole of my shoe," Ian said. "These are sport shoes, you see. Adela must have hidden that letter there while I was in the bathroom before I went to bed that Tuesday night. She didn't know I'd be putting them on and going out for a walk before morning."

"Oh lord!" Michael said. "I asked if your room had been thoroughly searched by the police. Carter must have searched it, too, after he killed Adela. But we never thought of the clothes you carried out of the guest room on you."

"Adela did such a neat job that it didn't bother me until just a while ago. But I put on a thinner pair of socks when I changed a few hours ago, and I suppose the paper had finally worked around until it made a lump. Well?"

"Will it help!" Sanders said expressively. "Listen. 'My dearest love, I'd hoped there would finally be a letter saying the Great Panjandrum had decided to go away again. Next week end is too far away but better than nothing. Darling, do you know how night after night—?'"

Obie stopped, looked at Antonia and Valerie, and blushed. "I won't read the rest of it aloud. It's pretty frank. That is, it defines the situation very clearly. There's nothing that would give any clue to the writer, though, except the handwriting."

"Freddie often called Bruce 'the Great Panjandrum,'" Antonia said. "You heard him, Michael. I guess he always had, even eight years ago. So Adela knew he meant Bruce and remembered that was Freddie's name for Bruce."

"Oh. That's a very nice point," Obie said approvingly. "Well, it ends up with 'Rapunzel,

Rapunzel, let down your hair and I will climb up without any stair.' That might bring Mrs. Ferrell's hair to mind."

"Freddie!" Antonia murmured. "Freddie wrote that! Ain't love the damnedest thing!"

Michael was frowning at his cousin. "I remember now when it was that you found that note in your shoe. You let me talk on and on and—¡*Por Dios!* Why didn't you produce it at once?"

Ian's grin was at once friendly and malicious. "I wanted to see if you could get along without this note. And I didn't want to spoil your act, *amigo*."

EPILOGUE

On the Sunday morning following Freddie Carter's arrest Mr. and Mrs. Dundas disagreed rather radically on a matter of foreign policy.

Michael had risen earlier than usual and was reading the morning paper. Valerie, waiting for him to hand over the first news section, remarked idly:

"I thought Toni would call last night. I wonder why she didn't?"

"Because she went to Carmel with Ian," Michael said calmly.

"She went to— Michael! Did Ian tell you before they left that they—?"

"Certainly he told me, my dear. He consulted me, since, being Ian, he had certain scruples."

"He consulted you and you— Michael, you put down that paper and listen to me! You know Ian probably would have taken your advice."

"He did." Michael folded the newspaper and threw it on the floor. "My love, Antonia is well past the age of consent, and she asked Ian to take her with him."

"Age of consent! Age of idiocy!" Valerie said forcibly.

"Really, Valerie, I never expected you to make noises like an outraged matron."

"But I'm very fond of Toni and I thought you were too. If you approve so heartily of this sort of arrangement why didn't we try it instead of getting married?"

"Because," Michael said with a wholly unregenerate masculine grin, "you never suggested it to me, darling." He ducked. "Take your hand off that vase, Valerie. That was a joke: look for the Union label. I wanted to marry you. The important point is that I had not just spent seven years with the wrong woman. Or just lost a wife and felt that I should mourn her decorously for a year."

"Would *you* ever have felt that you must?"

"We're talking about Ian. He is very conservative and he would feel it wasn't good taste to marry again for at least six months."

"Well, what's six months!"

"What, indeed, in the year nineteen hundred and forty-two?" Michael said ironically. "*Querida,* only a damned fool goes about saying today: 'Grow old along with me! The best is yet to be.' Toni's learned a lesson some military men haven't—not to give too little, too late. I think Ian's entitled to generosity from one member of your sex. If Toni wants to be generous—and Toni very decidedly does—"

"Oh," Valerie said, "if you're only thinking of Ian! I'm thinking of Toni. What does she get out of it?"

"She wants Ian on any terms, but ordinarily I would agree with you. However, it happens that what I prefer to call generosity will appeal to Ian more than anything else. Remember another of your Chinese teacake quotations? 'Virtue, with some women, is but the precaution of locking doors.'

"If Ian hadn't gone off with Toni that conservative streak would keep him from marrying her for quite a while. If he joins the army he may not be around to marry her six months from now. But one will get you ten that after this interlude in Carmel he will marry Antonia without bothering to mourn for Adela."

"Why?" Valerie said. "Why will he marry her?"

"Because that's what he really wants to do. He wouldn't have taken her to Carmel with him otherwise."

"Oh! He's so conservative, according to you, that he wouldn't marry Toni too soon after

Adela's death but not so conservative that he won't take her away for a week end—but after that he'll marry her because that's what he really wants to do, only he's too conservative to— Piffle!" Valerie said and left the room.

Michael grinned and let her go. When she comes back I'll have another try at it, he thought. She doesn't seem to understand that after seven years with Adela Ian is fed up with virtue, his own included. . . .

The doorbell rang. He opened the door on an elderly messenger boy, signed for the telegram, read it standing in the doorway, and laughed. Then as he glanced down the hill toward Jones his jaw dropped.

"*¡Madre santíssima!* Has Birnam wood come to Dunsinane?" he muttered and went to meet a tall old man, dry and brown as driftwood, who was coming slowly up the walk.

"*Buenos días,* Grandfather. You're looking very well."

"I wouldna say I'm no," the old man remarked conservatively. "I needn't ask how you are, Michael. And Ian?"

"You know that the police arrested Adela's murderer? Ian is cleared, and no Scotch verdict, either."

"I've read the newspapers, and Ian wired us."

"I know Ian wired Adela's mother that he was sending her body home for burial," Michael said, holding the front door open. "Sit down, Grandfather. You see, George finally arrived. He was," Michael recalled, grinning, "exceedingly trainsick. And there was nothing for him to do but attend the services for Adela in Berkeley and then get back on a train again."

"George Douglas was always a doited sumph," Mr. Maclean said scornfully. "But Adela's mother didna tak' it kindly that Ian sent George back alone. It was partly to get awa' frae her blether that I came out here. And I wanted to talk to Ian. I should have told him to go into the army when he wanted to a year ago. I could have dealt with Adela."

Michael grinned again. The old man would never cease to consider himself a clan chieftain, responsible for the well-being of all his tribe. Then he thought: Here's another perfectly good grudge dead of malnutrition. He doesn't irritate me any longer. I must be growing old. . . .

"I might as well tell you, Grandfather: Ian isn't coming back to Wisconsin," he said.

"I didna expect he would when I read his wire. But if he enlists in the army out here we dinna ken whaur he'll be sent. And I wanted to see the bairn."

"Ours, you mean? Did Ian wire you that you have a great-grandson? Don't tell me ours is your first?"

The old man nodded. "But weren't you informed of Roderick's birth? If you weren't that detective agency you employed to report on me isn't earning its fees," Michael said blandly. "In fact, once they located me, thirteen years or so ago, they didn't earn whatever you paid them. But I appreciated the rake-off they gave me for co-operating with them. However, for some years my activities have been public property."

Mr. Maclean smiled acidly and in that instant strongly resembled his grandson. "I paid off that agency a good many years ago."

"As soon as you were certain that I hadn't sunk but was swimming very nicely?" Michael said.

"You were ower young to be cast afloat in a strange city with no life line. Well, is Ian here with you or—?"

Michael looked at the telegram he still held in his hand and chuckled. It read:

> TONI AND I ARE GETTING MARRIED
> AS SOON AS WE CAN GET A LICENSE
> IN THIS MISGUIDED STATE CAN YOU
> AND VALERIE COME DOWN FOR THE
> WEDDING
>
> IAN

"I'll tell you in an instant where Ian is and call my wife and produce the great-grandson," Michael promised, taking the stopper from a decanter of scotch. "But first I think you should have a drink because I'm afraid you are due for a slight shock. Will you drink before noon?"

"Oh," said Mr. Maclean, "I wouldna say no."

COACHWHIP PUBLICATIONS
COACHWHIPBOOKS.COM

VIRGINIA RATH

DEATH AT
DAYTON'S FOLLY